An Untold Secret:

(A Journey Home to Walkamile, Texas)

A Novel By

Henry Wyath Gurley

Published in the United States by
HEADLIGHT PRESS
6500 Clito Road
Statesboro, Georgia 30461 (USA)

LIBRARY OF CONGRESS
CATALOGING-IN-PUBLICATION DATA

Gurley, Henry Wyath
An Untold Secret: A Journey Home To Walkamile, Texas/Gurley, Henry Wyath

p. cm.
ISBN: 1-58535-159-8

Printed in the United States of America on acid-free paper.

Book Design by Charles E. Cravey

❧ *Introduction* ❧

Whatever our true origins—there is a bit of "Walkamile"
in all of us. For those who would deny this as fact—
they are, in the long run, the lesser for it.

The admission of such an ownership is the inner
heart of the Southern pathos in all of its
intricate patterns. Thus, these adherents are,
in the long run, the greater for it.

Henry Wyath Gurley
Montgomery, Texas
January 2008

untitled

'One for sorrow,
Two for joy;
Three for letter,
Four for boy.

Five for silver,
Six for gold;
Seven for a secret
That'll never be told.'

By Anonymous

❧

Chapter One

Mavis Murray:

'Tis one death a-plenty . . .'

"I can only imagine parts of what I am going to tell about my family. Lots of it I heard from my family members, some intended or some unintended. Lots of it I'm guessing at. But I suppose it should go like this:

"It rained—pure, plain and simple. Not the expected April showers that farming communities await with a sure conviction from the Good Lord. It was May, and the rain in banding torrents repeated itself across the greening fields and woods of Walkamile proper. Birds had long ceased their vibrant mid-spring songs; wild animals, quite used to roving about in the broad daylight of spring, sought drier shelter from the incessancy; domestic cattle, appearing baffled by the near intolerable conditions, huddled under a lone tree in the middle of a pasture or unintelligently massed together near the edge of the pasture in a crude circle, heads bowed and oddly facing each other as if in a learned ritual toward the center of the circle. Plow horses, disquieted in their unaccustomed suffering, stood forlornly in their wet, unprotected stalls and snorted as if in derision of their uncaring masters at their shabby treatment. Their large liquid eyes spoke volumes as to their confusion. It was not cold, but the inclemency made it feel so to all creatures, including the folk of Walkamile, especially our Philbin family.

"This rainy day in particular was the day of Joshua Philbin's funeral. Joshua Philbin was my Grandpa though I never knew him because I wasn't even born when all of these eventful things happened. Old Brother Billy Heart was to conduct the graveside services. Our family couldn't wait for the weather to improve because the body would begin to smell, according to what my Mama told me. I don't think they embalmed bodies in those days unless they were townsfolk with money. They had eschewed a church funeral for the very basic reason that Joshua Philbin had never professed any acquiescent degree toward a committed Christian belief. He had often said that mankind sprang directly from the apes and a god couldn't have a thing to do with any of it.

"The remaining Philbin family members had relied heavily on Brother Heart's kindness of spirit in his agreement to conduct the rite of burial. Jeremiah had walked at least two miles to the Heart place to get Brother Billy Heart to do the service. *'Nothing Christian needs to be involved in placing the old coot in the ground,'* they had privately argued, discussed and finally agreed among themselves. Wife, son and daughter—they all despised him. Even nearby neighbors avoided Joshua Philbin like the plague. They, too, had learned to hate him over the years and shy away from him at all costs. Though he was my Grandpa, he had to have been a monster in the eyes of those about him—relative or neighbor.

"Right before Joshua Philbin had died, Leah Philbin, my grandmother, had sent her son, Jeremiah (my uncle) out on horseback to look for old Doctor Goldman. His search was fruitless, but he did talk to Jessup, Doctor Goldman's nigger. Jessup, who usually was the epitome of exactitude and knowledge of the doctor's whereabouts, was either not forthcoming or was, especially if he had been instructed to be, evasive. All of the Philbins hated niggers to the core. And Doctor Goldman's nigger, Old Jessup, was no exception. They called him a *'white nigger—a uppity white nigger.'*

"When Jeremiah returned home, drenched by the rain storm he had endured, Leah Philbin, with the assistance of Jeremiah and Ruth (my mother) suffocated Joshua Philbin with an oversized feather pillow. They had planned the murder to happen even if old Doctor Goldman had shown up to examine the *sick* Joshua, who, in reality, was not ill but was so inebriated that he was nigh to comatose. The suffocation event was not difficult in that there were six different hands applying pressure with the big pillow. It must not have took long.

"The weather grew so foul that Leah Philbin decided not to send Jeremiah out again to look for the Sheriff or the Justice of the Peace. He'd already made two trips: one looking for Doctor Goldman and another looking for Brother Billy Heart. If it cleared up the next day she might decide to send him off on such another fool errand.

"She had reasoned that the Sheriff probably wouldn't be able to make it out to their place in his low-slung car; and the JP, who had a reputation for being squeamish about dead bodies, likely wouldn't overtax himself in trying to come out while they were having these gully-washers. *'All of that in time,'* she is apt to have said. I don't know this for sure, but it's a fact that the three murdered Joshua Philbin and got away with it—like a big fish—hook, line and sinker!

"So it was on a rainy day in May, 1936, a Saturday to be exact—May 23—that our Philbin family loaded up Joshua's corpse on the back of their farm wagon, covered it with a dirty, stained tarpaulin, hitched up Jick and Jack, their two spooked mules, and made their way in the rain to the Cedar Grove Cemetery a mile or so out of Walkamile. As they neared the cemetery they saw, on either side of the broken-down gate, straight rows of cedar trees. It would have been apparent to them, had they noticed, that the trees must have been planted years before by caring hands. Even in the steady rain and the paucity of light, the trees stood like sentinels, erect and alive, in this space which was an introduction to many souls' eternities. The silvery gray of the cedars' limb tips glistened in the otherwise dreary atmosphere.

"Brother Billy Heart came on the scene within five minutes of the family's arrival riding his gentled old mare, Felicity. He had promised that he would be there come *'Hell or High Water'* which he had said. He rode up slowly, soaked to the bones in his black suit and a black hat that puddled water around the brim. A rubberized cape loosely graced his upper body, but it too had absorbed copious amounts of the falling moisture. Had the weather been worse, his coming to the gravesite may have been interpreted as having taken on an even more ominous note, especially with his awkward attire, all black.

"There were three Philbins in attendance: Leah Philbin, Joshua's wife of forty years, who was my grandmother as I've told you; Jeremiah Philbin, Joshua's and Leah's oldest son now an unmarried thirty-six, and my uncle, (which I've explained), and Ruth Philbin, their only daughter, an old maid at twenty-four years of age, my mother-to-be who would give birth to me in her 30s, late in her life as far as she was concerned. They too, despite their most valiant efforts at keeping dry, were hopelessly wet, their clothes clinging to their spare bodies. Their countenances gave off the impression that the sooner the better when this whole thing was over and done with. To a person they would have as readily tossed Joshua Philbin's body into The Gully, a washed-out crevasse at the back of the Philbin pasture, and left it to rot on its own accord and to be devoured by the countless scavengers known to inhabit those environs. The Gully was said to be a *hainted* place long avoided by local children and overly superstitious adults.

"A lone figure, hatless, in wet attire and splattered with a red mud stood in obvious discomfiture near a hole in the ground which appeared to be half-filled with water. This hole over which he stood was to be the site of Joshua Philbin's final resting place. Jeremiah called out to him, *"Stace! Come here and help me with Pa!"* The figure, Stace Wellborn, tossed his shovel aside and strode toward the wagon. There was no sense of formality as the two men lifted the body of Joshua Philbin and carried it head and feet in its advanced state of *rigor mortis* to the hole in the ground. With an assumed semblance of some delicacy and respect, they lowered the tarpaulin-wrapped corpse into the opening and dropped it as gently as they could. Despite their unrehearsed, cooperative efforts, those gathered there heard a splashing sound as the corpse hit bottom!

"Stace Wellborn came close to yelling out, *'Ready for you, Brother Heart! Ready!'* He repeated the last word nervously as he tried to catch his breath, now shallow and uneven. Stace Wellborn's muscular frame belied the near-innocent guise of his face—a cross between a man and a mere child.

"Brother Billy Heart stepped forward and motioned the Philbin family to gather around him so they could hear his words. He waited only a moment for them and then began. He had not bothered to bring his leather-bound Bible which was his usual accompanying guide at weddings and funerals. Too messy to have a good Bible ruined, I suppose he had reasoned. In the wetness his face seemed drawn and haggard, each line etched deep as the rain flowed down his cheeks.

"With an exaggeration of humility he began, *'Dust to dust and ashes to ashes don't sound too good on a day like this. Mud to mud might sound more fittin' but our brother Joshua Philbin didn't believe in a Christian God anyhow. So be it! He is facin' his Master now as I speak, and him and God can settle that issue. Not you and me. That ain't for us to be involved in. I'm a bit inclined to say that Joshua Philbin in his own way was a good and decent man and a good neighbor. Many I know would disagree with that. That is the way of all mankind. He treated Leah with good humor, I believe, and he helped her raise two decent children. Beyond that, I can't say much else about him since he never darkened the door of my church. God rest his soul! God accept him into eternity and deal with him fair and square. We would be greedy to ask for more.'*

"Brother Heart ignored the guttural harrumphs he heard during his homily. He had to say what he had to say and not get entangled in the Philbin family's fracas.

"Brother Billy Heart then patted Leah Philbin on her shoulder as did he with Ruth. He then shook Jeremiah's hand and accepted the dampened dollar bill from Jeremiah. *'Many thanks!'* Jeremiah spoke softly. *'It had to be done like this, I guess. We are civilized people.'*

"Jeremiah then nodded to Stace to start shoveling the dirt, now a mud the consistency of a brownish-red paste, into the grave. He returned to the wagon to get his own shovel to help Stace. Leah Philbin and Ruth got into the wagon, Ruth grabbing the reins. She turned the wagon around deftly and they departed behind Brother Billy Heart who was several yards ahead of them.

"Leah Philbin's voice carried on the damp air, *'Supper'll be ready for you and Stace when you're done here.'* She then called back to Jeremiah almost as an afterthought, *'Hurry home! We don't want you a-dyin' on us now in this dampness. 'Tis one death a-plenty but soon enough in God's own time—in God's own good time.'*

"The wagon made little noise as it slowly moved over the wet ground off into the rainy distance. It soon merged into a sheeted mist with only the protestations of Jick and Jack carried on the wind. Brother Billy Heart had been swallowed up by the mist without notice scant moments before Leah and Ruth disappeared into the same murky depths of the nearby woods.

"This is the best I can do in piecing together how Grandpa Philbin's funeral might have been carried out. Remember, I just heard bits and pieces here and there and another sketch at another time. Odds and ends, and bits and pieces—that was about the extent of it. Nobody ever sat down and told the full story or the full truth. That's for sure. I had often thought that I would talk to Stace Wellborn in later days, but he got sent off to a place for crazy people. He finally got to where he couldn't even talk."

❧

Chapter Two

Robert E. Massey:

'Rich, rich, rich!'

"Etta Dykes was in a state of absolute bliss. Bruno Richard Hauptmann was dead at last! He was electrocuted on April 3, 1936, at 8:47 P.M. somewhere in New Jersey if she, indeed, had heard the radio newsman correctly. He had taken his last breath on a Friday. That was all right with Etta Dykes, quite all right. He didn't deserve to live over another weekend. What he had done to an innocent babe was unforgivable in her books, and no punishment, including a slow and agonizing death, could fully repay society for his dastardly crime. But he had to pay. She wanted so badly to tell someone of the news she had just heard on the radio. Clayton, her husband, would have chided her for her silliness had she broached the subject to him. She'd have to wait and talk to Elbridge Massey about it during his next visit. He'd listen even if he wasn't interested one iota.

"Over four years earlier Etta had started following the news of the kidnapping of the little Lindbergh baby, a twenty-month old son of the famous Lindberghs: Charles Augustus Lindbergh and Anne Morrow Lindbergh. She had often hunched her body over to be near her battery radio so that she could listen for the latest news on the hunt for the kidnapper. The reception was hit-or-miss at best, and she had noticed on bright, sunny days she could barely hear the voices or the music on the radio. She had begged Clayton to have the aerial fixed outside the window and to have the grounding checked. He'd nod and go on about his business. She read every copy of *Grit* that she could lay her hands on; she finagled copies of *The Houston Post* from the rural postman, Elbridge Massey, some of these copies a day delayed. Her finagling came at a price, however. (Elbridge Massey was my Grandpa).

"Around 10:00 o'clock each weekday morning, Elbridge Massey would pull up to the Dykes' mail box in the front of their home in his old Ford truck. If he noticed Clayton Dykes' truck (Clayton was Etta's husband) parked at the back of the house, he would honk his horn which signaled that he had delivered some mail which usually included one of the Houston newspapers. If Clayton Dykes' truck was absent from the premises, Elbridge Massey would personally deliver the mail (or newspaper) to the front door. At least once a week he was invited inside if the coast was totally clear, and he would receive his payment: a sexual favor from Etta Dykes. If, by chance, Clayton Dykes, Etta's husband, drove up at this importune moment, he and Etta could always use the excuse that he was picking up Etta Dykes' charity packages for delivery on his route for a distressed family in need. Etta was celebrated in the county for her charitable deeds. On the few occasions that this had happened, Etta and Elbridge had to do some Fancy Dan footwork to quickly get dressed and not look too frowzy in the much-hurried process.

"Their liaison had begun shortly after March 1, 1932, when Etta Dykes had first learned of the Lindbergh baby's kidnapping. She had met Elbridge Massey at her mail box to inquire about subscribing to a Houston newspaper. He had told her that he could always provide a paper for her during the week at no charge and that she could talk her husband, Clayton, into picking her up a Sunday copy at the little grocery store just outside Walkamile. Etta had not suspected that there would be strings attached to such an arrangement, but she was grateful for Elbridge Massey's kind consideration and quite receptive to his attentions.

"Etta Dykes read of various ransom notes related to the Lindbergh kidnapping; she read that the Governor of New Jersey was personally getting involved; a radio newscast cited a mysterious "John" who got away with a paid ransom, never to be seen or heard from again; Gabriel Heatter, the famous newsman, (or perhaps it was another radio newsman) had reported that the Lindbergh's nurse had found the little boy's thumb guard near the vast Lindbergh estate. This, in itself, was intriguing news. Titillating news was overly welcomed by Etta who felt isolated and suppressed in the Walkamile community. The unreliable battery radio and her now almost weekly romp with Elbridge Massey were the stellar highlights to her otherwise boring existence.

"Etta Dykes exulted in all these happenings. Her life in Walkamile no longer depressed her; her marriage to Clayton Dykes could now be tolerated. She and Clayton had long before this time agreed to disagree on matters of sex. She despised contending with his animal desires and had told him so. He had wanted to do some *unusual* things on several occasions when he had finished his noonday lunch. Etta had told him to go milk the cow down the road, not the cow at home. He got the message and bedded every available female who fell under his charms. There were reports that he had even found compliant young boys to his liking when he was unable to avail himself of the feminine persuasion.

"Etta had reached the point where she no longer cared one way or the other. What she really could not tolerate was his physicality: when he undressed in preparation for the sexual encounter, he looked like a horse. His private parts were huge, and each time that they had had a romp, Etta had felt violated. There was no joy in the act. In fact, the act itself hurt her. Even the anticipation of having to be bedded by Clayton brought on a case of nerves. As she was to learn later with Elbridge Massey, a man could receive pleasure himself and still be gentle with the accommodating woman. And, much to her surprise and gratification, Etta discovered that she actually enjoyed the sporadic encounters and found herself looking forward to the next one. The news surrounding the Lindbergh baby, the dalliances with Elbridge Massey, and the staccato rendering of the trial news by Gabriel Heatter when the battery radio cooperated: Etta Dykes' life seemed to be more complete and fulfilling unto itself for a change.

"The days, the weeks, the months rolled by as a reality in a diffused light. Etta now realized that Clayton Dykes had married her for one reason only: her land and her money. She had inherited the existent estate from her father, Winslow Harris. Along with the vast acreage spread far and beyond Walkamile along the Trinity River, came 'buckets of money' as the lawyers called Winslow Harris' investment certificates and ready cash. It became a standing joke in the county that no less than a half-dozen lawyers were reconsidering their own marital arrangements of the moment. Their change of heart as to their own situations: Etta Harris was a prime catch. Any of these lawyers, if ultimately successful in their pursuit of Etta Harris, would not mind being called a *gold-digger.*

"But Clayton Dykes arrived on the scene with a proper degree of bravado, not excessive, that caught Etta's immediate attention. Hardly a year after they met at a church social, Etta and Clayton were married—each astride a horse—by Reverend Franklin

Goodenough! The jokesters in the community, always seeking that which would titillate and amuse, questioned if the marriage was legal because the couple had not had their feet on the ground when they took their marriage vows! *'Eight horse legs on the ground do not a marriage make,'* they had bandied about. The same county gossipers were agog with talk about Clayton Dykes' proclivity for a wandering eye. Without a doubt his reputation had preceded this latest action. Now the same gossipers could add to their litany of reproach of his activities that he was a dyed-in-the-wood gold-digger. And he had struck it rich. Rich, rich, rich. At this moment in time he would never again be unequal in shouldering the responsibilities he would face.

"Etta Harris and Clayton Dykes had married and the talk had stopped for the time being. It would be only a short time, however, before the same chain of gossip started up again in light of Clayton Dykes' inability to keep his own eyes on that which was his and closed against that which was not his."

❧

Chapter Three

Koskobe Renner:

'A real live palindrome . . .'

"My Granddaddy, Otto Renner, wouldn't have recognized a palindrome if he had met one on a sandy road leading in or out of Walkamile. Quite likely the average citizen of Walkamile would be subject to the same deficiency, a lot like me. But my Granddaddy, Otto Renner, did exercise a certain skill in his handling of the challenging nuances of the English language. He had, quite by accident, by love or by design, married Alla Perkins, and she had become Alla Renner when the marriage rites had attached his moniker to her first name. Otto Renner had recognized that oddity at first blush but had cast the occurrence aside as a circumstantial quirk that likely would not happen in another hundred lifetimes. At that moment his awareness of this coincidental happening had minimal impact, if any at all, on him.

"I, however, should know all about this palindrome business. I am his grandson, and I have been stuck with an almost unmanageable name due to my father's distaste for the palindrome-naming scheme which infected all the offspring of Otto and Alla Renner. My father, their oldest son, received the name of Arppra

Renner only after Otto and Alla Renner had decided to continue the nonsensical palindrome-naming scheme. They still, however, did not know that the construction of words and names also had a name for that term: palindrome. It would be quite a few years before they learned of such a term. And they would learn of it from my father, Arppra, who would be introduced to it quite by accident in a school classroom.

"My father, Arppra, had advanced to the 8th Grade, and his teacher that year, a Miss Mildred Lohan, as she had transcribed his name into her roll books, had remarked, *'My! My! We have us a real live palindrome in our class. In fact, I'm aware of three palindromes in this person's family.'* She then elegantly swiveled her curvaceous body to the blackboard and chalked the names: *O T T O, A L L A, A R P P R A. 'Can anyone inform me what a palindrome is?'* she had asked. My father didn't bother responding because he was mortally ashamed of his name, preferring to be called *Arp* by his buddies. *Why should she mess around with my name?* he had thought to himself. The other boys in the class, casual in their desire to learn of such things, were more interested in Miss Lohan's physical attributes as viewed from the backside.

"No one answered Miss Lohan (so my father told me many times). Now she was in her element as she began to explain the root structure of the word *palindrome.* The 8th Grade class, made up of boys and girls who had already reached the shrieking hormonal demands of puberty or who were on the verge of crossing that sacred threshold a bit late, sat in silence until Alicia Woodman, a long-haired, mousey girl who had a brain the size of a small washtub, spoke up, *'It is so obvious! The names read front to back and back to front the same! Haven't any of you heard of the famous question: Was it a car or a cat I saw?'* Miss Lohan hurriedly wrote this question on the blackboard, but then Alicia the Brain spouted out another lulu, *'Able was I ere I saw Elba.'* The class, almost in a chorused unison, groaned aloud at Alicia the Brain's overt display of brilliance. Alicia had desired to inform the class of the Greek root *palindromos* but she had restrained herself. She had thought to herself, '*Oh, God! Why do You punish me with this horrid ability to remember such tripe that I may have seen while thumbing through a dictionary? Why God?*'

"But I stray. My sister was named Anna; I had a younger brother named Bob (such originality!); and even our pets were given palindromic names, many of which I am thankful that I have forgotten. The few that can't seem to escape my mind were *Tat*, an outdoor cat, *Gog*, a huge cross between a mastiff so Daddy thought and an unknown and probably unwilling female partner of some common yard dog breed.

"My name is another story, however. I won't leave you hanging for long, and I promise I'll get to the meat of the reasons why any parent on Planet Earth would name a child *Koskobe*. I suppose if you had been named *Arppra* anyone with a half-brain and a scintillating streak of compassion would forgive you for being engaged in such a travesty as giving your child a name that would hang about his neck like an albatross for the rest of his life.

"My Daddy had lived through World War I. He had heard stories of families worried sick to the core of their hearts about their sons fighting in Europe—whether they were alive or dead or maimed for life. If they ever saw a list of those soldiers killed in action, they hurriedly traced their trembling fingers down the list, pausing at the letter of the alphabet of their last name. The Browns, the Smiths, the Johnsons, the Williams and those others with common last names suffered mightily until they could go through the list to see if their son, or relative, or friend or acquaintance was on the list. This practice, I think, was in effect in the Civil War and probably even in earlier conflicts.

"Daddy insisted that I be named Koskobe Renner, and he wouldn't have to suffer at all if a war came up and he had to look at a list. If he saw a Renner on the list, then he was certain it was one of his relatives. It seemed that no one other than our family had Renner as the last name. If it didn't have Koskobe as the first name, then he wouldn't go to pieces. Thus, the origin and continuing history of my pitiful name. *'Damn their hides for naming me like that!'* I always say under my breath to absolutely no avail.

"Just as my Daddy tried valiantly to be called *Arp* by his buddies, I have, over the years, urged my friends to call me *Kos* or even *Kobe,* though Kobe quickly went out of style after Pearl Harbor when people started to recognize names of Japanese cities. When my truest friends wanted to piss me off royally, they would call out in their loud booming voices: *'Koskobe! Where are you? We're here, Koskobe!'* I could have killed them one and all, both girls and boys—shit asses that they turned out to be! But I didn't, and I just let well enough alone and went on in life being called whatever whoever wanted to call me. There was an old saying back then that always brought a smile to me: *'You can call me anything you want as long as you call me to supper.'* True words of wit!"

෪

Chapter Four

Anastasia Woodman:

'A grand day to be walking . . .'

"My aunt, Alicia Woodman, wandered through her fascinating life in a proverbial fog that only she comprehended, I am told. Her brother, Murt Woodman (my father) often spoke of his sister in the most glowing of terms as to her unbelievable intelligence. However, on the other hand, he would remark on many occasions in almost a matching breath that the poor thing even as a full-grown adult didn't have the sense God gave a goose when it came to the everyday situations which one confronts in life. If anything unusual occurred suddenly which was different to that which she was accustomed, Alicia Woodman would be in grave trouble instantly. She had no innate capabilities to sort out a common sense approach to change.

"My father once told me that Alicia, on her own terms, had often frowned in the deepest contemplation, but at the same time he said that she had laughed much in the company of those she liked. I had not understood the dual significance of this at the time, but as I learned the complexities of my aunt over time I think I grasped the meaning of his statement.

"He once told me that Aunt Alicia was sitting under a large cottonwood tree in their front yard reading a book when a violent rainstorm came up quite suddenly. *'Why! The silly goose did have the sense to put her book under her skirt to keep it dry, but after that action she sat there, arms spread wide, face lifted toward the heavens, lightning crackling in all quadrants of the sky, thunder a-boomin' like it was the end of the world. Mama called to her, but Alicia either didn't hear her or ignored her on purpose. Lightning could have struck the tree or Alicia, and that would've been the mortal end of her. But, perpetual fool that she was, she survived probably through God's good graces. She seemed to have savored getting wet, her stringy hair matted to her face and her dress plastered to her body. Mama could have killed her on the spot. When the rainstorm had ended, your Aunt Alicia is reported to have remarked,* 'How refreshing!' '

"My Grandma Woodman told many stories about Alicia and the vicious dogs in the neighborhood. *'We did live in town, you know, and Alicia could walk to school as a rule without any problems. She'd pass several homes whose owners allowed their dogs to run free in their yards. Some of the dogs were mean old Chows that'd bite at the drop of a hat. There might've been some aggressive pit bulls in the mix—guard dogs for lack of a better word. Neighborhood boys picked at 'em and made 'em meaner than they should have been. When they came roarin' out at Alicia, she'd stop, books in hand, and look at them without blinkin' an eye. They'd all, one after the other, tuck their tails between their legs and walk alongside Alicia until she had exited their domain. The neighbors never could figure out what she had done to the dogs to keep them from bitin' her. One of them asked her about it once at a church social. Alicia's explanation was real simple and almost came across like she might have been lyin' to the neighbor. She told the neighbor:* 'I just tell the dog if he's a boy dog that he is a handsome old fellow on this very beautiful morning. I then ask him if he'd like* *to walk with me and protect me from harm while I'm in his territory. That's all, really. They all are faithful in seeing to my well-being while I'm on their turf. They're my guardians, really they are. If it's a girl dog I use about the same saying, but I tell her how beautiful she is. When I can't tell if the dog is a boy or girl, I just tell them that it's a grand day to be walking in their territory, and I desperately need their protection. Really, that's all!'*

"Daddy used to tell me stories about dog whisperers and their uncanny abilities when it came to handling savage, near untrainable dogs. He said that often the dog whisperer was the seventh son of a seventh son or the seventh daughter of a seventh son or a seventh daughter. My Aunt Alicia Woodman was none of that—in fact, she didn't even come close to meeting that exacting requirement. Daddy thought perhaps that Alicia lived on a mental plane removed from the average person. She was smart. Boy! Was she smart! Her head was in the high clouds a large part of the time, far, far above and away from the reality of our little Walkamile community. And she treated all animals as equals to her and felt that all a person needed to do was communicate with them on their level. Imagine her asking a dog that's getting ready to bite her to accompany her while she's in that dog's territory and having the gall to tell him that he is a handsome old thing. What fool on earth would think of such poppycock? But her stratagem apparently worked—fool that she was (as Daddy had said a thousand times).

"In later years my Grandma Woodman told me of the difficulties she had when Alicia came into this world. *'Bless her heart! Her head was so big that I had to struggle for over twenty-four hours. I prayed to God to let the little one live but to take me out of my misery. That's how bad I was hurtin'. God didn't see it my way at all, and I always remember the words from the Bible that He won't give us anything that we can't bear. That was a consolation, not then, of course. I was bedfast for over a month after Alicia was born, too weak to even sit up in bed. I'd look at the little creature with a big head and think to myself that she was, indeed, an ugly thing. But her eyes were bright, and she smiled all the time. I thought maybe she had been born daft. It would not have surprised me if that had been so because of what she and I both went through with.'*

"Grandma had continued with her iteration of the events of Alicia's birth and her toddler days: *'You know, we lived next door to good old Dr. Goldman who had been with me during my sufferin' of delivery. He had told your Grandpa that he feared that the little one, Alicia, may be a water-head baby. He said only time would tell. If the head continued to grow, he said, that would be his diagnosis. Your aunt's head was large from birth, but thank God, it didn't grow disproportionately with the rest of her body as she entered toddlerhood. Yes, she was awkward in her movements, almost spastic at times as Dr. Goldman had pointed out to us. He had warned us to watch Alicia real close because if she showed any form of the Three Ws, we had to be concerned. He told us that the Three Ws was WACKY, WET and WOBBLY. She did take on these characteristics right away. But, oh my dearie, she was smart. What a smart kid! She was reading simple books by the time she was three. We really didn't know it at first; we thought she was pointing at the words from memory as we told her what the pictures and words stood for. But we were wrong! She had somehow managed to capture the sounds of the combined letters which formed themselves into words—all on her own, so it seemed. And she peed at the drop of a hat! Lord, could she pee! She could hear the sound of water bein' poured from a well bucket or be near a gurglin' stream, and she would pee. And what made it all the more concern for us was that she waddled about like a duck—lean to the left, stand up teeterin' in the middle, and lean to the right. But thank the Good Lord, she outgrew the peein' and the waddlin', but her wackiness increased and we thought of that as just raw and pure intelligence. All in all, Dr. Goldman observed the whole thing but would never come out and say that the poor little thing had hydrocephalus (that's the fancy word for water on the brain). I looked it up in a medical dictionary and memorized it because I was so afraid that that's what would happen to my Alicia.'*

"My Aunt Alicia never did become what you could call pretty. Her head, elongated like that of a praying mantis, jutted forward on a skinny body. And her hair was wild like stalks of fine straw blown askew by the wind. Her face was flat, smushed in almost, and the top portion was overly accented by large, round-lensed black framed glasses which gave the praying mantis face a severe, owlish look. Regardless of the clothes she wore, it always seemed that none of them fitted her properly, despite the exhaustive alterations my Grandma attempted. She couldn't help it that she was ugly just as a pretty girl can't help it that she's pretty and attracts the boys like flies to syrup.

"Aunt Alicia's teachers in the small Walkamile School dreaded the thought of having her in their classes as she advanced from grade to grade. They could not keep up with her thirsty demands for knowledge far and beyond what they could offer. If the teachers attempted to conduct games in the classroom for the students' diversion, based on their age and skill levels, the results were always disastrous. Aunt Alicia would blurt out the answers, as a rule, before the questions had been completely asked. And spelling bees were impossible to conduct. She won them all, hands down! No one student stood a Chinaman's chance against her. The usual arithmetic exercises in which students went to the blackboard to work out problems of addition, subtraction, multiplication—Aunt

Alicia would scan the blackboards once, and then she would begin to call out the answers left-to-right much to the teacher's chagrin. She had been double promoted on two occasions: from the first to the third grades and from the fourth to the sixth grades. This action by the school officials made her two years younger than the average student, and she had graduated at the top of her class at the age of fifteen. And sadly, the two-year age difference might have taken a toll on her social development in blending in with the other students.

"When she had graduated from high school as the top-ranked student with a grade point average so high that the school administration chose not to release it, she had to have several wooden risers placed behind the dais so that she could be seen as she gave her valedictory. Even then, she appeared childlike as she delivered her prepared speech in her sing-song, childlike voice. When she had finished her crafted speech, she had not waited for the applause. She had simply turned to the left, walked off the stage and joined her non-senior friends in the auditorium's audience. Daddy always said that my Aunt Alicia marched to a drummer that no one else heard. Likely or no, he was right on. She should have returned to sit with her classmates at the back of the stage.

"Dr. Goldman, realizing her unparalleled brilliance, had made quiet contact with old friends and associates in Houston regarding the need of a scholarship for Aunt Alicia. With their influence and financial assistance my Aunt Alicia ended up at Rice Institute as she barely reached age sixteen. Even as she caught the bus for Houston and her new life at Rice Institute, she was as wacky as ever. Rice Institute and the big city life in Houston were to change her forever, but she would retain her inability to possess any degree of common sense. Her eccentricities would be enhanced by the academic milieu among students and faculty as wacky as she; her life after four years at Rice would consist of a series of harmless conflicts which, to some degree, would add to her idiosyncratic charm, a trait which made me adore her on the occasions I was in her presence.

"She was a joy to have as an aunt. There were numerous times of which I thought that she did not even realize that I was in the same room as she; but then again, she would surprise me by pulling out some trinket from her jewel box or her armoire and informing me that *'This will look darling on you. I just know it will!'* Or she would produce a book from her bulging satchel, scan it momentarily, and then hand it to me with the admonition, *'I thought of you when I read this. You must read it and receive the same pleasure I received as I read it. It is so illuminating!'* Or she would toss out one of her aphorisms which usually came across as thought-provoking challenges, *'You never get a second chance to make a first impression!'* These precious instances always caught me off-guard what with her spontaneity and her total lack of guile. Over the years I learned that my dear Aunt Alicia possessed not one mean bone in her body. She was kindness personified, and she would forever remain a guiding star for me and would consider me a real jewel-in-the-rough as we continued to hone our friendship."

Chapter Five

Patrick A. Goldman:

'And son, you wonder why I drink?'

"My lovable old grandpa, Dr. Kristian Adolphus Goldman, was a drunkard who somehow managed to see to the physical ills of several generations of residents of the community of Walkamile while ignoring his own physical and mental ailments. How he was able to perform on-the-spot surgeries on old men and women, children from infancy to boisterous teenagers, young mothers who were screaming and writhing in arduous pains of childbirth—and yes, even some much-loved animals—is still not clear in my mind. Why? Because he stayed drunk with a big, open smile most of his waking hours and definitely a large number of the hours that he slept fitfully in a stupor. All of this is fact according to my father, who, by the Grace of God, never touched spirits.

"My equally lovable old grandma, Miriam (Wexler) Goldman, was a pill head and a regular sipper of paregoric who somehow managed to live with the ever-perplexing drunkard of a husband! She had been a Registered Nurse when Grandpa had met her, and my Grandpa became an absolute idiot around her, besotted to the point of declaring his eternal love and admiration for her. Grandma had brilliant red hair and just the hint of freckles on her nose, and she had an associated temper to match the red hair.

"Grandma at that time lived in a dormitory-style facility at the Tulane Medical School where she was in charge of nursing students who were attending certain classes affiliated with the Medical School. She had related on those occasions, when she was not experiencing the pain of withdrawal from either her pills or paregoric, how Grandpa would, when three sheets to the wind, park himself outside her bedroom window and extol the virtues of her beauty and his undying love. He would sing love ballads, and poorly so. He would recite Shakespearean love sonnets, and poorly so.

"Once he even attempted to strum a guitar he had borrowed as he sang:

> 'She sat by her window and played her guitar,
> Played her guitar, played her guitar;
> She sat by the window and played her guitar—
> Played her guitar-ar-ar-ar!'

(Plus the dozen other verses of this silly song).

"School officials discretely requested Grandma to tell him to cease and desist his amorous blathering, but try as she might Grandpa continued his promotion of his love for her with a deliberate clumsiness—night after night, so I understand. Grandma always wondered how on God's Green Earth he could make a passing grade in the exacting classes he was taking at the time. But he could, and did, and graduated in the Top 10% of his class. And he finally captured Grandma's heart when he graduated from the medical school. They were married in New Orleans shortly after.

"My father told me that he had not learned of Grandma's addictions to pills and paregoric until he was in high school. He learned that she had been caught falsifying prescriptions which she had taken to Carter's Drugstore. The pharmacist, a friend of both Grandma and Grandpa, had not wanted to let the cat out of the bag because he too had exercised a degree of incaution on several occasions as relates to proper dispositions of prescriptions. What really had bothered my father was the incident when two of his high school classmates, best friends of his, had informed him that his mother was paying young men to go to the drugstore and buy paregoric for her. That was the one lulu that caused my father to go to a sober Grandpa and tell him to so something. *'Mama's killing herself!'* he had screamed out to Grandpa.

"My father, Adler Goldman, once talked to me about the downfall of good men who relied on the temporary bliss they received from a bottle of whiskey. He told me that my Grandpa, once in a drunken state, related to him how the bottle would assuage his angst and bring him a relief, be it temporary in nature. Grandpa had said, *'Adler, you're young. You tend to look at the world through the proverbial rose-colored glasses. Adler, my son! That world does not exist. The real world is a clear and stark series of pictures of broken lives; limbs of able young men are broken and crushed; dead babies arrive on the scene and the grieving parents bury them in the family plot and have a tombstone erected with a sculpted angel or lamb on top and the engraving reads OUR LITTLE ANGEL, and the dates of birth and death are the same; old people who should have been dead months before hang on to life, and they shit in their beds, and they pee willy-nilly, and the rooms they are imprisoned in stink with the acrid scent of urine and the overwhelming smell of human excrement, and the overpowering scent of death is all about; and, the least understood of all pictures is that one utterly final one when the lawmen call you to a residence where a multiple murder-suicide has happened: bodies in all states of disarray all over the house, bowels strung out on one corpse, a near-severed head hanging loosely on a torso, the bodies of small children on what must have been their beds, their eyes staring blankly into the distances of an unrealized space and, more sadly, an unrealized life; and then, in a dim corner, a face blown to smithereens with what appears to be a 16-gauge shotgun blast in the mouth of the murderer who lastly took his own life, perhaps to avoid the consequences of facing his final punishment. The shotgun rests to the side of what once was a man like you and me. And you wonder, Adler, why I drink? Oh, boy of mine, I drink because I seek to erase these pictures that go with me throughout the livelong day and the endless night. And yet the people still love me as they call me Good Dr. Goldman. Oh, they are so wrong. I am not good. I am weak. I am but a lowly man who sees their pain and then has to suffer my own pain the best way I can. I drink. I have another and another and another. During the day when I have office hours? Oh yes! My medicine cabinet is a handy place to hide my nipping flask. I once swore to the Hippocratic Oath, but now I realize that I should have sworn to the Hypocrite's Oath!'*

"Daddy has relished the memories of week-long planning he had made as a child with Jessup, Grandpa's *valet du-jour*, as he often called him, an old black man who had been a part of the Goldman family for so long that he was affectionately addressed as *Nigger* by each succeeding generation of the Goldman's. Grandpa would have promised Daddy a long, relaxing weekend on Brush Lake—a respite for him with the pole-fishing on the lake stretched out over the lazy summer days. Then Monday would bring a stark reality that all of this was nothing but a temporary foolishness—escapism of the worst sort. The silky green patina of Brush Lake caused by the heavy pollen of overhanging tree branches, hushed and velvet, its solitude shattered only by the squawk of a startled bird or the flopping of a large fish in the middle of the lake, was a panacea for all that ailed the human spirit. This world could not mask the over-riding angst of Grandpa, but Daddy felt that it was a fairyland for him: the sights and sounds of the night and the anticipation of the next morning—early rising with the smells of coffee and bacon—and biscuits baking in a black Dutch oven. If it had been escapism, my Daddy, only a young boy who adored nature, loved every facet of it.

"Daddy said the fishing trips would come off without any hitch, and Jessup would organize with the greatest flair of efficiency: the careful packing of many sleeping bags, the lanterns, their globes rubbed to a pristine crystal clarity, their wicks trimmed to perfection, the kerosene with its intoxicating fumes, (Old Jessup called it *coal oil)*, the long-stemmed matches in a waterproof packaging, (the smell of the phosphorus was intoxicating to my Daddy), the foodstuffs, mysterious in their colorful tin cans and exquisite paper wrappings tied up neatly with store twine, the careful selection of clean bales of hay from the Good Doctor's barn located on a small farm he owned (something for all of them to sit on around the campfire), shovels, hoes, rakes, over-sized enamel coffee pots with white backgrounds and mottled blue splotches, and a myriad of store tins, mosquito netting by the tens of yards, a snakebite kit and an emergency medical kit, and an ample supply of drinking water in large aluminum containers with spigots and dozens of canvas-swathed jugs of water. Daddy called them *'toe sack jugs.'*

"Daddy knew that there would be little or no bathing and this pleased him immensely. You didn't dare go swimming in the lake because at night you could hear the roaring and bellowing of alligators upon the night air, and you could see the trails where they had roamed about doing whatever they were doing at night. Daddy purposefully involved himself with Jessup in most of these preparations, and Jessup allowed him to piddle about up to a point.

Then he finalized whatever activity they were involved in at the moment, ensuring, of course, successful completion.

"Daddy has told me many times, *'We always arrived at Brush Lake after dark on Friday night. The usual campsite loomed ghostly and eerie, and I could visualize monstrous water moccasins crawling about, ready to bite the first thing that moved. Old Jessup gave none of this no mind, and within a good hour the campsite was nearing completion what with a roaring fire in the center of the site, bales of hay spaced about the fire in a circular fashion, and a coffee pot already bubbling as it hung on an iron stand over the fire. Daddy's dog, Rabbit, would be beside himself with instant and spontaneous reactions to every strange noise about him.*

"Daddy would pause, then smile at me as he recalled those times: *'Whoever the Good Doctor had invited would be stirring about, talking in loud voices which seemed to express their bravura. There would be remarks of: Wonder when the coffee will be ready? Oh, but I know it will be good when it gets ready. But I knew that not one of the grown-ups there would have the least interest in a hot cup of coffee unless they had something to lace it with, like a good dash of the Good Doctor's whiskey. In only a short time the voices would grow louder, the laughter would come more often in throaty staccato measurements, and the foofaraw would increase in intensity as Old Jessup fried bacon, Irish potatoes, and beef steaks on a second fire he had built. Even though the beef steaks had been iced down, Old Jessup knew they wouldn't survive the night without the potential of spoiling. He knew exactly what to do: feed them now before they get rip-roaring drunk.'*

"On one summer fishing trip Daddy related to me that they had all barely survived the first night when, at the very crack of dawn, a man on a horse had ridden up about the time Old Jessup was getting the morning coffee and breakfast going. He had yelled out:

'Nigger! We need the Good Doctor over at the Chambers' place, out in the field on the north side of their place. Need him bad! Matthew Chambers got run over by his tractor and we've had him out in the field since sundown last night. Can't move him 'cause one of the back plows has gouged him in the chest!'

"Old Jessup got a pan of water and a cloth and walked briskly over to a bale of hay on which sprawled the body of a still-drunk Doctor Goldman. At first he began to wash the doctor's face with a degree of care, but when he met resistance he splashed the doctor's face with the remainder of the water in the pan and then proceeded to dry it off as best he could. *'What the holy Hell?'* came the screech from Grandpa as he protested the rough and unexpected treatment from hands which usually brought him comfort from his pains and nightmares.

"Nigger calmly told him he was needed at the Chambers' place, that Matthew Chambers had got himself run over by his tractor. *'He's still under the plow, been that way since sundown yesterday.'* Nigger stressed to him.

"Grandpa never did return to Brush Lake after this incident. In fact, the tradition seemed to have faded into the mists of the lake. He did tell Daddy many years later that when he got to the field, Matthew Chambers lay under the plow, gouged by the point of the plow, and there was hardly any blood evident. His eyes were glazed as if frozen in a moment of unrestricted horror and pain. *'Thank God! I had something to give him and when it started to take effect, a smile came to Matthew's face. The neighbor men then dug him out from under the point of the plow. He let out one long sigh, and he was gone. We all removed our hats and looked skyward. I couldn't believe what I saw above: two buzzards already circling in the morning thermals, and I thought of the old rhyme that my Mama had taught me as a child: 'One for sorrow, two for joy; three for letter, four for boy; five for silver, six for gold; seven for a secret that'll never be told.' Why there were two buzzards circling, I don't know. They represented joy, so I suppose Matthew was flying to his Maker. And son, you wonder why I drink? Now you know, my boy!'"*

❧

Chapter Six

William Beatty Heart:

'His sins upon the altar of confession . . .'

"My great grandpa, Brother Billy Heart, was a poor, illiterate farm boy who realized early on that he had fifty or more years ahead of him that would be filled with back-breaking labor. His papa had scrabbled out a bare bones living on a patch of land outside Walkamile, and this *eking out a dollar with a gallon of sweat,* as he termed his hard-scrabble existence, had taken an inexorable toll both on his physicality and his mental attitude toward the world about him. At forty-plus years of age his Papa had assumed the appearance of a crotchety old man—the skin on his face and neck and the topmost part of his hands was leathery; the once bright blue of his eyes had faded; his shoulders were hunched in a manner which portrayed a total submissiveness to his environment, a complete failure in life, perhaps. I've heard family stories that my great grandpa, Brother Billy Heart, wanted no part of the world into which he had been thrust.

"Having neither the means to escape his obvious servitude nor the urging of any of his family members to do so, Billy Heart found Jesus one summer long ago at a brush arbor revival. Finding Jesus was the avenue which would lead him away from the hoeing, the chopping, the plowing and the subsequent reaping, year after year, of the crops that his papa had said from time's oldest memory *eked out a dollar with a gallon of sweat.* It had not been too difficult for Billy Heart to walk down the pine-needled covered aisle and accept Jesus Christ as his Savior. For the last couple of yards he had prostrated himself and crawled the remainder of the way to the makeshift altar where he loudly proclaimed that he was a sinner and he needed Jesus Christ to come into his life that very night. He might be poor and illiterate and without means, but he never accepted the fact that he might also be dumb. If all there was to a goal of Salvation was to put yourself in front of a bunch of other sinners and say that you were one of them . . . then Billy Heart could do that without a second thought. He had perceived in his own selfishness that when he crawled the last few yards toward the altar that that act, in itself, would open up the doors of Salvation without any hitch whatsoever. On that same night when others came forward to accept Jesus Christ, they had appeared to walk hesitatingly toward the altar with little or no conviction in their decision. Not Billy Heart!

"Now, all he had to do was to quit his papa's farm and hit the road to preach the gospel. He would have the hat passed at the tent revivals he would be invited to, and the hat would overflow with green dollars and shiny silver coins. And he would wear a white shirt and real dress trousers, and the young ladies would ogle him and whisper to each other: *'Now, isn't he a fine specimen!'* Billy Heart's immediate task, however, was to insinuate himself into the good graces of the brush arbor evangelist, Brother Andrew Cole. Deep in his craw Billy Heart knew that this might present itself as an entirely different kettle of fish. Brother Andrew Cole did not seem to be the type to suffer fools in their pursuit of the Kingdom of Heaven.

"Brother Andrew Cole had the persona of a serious-minded taskmaster. What he preached was black and white: you had to be saved and born again or you would burn in an Everlasting Hell. He emphatically preached that there were no routes other than this route to Life Everlasting through God and His Son, Jesus Christ. The path was straight and narrow. One's faith must be a total and obeisant acceptance. What Billy Heart ultimately had to do was to win the confidence of Brother Andrew Cole over the next several days remaining in the brush arbor revival. Billy Heart's early acceptance of the Way of the Lord was only a first step in what might drag out as a long process—and worse yet, a process that might fail.

"Family tales relate that there must have been some sort of Divine Intervention several days after Billy Heart had professed salvation. Billy Heart never received the Holy Ghost at the brush arbor revival. The brothers and sisters who prayed with him on his acceptance night and the nights thereafter repeatedly told him that he had to let himself go into the arms of Jesus. If he would do that, the Holy Spirit would come over him like the comfort of the Balm of Gilead. It never happened, but another event brought about the desired result Billy Heart had been seeking since the first night.

"Brother Andrew Cole had fallen violently ill and had to remain in the temporary care of the family where he was staying. He was so sick that he couldn't get out of bed. Billy Heart took it upon himself to take Brother Andrew Cole's place until he was back on his feet. Brother Cole agreed to allow Billy Heart to proceed with some reluctance and more than a tinge of doubt. For three or four nights Billy Heart conducted services that were filled with powerful singing, heart-rending confessionals, soaring testimonials and Bible readings from many revived congregants. Dozens of sinners came forward at altar call and accepted the stringent dictates of faith that Billy Heart and the others had laid down. Some of them had crawled all the way from the back row of seats in an attempt to throw their sins upon the altar of confession.

"When Brother Andrew Cole was able to return to complete the revival, his own offering hat once again began to fill with lucre. The sight of greenbacks in the hat filled his heart with a great love for the congregants. Surprisingly, those attending the nightly revival sermons had praised Billy Heart's valiant efforts to High Heaven. At that moment Brother Cole asked Billy Heart to travel with him to Hardin for the next brush arbor meeting. Billy Heart had, of a sudden, become Brother Billy Heart even though he could neither read nor write, and his only purpose in accepting Jesus Christ in the first place was so that he could escape forever the bondage and defeating atmosphere of farm life. This, indeed, was the ticket he was waiting for—a ticket out of Walkamile. The two Brothers closed the revival on a Sunday night, two weeks after they had first met each other. Brother Billy Heart still had not received the Holy Ghost, but no one, including Brother Andrew Cole, seemed to take note of that fact. The golden glow of an early Monday morning sun shone in their faces as they headed out— eastward to Hardin."

❧

Chapter Seven

Micah Abraham Jessup:

'A little bitty fish in a great big pond.'

"The white folk called him *Nigger* most of his life and, if not that, they showed a scintilla of affection and called him merely *Old Jessup*. Old Jessup was my grandfather. I loved him too much, I suppose, but he was all things to me as I grew up in a world of white folk and my own color who often did not accept me and my different ways. My own kind told me in the way that a brutish person yells at an animal that I was *uppity* and a *white nigger*. Grandpa Jessup always told me to let it roll off. *'It's one of them never-mind kind of things,'* he would say to me as he rubbed my head as he was wont to do when he needed to let me know he loved me. His serenity when untoward aspects of other folk reared their ugly heads was a lodestar, an asset, and he withdrew emotional funds from it quite often. His manner of showing his love and affection could be a light touch, a wink of an eye or a faraway smile. It could even be a deep silence. I liked it best when he rubbed my head hard.

"Abraham Jessup, that was Grandpa's full name, told me stories about his own grandpa who was born into slavery. The stories were not pretty by any stretch of the imagination, but I had to hear them. These stories were our oral histories, links to a turbulent past from which we were still trying to escape. They were my heritage, irredeemable, like it or not. My Grandpa Jessup was a prime example of the ongoing notion of slavery, but there was little of nothing that any of us could do to remedy the situation. Grandpa taught me that the condition could be alleviated, but not completely done in one fell swoop. Grandpa Jessup, along with my own father—his only son—had urged and pushed and shoved me to get all the book learning that I could. Education and patience, they both preached. Then my own Daddy, Isaac Jessup, died suddenly in a tragic drowning. In another environment I could easily have given up and dared to challenge the necessity of my planning for my own future. My future of a sudden had run a course that I had not expected. But Grandpa Jessup, as always, stayed the course and ignored the *'bump under our wagon wheel'* which he used to describe an unanticipated problem.

"Bereft, I focused my full attention on my Grandpa Jessup. He became my beacon as I muddled through my difficult teenage years made even more difficult by the loss of my father. I buried myself in books; I read everything within my reach, whether I comprehended it or not. The teachers I had at our *colored* school were not trained sufficiently to provide the academic atmosphere that we all required if we were to get ahead and break out from the repressive prisons guaranteed by a poor education. My mother, Matronella Jessup, was always in the background in her quiet, yet noble, manner. She realized her own limitations, but she could, and would, encourage me to be the one who stuck to his goals. She was never embarrassed by her shortcomings, and she was probably the first goal-oriented person I ever met, though I was not aware of it at the time. She told me once that she heard Mrs. Goldman call this good thing of setting a goal and sticking to it *stick-to-itiveness.* I was to set aside that word as my mantra in years to come and use it to beneficial effect on many occasions.

"When I completed the 8th Grade at the *colored* school, there was no high school for me to attend. Mama had a sister who lived in Houston, and they made an agreement that I would go there and live with her so I could attend one of the big Negro schools there: Phillis Wheatley High School. On the late August day that I departed by bus from Walkamile, my mother and Grandpa Jessup went with me to see me off. I only had a cardboard box with two changes of clothing in it. My two shirts had been washed, starched and ironed; and my khaki pants had been ironed to perfection. The box was tied with twine. And Mama had packed me a lunch of biscuits, fried bacon, a green onion, and a baked sweet potato. I carried it on the bus wrapped in a Mrs. Baird's bread sack.

"As the bus drove off I watched both Mama and Grandpa waving at me until they were nothing but a tiny speck on the horizon. Dear, dear Lord, did I feel lost! My rock and my anchor, respectively, would no longer be present, near at hand, to guide me as I was buffeted about. But when I arrived in Houston my Aunt Audie met me and we rode a bus all the way out to Denver Harbor to her home. That trip on the bus and the transfers we had to make alone proved to me without any lingering doubts that Aunt Audie was going to be my emotional safety net should I need one. The city of Houston didn't seem to intimidate her in the least. She had whispered to me as we sat in the back of the bus, *'Houston is just a bunch of Walkamiles laid out side by side.'*

"When I enrolled in Wheatley High School in September, I was aghast at the sheer number of students. They were everywhere! Once my classes started I found out, much to my delight and relief, that my previous eight years of study would pay off handsomely for me. I was admirably prepared to meet the challenges of a big city school. I adored my teachers, especially the calm and elegant older ladies who exuded an aura of total confidence. Their gray hair provided them with a manifestation of authority and grace. And their tortoise shell glasses were attached to lovely chains around their necks which allowed them to take them off to clarify a point of discussion during a lesson. God! I loved them all! I had one male teacher the first year. I've never forgotten him because he stressed elocution to the extreme. When he spoke, the words which came from his mouth sounded as if they all had ten syllables and one hundred letters. I had not realized that the language we uttered could sound so divinely. To hear him orate formally was a rare pleasure, and chill bumps would form up and down my spine as the prose flowed from his silken throat. My first month in the 9th Grade was what I have jokingly referred to as *Micah's Enlightenment.* He was demanding to the extreme, and if he asked a student a question that student was expected to provide him with a correct response. In addition to the correctness of the response, that student would face a thousand firing squads if he gave a mumbled response. *'El-o-cu-tion!'* he would scream, and the class would suddenly come to a stiff-backed attention.

"My mother and Grandpa Jessup traveled to Houston by bus to watch me graduate with highest honors from Wheatley High School. I'll not soon forget the tears they shed, as did I, as I walked across the stage to receive my diploma as Valedictorian. Ignoring the preset rules, I waved to them and to my Aunt Audie as I turned to join my classmates lined up on the stage. Dr. Gresham, the Superintendent, glared at me for my blatant misbehavior, but there was a twinkle of merriment in his eyes as he did so. The floodlights on the stage felt warm and fuzzy and bathed and caressed me lovingly on that May night. I knew then that education was the route I should take in my pursuit of absolute freedom. I also realized, likely for the first time, how Grandpa must feel each time one of the white folk addressed him as *Nigger.* At that moment I silently wished that I could free him. Nobody could call me *Nigger* after tonight because I was on my way to equality (or so I thought!).

"A pleasant summer at home in Walkamile where I reacquainted myself with all the pleasurable and relaxing aspects I had long taken for granted—a monstrous change from the city life with which I had become acclimated with my Aunt Audie. Those years at Wheatley High had been eye-openers for me; and I knew how blessed I truly was to have a parent and an insightful Grandpa who saw the need for a continuing education. Then came Dillard University in New Orleans and a full academic scholarship to speed me on my way. I would have to live in a dormitory (they called them *halls),* and that experience would be a novelty for me. *'Oh Lord!'* I thought with a cold touch of dread, *'I'll be a little bitty fish in a great big pond.'*

"In the truest sense of the word, if I am ever to comprehend the tangential forces which propelled me toward each plateau of my advancement, I have to view each of my actions as a stepping stone. There is no other way to analyze them. Eight grades in the humble little *colored* school in Walkamile—which seemed, at the time, like an Everest, was the initial stepping stone though I did not know it at that time. Then the major step to Wheatley High in Houston and the unanticipated trek to Dillard University was, what I surely thought to be, the final stepping stone. But as it turned out, it was not. I discovered along the circuitous pathway that the multitudinal processes of education are never-ending. Life itself becomes the final post-graduate school, and it offers no engraved and embossed diploma. As I was to appreciate from the Dillard school song, *'Thy halls where men are men and free.'* My thoughts always returned to Grandpa Jessup when I sang this line, and I knew I had loved him more than I could ever express. Perhaps I was obtaining Abraham Jessup's freedom with each unpracticed step I took."

❧

Chapter Eight

Robert E. Massey:

'The part of a pitiful old man.'

"My Grandpa, Elbridge Massey, sat me down one time and told me that he would like to have a talk with me. I was grown at the time, and I'm sure he felt comfortable in confiding in me. It had not been necessary for him to tell me his most private regrets, but he did. And it had greatly endeared him to me all the more.

"Grandpa was getting on in years (or so I thought), and what he revealed to me during his "talk" with me made me appreciate the fact that perhaps he wasn't getting on in years as much as I had thought. In fact, what he told me surprised me for a couple of reasons: Number One—why would he tell me such things? And Number Two—did any of it really matter in the grand scheme of our lives? Regardless, the following recollections have remained with me. You must remember that this was many years ago, and everyone and anyone who would be unjustifiably hurt by my revelations are long dead, I would think.

"Grandpa spoke as if these past events had only happened yesterday. He did not speak as if in an atoning confessional, more so as a modest narrator of pertinent historical events which involved our family. He began in a soft voice, tremulous at times, and then his voice and his mannerisms seemed to drift back to another time, but took on a commanding timbre with resoluteness in each of his movements. In the beginning a pensive, if troubled, look captured his outward countenance, but in a reflective moment both his facial expressions and his voice took on the aura and resonance of a happier time. Or that was my assumption, rightly or wrongly.

"He began: *'I will never make disparagin' remarks about your Grandma. When I married her, she was a fine, upstandin' young woman. And when she died after our happy years of marriage, she remained one of the finest human beings that God put here on the face of the Earth. None of what I am about to tell you should lessen your love and respect for that good woman. She had nothin'—absolutely nothin', not a whit—to do with what I did. I was fully responsible for my actions, and they was never motivated by any thought of revenge to get even with her for any transgression she may have aspired to against me. She was not a helpmate of that sort.'*

"He had continued after some additional thought: *'I was cursed in a way with my job as postman for the rural route in and around Walkamile. I got to know people intimately, too intimately to suit me when you get right down to brass tacks. But that was part of the job—being a good, helpful neighbor. For some I was the lifeline: pickin' up a dose of medicine prescribed by Doctor Goldman at Carter's Drug Store and takin' with me on my route and deliverin' it to a sick person on my route. Another would meet me at their mailbox and ask me to deliver a mess of squash to Old Mrs. So-and-So who needed more than squash. And there was the lonely old souls who used my assured presence as their company each weekday about the same time. They had no one else in their lives, and I kept a passel of junky mail so that I could hand them somethin'—anything to bring them a bit of pleasure in their miserable existence. The requests went on and on.*

'*Then one day in the early 30s I was met at her mailbox by Etta Dykes. This didn't figure out at all to me. Etta and Clayton Dykes had everything material. They lacked for nothin', and here she was at her mailbox requestin' information about subscribin' to one of the Houston papers. Then one passin' thing led to another passin' thing. Etta Dykes used her charity givin' as an excuse to get me into her house. Before all of this started her charity bundles had been delivered by one of their flunkies. Now I was involved for whatever reasons. The handwritin' on the wall should have screamed out at me, but maybe I didn't want it to. Maybe I wanted to get involved, I've told myself a hundred times over. Maybe things at home wasn't what I thought them cracked up to be though I thought I was happy. Maybe I wasn't.*'

"I had not said a word as the old fellow was relating this to me in his roundabout way. As I listened, I had no inkling where any of this was going. Then he broke the silence: '*The Old Devil works in more mysterious ways than the Good Lord. First thing you know, Etta Dykes and I began participatin' in a dance-with-the-Devil. At first, our entanglements happened every couple of weeks. Then I think the Old Devil really took over, and we just had to see each other at least once a week. It was do or die. Etta's charitable works picked up quite a bit for more than obvious reasons. We were in too far, too deep. We couldn't reverse the course of our actions and return to what we both had once known even if we had wanted to. I don't think Clayton Dykes never smelled a rat, but we did have some close shavin's. He probably wouldn't have cared even if he had 'cause he was so busy with his own shenanigans. His dalliances was known all over the county. But—let me make a point: this give me or Etta no right to hurt our own partners in life and carry on as we did.*'

"I was bursting to ask a question, so I interrupted him, '*What happened to bring an end to all of this?'*

"His voice broke a bit as he answered: *'Etta died suddenly during the war, close to the end of the war, and it didn't take no time 'til her corpse was hustled off to Houston to be buried. I had been with her just the day before she died, and it was hard for me to believe that anything was wrong with her. She was alive and well on that day, not sick at all. And I've never heard what the reason for her untimely death was. Clayton Dykes has influence enough to keep stuff like that closed to the public, I suppose. And even if you had wanted to know and could find out, somebody somewhere would get word to him that you had been snoopin' about. My thought is that she was murdered by Clayton—or he had the deed done for some reason other than her and I bein' on such good terms. I see dollar signs in the picture somewhere. You and me will never know. Dollar signs carry weight, lots of weight—lots of weight!'*

"Why are you telling me this, Grandpa?" I had to ask.

"He looked at me for the longest moment. Then he almost whispered, *'Son, I want you to know that everyone you will meet in life is an imperfect creature. Everyone you know and will get to know as you walk the pathway of life is a sinner. Some are bigger sinners than others. I'm a big sinner. Your Grandma, who I believed to be a saint, was a woman who prayed to God to forgive her of her sins on a daily basis. I never knew what her sins could be. I didn't witness any. Oh, on a rare occasion she would have a hissy—I called them shit hissies, not to her face, of course, but when it was over, it was over, and she went on with her daily life. But she still asked God to forgive her. I have never asked God to forgive me, but I can ask you to forgive me for doin' what I did and for burdenin' you with the details of my misspent ways. Will you do that?'* As he asked the last question, he slumped over in the recliner, and he looked the part of a pitiful old man.

"There were tears in the old man's eyes. I reached out with both of my arms spread wide open, then encircled his head and shoulders with my arms and pulled him from his slumping position and held him to my chest. He sobbed, noticeable guttural sounds coming from deep within him. I continued holding him until he calmed. I then whispered to him, *'I love you, Grandpa. Thank you for sharing your problems with me and asking me for forgiveness. I have nothing to forgive you for, but do know that I love you and I loved Grandma as much.'*

"That meeting seems so long ago. It comes back to me blow-by-blow each time I stand at the foot of their graves each year at our Cedar Grove Cemetery working. I could swear that as I am standing there, I can hear both their voices on the wind. It is a reassuring sound I hear. There are isolated moments when I can almost sense their bodily presence, but I am brought back to reality by knowing that this cannot be so. By the same token, I feel compelled at times to reach up and thrust my hands into low-lying clouds seeking out a physical indication that they are near."

◎

Chapter Nine

Charity Chambers:

'I'm sorry I called it a nigger shooter.'

"Stace Wellborn was my bachelor uncle who continued to live on his family's place after his folks, my grandparents, both fell victim to the ravages of a virulent flu. He was eighteen when they died within two days of each other, and my Mama, Verity (Wellborn) Chambers could not, by hook or crook, talk him into coming to live with us. Even my Daddy, Matthew Chambers, assured him a paying job on our farm and promised him that he would teach him how to drive our tractor. No amount of coaxing would budge him from his decision, and he remained alone on his family's place. There was no way that he could farm what land his folks had under cultivation, tend to the cows and hogs, maintain the garden that produced a substantial portion of their livelihood and see to the constant demands of their orchard. And the paper shell pecan trees that Grandpa had treasured and coddled as if they were helpless children were an entirely different matter and were, in effect, a full-time job.

"Three years after Grandma and Grandpa had succumbed to the flu my Daddy, Matthew Chambers, was killed by his own tractor. He had lain under the back plow from near sunset until a little after daybreak when neighbors were finally able to find Dr. Goldman.

Stace had sat on the ground throughout the long night as close as he could to Matthew. As the night wore on he would whisper into Matthew's unhearing ears, *'This woudna happened if I'd-a took you up on your offer. It's all my fault, Matthew. It's all my fault! Somewhere there was a voice tellin' me to move in with y'all. But oh no! I'm a stubborn one. I'm a stubborn one, and now look what my stubborness has brung on. God forgive me! God forgive me!'* Other neighbors gathered about the accident scene chided Stace gently with *'Hush, Stace! What happened was an accident. It's not your fault! Matthew don't need to hear none of that kind of talk right now. Be cheerful with him, talk to him about all the good times y'all have had.'*

"In the darkness of the poorly lighted background, Verity Chambers, Matthew's wife and my mother, held on tightly to my hand. A lantern's light, fluttering in the soft night breeze, showed a face stretched taut in disbelief. Neighbor women had begged Verity to let them take her home where she could get some rest. *'The Good Doctor Goldman will be here in a little bit. He'll fix up everything just fine, and you'll need to have your strength to see to Matthew. He's in a shape that he's goin' to need your special care for a long, long time.'* They all knew they were lying through the teeth, but reassuring words were all they had in their empathy arsenal at this time. Verity had not cried one tear, her shattered spirit long spent from the outright shock of seeing someone she loved so much dying by slow degrees right before her eyes. And she was helpless to do anything. Her friends had done all within their power to keep her away from direct exposure to the tableau that was being played out just a few feet away.

"When my Mama and Daddy had married, they felt that they could conquer the world as long as they stuck together. They were a team, united by each other's heart. All of their personal, financial decisions were jointly made. One partner would never commit to any action without consulting the other partner. Some of the neighbors thought my Daddy was henpecked, but little did they know that he was a fifty-fifty partner in all aspects of their lives. It was never a consideration that something was a *Matthew thing* or a *Verity thing;* it always had to be looked at, regardless of what it was about, as a *Matthew-Verity thing.* They were teammates.

"When Nigger and Dr. Goldman, along with their hung-over but subdued entourage, drove up the road adjoining the Chambers' property, a sustaining murmur of relief went through those gathered around the tractor. Dr. Goldman approached briskly, took my mother's hand and spoke softly to her, *'I'll see what I can do, ma'am.'* From only a few feet away he could easily determine that the situation was hopeless. *'Hand me my bag, Jessup.'* While he waited for his bag, he chose not to betray any preconceived medical assessments he may have already concluded. Old Jessup, with the tactful delicacy of a practiced professional, placed the black bag to the Doctor's right and unsnapped the latch at the top of the bag as quietly as he could. Doctor Goldman knelt on the soft ground and proceeded to find a needle and a vial sealed in a sanitary packaging. He next poured alcohol on both his hands, and Old Jessup tore open a second package and, without touching the heretofore undisturbed contents, held the white cloth so that the Doctor could wipe his hands. Old Jessup then ripped open another package, and the Doctor pulled the two rubber gloves out and onto his hands, struggling with getting the glove on his right hand. He next tapped the vial and inserted the needle into it, slowly drawing out the viscous liquid. Wiping Matthew Chamber's left arm with alcohol, he inserted the needle which released the liquid slowly. In an instant a wan smile came to my Daddy's face, and he looked around his newly-found environment with unseeing eyes.

"Doctor Goldman gave instructions to the men to dig my father out gently. *'Use all the caution you can muster to see that Matthew is not damaged any more than is absolutely practicable. Think of it as using kid gloves.'* When all of the surrounding soil had been scooped out by hand, several pairs of hands pulled my father out from under the plow. Stace was at the forefront of this agonizing activity. When my Daddy was cleared from a pinned and gouged position that he had been in for over twelve hours, I noticed a faint smile on his face. He seemed to sigh just as Mama and I approached him, and then he was gone—finally at peace. The men about removed their hats in a show of respect and stood silently. I even heard a manly sob coming from one in the group of men. There were several stifled gasps from some of our neighbor women. Doctor Goldman looked skyward and commented in an aside to Old Jessup about seeing two buzzards which he said were a sign of joy. I had no idea what he meant by his remark. I was not capable of experiencing any trace of joy with what I had witnessed throughout the long night. And the scene now brought no sense of joy to me.

"Doctor Goldman walked to where Mama and I were standing rigid like stone sentinels. He took Mama's left hand and my right hand in his own large hands. He held them for a long time, pressing them perhaps to impress upon us that he had tried mightily but had failed miserably to save Daddy. *'Matthew was too far gone. The finest medical team in our great country could not have saved him. I did all I could and wish that I could have done a lot more. I must reassure you that Matthew was in no pain during the long night. Our Great God was a marvelous Creator when he designed the human body. Your beloved Matthew went into a state of shock within seconds after the accident. His system protected him against what would have been an insufferable pain. God bless you all. Feel free to call on me if I can help any of you.'* He then handed Mama a small bottle of pills. *'Each of you take one of these tonight when you go to bed. It's a sedative to make you rest. And you both need rest.'* He motioned to Old Jessup, and the two walked off in the direction of the Doctor's car parked on the road at the end of the field. Their exit had all the appearances of a practiced ritual which the two of them must have done a thousand times before.

"After this terrible accident Stace, with some reluctance, agreed to come live with us and help us. He had protested, *'I don't want to be no burden on y'all.'* Mama gave him a room all to himself, and he seemed to fit in real well at the beginning. In the next several years he deteriorated, slowly at first and then more rapidly, both in mind and spirit. Where he was once robust, a strapping specimen of a young man, he became oldish in many ways long before his time. His attention span became erratic and at times almost non-existent; he became unreliable as to our expectations in the performance of assigned duties. In essence, he became a burden, heavy and constant, to my mother and me—the very thing that he had worried about when he made his decision to come live with us.

"He let his hair grow to the point that he looked like a mountain man, and he refused to shave. Mama teased him in the way that sisters can tease brothers, *'Stace, you look like a woolly mammoth. And I thought that they had become extinct millions of years ago. If you start growing ivory tusks I'll have to think about sending you to a museum in some big city.'* The slightest smile would crease what little part of his face that could be seen, and then he would assume his regular blank pose. His decline seemed to pattern itself against the hands of time—a languid spiral of complexity unraveling before our very eyes.

"The final blow was when he refused to bathe, claiming vociferously that he was afraid he would be drowned by the spirits in the water. *'I can see them in the water and they are a-starin' at me with eyes as big as goggle-eyed perch,'* he told us as if he were reciting the first line of a child's fairy tale. My mother and I knew something ominous and unexplainable was happening to him, but we hardly knew how to help him. When he started seeing tiny, sparkling angels hovering in all the trees during the day and red and black devils flying through rings of fire in his room at night, we both decided that professional assistance had to be sought. He needed help that we could not even attempt to offer, and he needed it soon. We both recalled Doctor Goldman's offer to us to call on him if we ever needed any help. We desperately needed him now.

"Mama and I went to see Doctor Goldman. We told him everything we knew about Stace, not holding back one small detail. To make sure that we did not forget anything, both of us made lists to remind us when we met with Doctor Goldman. And Doctor Goldman listened attentively, taking extensive notes, and then he told us what we expected to hear but had prayed we would not: *'Ma'am, it's likely your brother is insane. Whether this is circumstantial from what has happened to him up to this point in his life or whether it is an inherited trait is open to supposition.'*

"Mama had asked the Doctor what he would recommend. The Good Doctor Goldman had been blunt in his answer: *'Ma'am, I am not a psychiatrist. I'm a humble country doctor. But you and your daughter can't take care of Stace based on what you have told me. I'd highly recommend that you pursue having him committed to a state mental facility. I can get the process started for you, if you like. Whether he can be helped by them or not is beyond my scope of practice. We can hope that he can be helped. We can hope this together and also hope that we live to see the day when he can be returned to you a well man. Just let me know when you've taken the necessary time to make a decision. Don't rush it unless you feel that you are being threatened, which I don't think you are.'*

"The Good Doctor's words were like a thunderclap on an otherwise clear day. Three weeks later, after Mama had cried, cursed, prayed and stayed awake for nights on end, she had made her decision. There were moments during this period that she had come close to cursing God for her troubles and everything that He represented. She had screamed out, *'First You take my Matthew, allowing him to suffer way too much, and now You burden me with sending my own baby brother to a nut house. What kind of God are You? Tell me, God!'* Her brief screaming session over, she bent double in her chair and sobbed until she had no more tears to shed. When she reached the point of not being able to cry anymore, she sat in her chair and shook all over. Then her entire body stiffened as if to signal to the world about her that she had spent her last traces of emotion.

"Two weeks after her screaming tirade against God, the Sheriff and a Deputy had driven up with Doctor Goldman, and they had taken an unresisting, dirty, disheveled Stace Wellborn away. As he was placed in the back seat of the Sheriff's car, I looked at him, tears streaming down my face, and I saw a completely broken young man who looked twice his age.

"So many thoughts raced through my mind: Was this the same uncle who had taught me how to shoot a rifle? Was this the uncle who taught me everything I could possibly know about fishing for catfish? Would this be the uncle who taught me how to play dominoes and somehow always let me beat him badly when we were playing for matches? Was this the same uncle who taught me how to make a nigger shooter? And when I had successfully made one, I reminded him that Mama said we should call it a slingshot and not embarrass our family by using that other word. He had grinned broadly at me and had apologized inappropriately, *'I'm sorry I called it a nigger shooter.'* We both laughed at his slip-up.

These fleeting thoughts now passed, and I realized that this was my Uncle Stace being taken away from us—a mere child-like being in a man's body.

"Try as I might, I could not picture Stace when he had been in fine fettle. I had a fear that picture would never return to me. And I looked at Mama and saw an abject look of total loss on her countenance that came close to matching the look on her face when my Daddy had been killed by the tractor. Mama's eyes were dry as she watched the three men drive away with Stace. Mama had cried her heart and soul out long before this moment. She had no more tears to shed now that she had committed the final betrayal of her baby brother. Her emotional well dry, she took one last look at the disappearing car and then went into the house and sat in her chair, both of her hands tightly clutching the arm rests. *'I have failed twice, my child,'* she mouthed to me as she held on to the arm rests even more tightly. In the desolation of my own inner spirit, I discovered that I could come up with not one word of solace for my Mama or myself. I, too, had failed."

❦

Chapter Ten

Mavis Murray:

'*Krauts are Germans . . . because they eat so much cabbage.*'

"When I was a little girl, six or seven years old I suppose, I seem to recall that I had always been called Mavis Philbin. Even before I started school, my mother and grandmother had taught me the alphabet and how to print and spell my name, and I could count to a hundred frontward and backwards. My mother had hardly enrolled me in the first grade when I was confronted with learning to spell my new last name: *Murray.* Whatever it was that transpired between my mother and my first grade teacher, Mrs. Oostrook, all of it happened behind the scenes. I was suddenly (one Monday morning) moved from the Ps to the Ms in the seating arrangement of our first grade class. Mrs. Oostrook did not bother to offer an explanation to me or to the class. I suppose kids that age pay little attention to changes which do not affect them directly. So . . . I became a Murray with little or no fanfare. I had this terrible feeling that I should start acting like a different person since I had a new last name. Inside myself, I didn't feel different. My clothes and shoes were the same as they had been when I walked into my first grade room to my regular seat. My hair felt the same on my head. Everything I saw as I looked around, looked the same as it had a few minutes before. The only change I really noticed was that the girl in front of me now had on a red plaid dress where only a while ago I had been staring at a boy's back that was covered with a blue shirt.

"And at home I was suddenly and efficiently moved out of the comfort and security of my mother's bedroom to a tiny elongated cubicle off a hallway leading to the back porch. A cot type bed with a thin mattress and an ugly green blanket greeted me. I had to place my extra clothes in a box beneath the bed. There was no storage space for anything else unless you could count a big old nail for hanging my coat in a nearby corner. And worse yet, a man moved in with my mother. His name was Adrian J. Murray. He had not taken the room I always called *Uncle Jeremiah's Room.* That room remained empty until Uncle Jeremiah came home for short visits from his oil field job in Kilgore.

"My mother finally took me aside one day and suggested that we go out on the porch for a little girl-to-girl talk. We both sat in a double swing which wouldn't swing anymore if two people were occupying it. I was surprised and a bit perplexed (as would any seven-year old child who had been suddenly uprooted from a status quo environment). The news, if you can call it that, was terribly, terribly confusing to say the least. I have to stress that I was a frightened seven-year old kid at that time, and my recall of what my mother told me will, of necessity, be embellished by my own childish interpretation of that talk. But do let me tell you, I can remember it—most of it—because I was scared to death that my mother was going to tell me that she was going to send me away to a home for orphaned children because I thought I had suddenly become one.

"With some delicacy, my mother began to talk to me: *'Mavis,'* she began, *'a child your age should not be expected to understand everything about their short life. I'll try with my best efforts to explain to you why your life and mine have changed with the arrival of Ad'* (I learned later that this was my mother's affectionate nickname for Adrian). This is the moment that I almost started to shake, cold-like chills coming over me.

"She had looked at me with a piercing stare and then continued her talk: *'It happens, child, that your mother made a mistake seven years ago. At least that's what our society calls it, but I don't agree because that mistake brought you, my sweetheart, into my life. I don't see how you could be called a mistake. And I've never thought much about what this tacky little society in Walkamile thinks. They hoot and holler at the drop of a hat, ready to criticize everybody but their own little knittin' club. Ad and me used to date many years ago, and when we realized that he was to be drafted for the war, our lives changed almost overnight. We knew it might be years before we saw each other again, especially if Ad had to be shipped overseas to fight the Japs or the Nazis. I had prayed to God that Ad would not have to go to the war 'cause he never did learn to read or write or even learn his sums. But I don't think God pays much attention to greedy prayers like I prayed. We were madly in love, me and Ad, and in the confusion of the moment, we both allowed our weaknesses to take charge. We couldn't hold back. No, we couldn't hold back at all even though both of us heard a little voice tellin' us to.*

'Darling, I can't come out and explain it to you in plain old black and white, but that's when you come into the picture. Ad and me had agreed to be married when he got his guaranteed leave after his basic trainin' in El Paso, but due to some foul-up he didn't get leave and ended up gettin' shipped overseas to England without bein' able to come home. That's the Army for you, dead sure. There I was: gettin' ready to have you and I wasn't married. This little community of Walkamile don't take kindly to unmarried women havin' babies without a professin' husband about. But I said to

your real unhappy grandmother, what the heck! I'll have the child, and to Hell with them all and the horses they rode in on and the Injun that followed! And then you arrived. Your own grandmother and me both were overjoyed to have a beautiful little girl in the house with us.

'Your grandmother was not a pleasant person when she first learned of my condition, but when you come on the scene, she was as happy as a springtime lark. And Ad, your Daddy, didn't even know about you. I tried to get his military address but his Mama wouldn't have no part of it. She did tell me that Ad had been sent to England, last she heard, and I could start lookin' for him there. Now tell me, dear child, how was a poor soul like me goin' to go to England to look for a soldier boy? The higher-ups would most rightly laugh their behinds off if I had dared to try!

'And Ad wouldn't write because he didn't know how. I guess he was too proud to get one of them USO ladies to write for him. I don't know. Maybe there was no USO lady where he was. I don't know, but you come into our lives and I give you our last name: Philbin.

'Oh, dear child, the neighbors talked blue streaks about me, but I've got tough skin like my own Mama. The silly old bags was all about and looked at you and clucked like a bunch of old settin' hens long past layin' age and said foolish things like, 'Oh, what a pretty one! You know she looks just like you. I couldn't tell for the life of me who her Daddy was. She is a Philbin out-and-out, that's for sure!' I could've spit nails at them, but I didn't. I just give a ignorant lookin' grin to the old witches. And your Uncle Jeremiah would beat the livin' Hell out of any man that had any designs on bringin' up the subject. So at this point you become Mavis Philbin.'

"I had sat through all of this in a fog (as would any child); her ramblings seemed to swallow me one moment, and then they would lift me at another moment and give me hope; and I would think that I understood some of what my mother was telling me. But I know I was not understanding everything she was telling me. Deep down, I wished that she wouldn't tell me anything. I felt that it might be easier that way. If I didn't know anything, I didn't have to understand anything. I'd be a real happy little girl if I could just return to our lives before any of this started up. Much later in life, I was to learn that familiarity brought a degree of comfort to me. As this innocent little child hearing all of this, I could not even try to find my earlier taste of security and comfort which had been the cornerstones of my short life.

"Then my mother continued her confusing, often rambling, story: *'Not long ago I got a letter from some government official who had a Washington, D.C. address, Department of Something-or-the-Other. Real official lookin' letter. This man, a Mr. Albert Switchman, informed me that Adrian J. Murray had asked him to contact me to inform me that he had been a prisoner-of-war in a German Stalag (I didn't know what that stood for) and had underwent mental and physical rehabilitation successfully. My name had been entered on the records as his wife. They was wantin' to release him to his next-of-kin. That was me, I guess. This was all a bit puzzlin' to me 'cause when Ad went to the Service I know he knew that he didn't have no wife. And the uppity-ups must have his records and would know that he was a single man.*

'Dear child, it is no wonder that Ad didn't write to me. I found out that a stalag was a prison camp, and I can't tell you how bad Krauts can treat prisoners. Krauts are Germans and they're called that because they eat so much cabbage. I read that somewhere. I wrote this Mr. Albert Switchman the best letter I could and told him that I was happy to finally get some news of my husband. Would he be so kind to get Adrian home to me, I had wrote. Three weeks later Ad showed up at the bus station, and to me it seemed just like it was

*yesterday all over again. This Mr. Switchman had sent a telegram
to me in care of the Walkamile Post Office informin' me of Ad's trip
home and when he would arrive. I wanted to go to the bus station
ever mornin' but good common sense made me stay put until the
right day.'*

"The mental fog was getting thicker as I understood less and less
of what my mother was attempting to tell me. She had used words I
had never heard of: rehab-something, mental, Krauts and so many
more. Then she started to talk again: *'When I got over my cryin' jag
at the bus station, Ad and me went inside and got us some coffee.
We sat there for hours just talkin'. Poor Ad was flabbergasted when
I told him he was the daddy of a pretty seven-year old girl. He kept
sayin' No! No! No! No! But I kept tellin' him it was true. He was a
real-live daddy, and didn't even know it. I think he was real happy
to learn about you—in fact, I know he was very, very happy. I could
see it in his eyes—they sparkled when I talked about our little
Mavis. We kept orderin' more coffee as if that would solve all of the
problems in our new-found lives. I was surprised Ad didn't smoke,
'cause if he had or if I had smoked, we'd have lit up that place with
trails of smoke.'*

"My mother sat very quietly for a spell, and then she began her
ending comments: *'Ad and me wanted you to have a real Daddy
and a real last name, so a bit later we went to the Courthouse and
got our marriage license. We waited several days and then had a
J.P. marry us. It was a quick thing for us—not quick when you think
that it took over seven years! And I had lived in sin for seven years
accordin' to the old bags here in Walkamile. Then Ad started askin'
about how we get your name changed to Murray, and we got the
County Judge to help us with that. The Judge speeded it up when he
found out that Ad was a prisoner-of-war—a "hero" he called Ad!
So child, Ad is your real Daddy, a real hero, and I hope you can*

learn to love him as much as I do. I know you will.'

"At that point in time I gave no fragment of a thought to loving a total stranger. He had arrived on our happy little scene and had severely interrupted our lives—all of us. I was going to be uprooted from my happy little nest that I shared with my mother; I had been moved from the Ps to the Ms in my first grade class. And my mother wanted me to love this stranger: my real Daddy, a war hero. Before any of this happened, if I had come face to face with him on the dusty little streets in Walkamile, I wouldn't have paid no mind to him at all. But he was my Daddy! This was going to take a lot of getting used to on my part. Remember, I was only seven years old at the time, and my mother had, like it or not, placed this heavy, heavy burden on me.

"Next thing you know—that's when I got moved pretty quick to the little bed near the hallway to the back porch. I now had a Daddy. The mental fog around me was still as thick as ever. I thought to myself, *'How can you go seven years without a Daddy and then wake up one morning and have a Daddy?'* There was something strange going on in our house, and I didn't understand any of it. My mother and Ad whispered to each other most of the time, and they giggled way too much when they thought no one was paying them any mind. My grandmother moved about the house nervously at all hours of the day and night. It seemed that she shuffled her feet to let us know she was approaching. And she forever looked over her shoulder with a frightened look on her face if she heard a sudden, unrecognized noise.

"And when Uncle Jeremiah came home from the oil fields, he would huddle with my grandmother and then my mother (when Ad was not present), and they would whisper to each other for long periods of time. As a child in the middle of all this whispered secrecy, I had no idea what they were talking about, but I felt uneasy and uncomfortable because I had sense enough to know that they were talking about something very strange and foreboding—and truly something they didn't want me to know about at all. I worried that their whisperings was about me, and that perturbed me even more than it should have. It would develop that many years would pass before I learned of the nature of their horrific whisperings. What I would learn would not even be believable under the best of circumstances. Too bizarre to accept at first blush, it would color my own existence in a manner that would eventually push me in a spiraling whirlwind to the edge of my own sanity and well-being."

ॐ

Chapter Eleven

Robert E. Massey:

'Oh, the humanity and all the passengers.'

"Etta Dykes had followed the Hauptmann trial almost religiously to its conclusion, but yet she hungered for more news of the famous Lindbergh family. She subscribed to those news magazines which she felt would provide her glimpses into the lives of the many famous Americans whether they be movie stars or just rich, well-known personalities. She found, much to her dislike, that the Hollywood stars were too controlled by the big Jewish movie companies. Any tidbit that affected their leading stars would be manipulated from the time it was approved for release until the exact moment the same was to appear in a news publication or one of the popular movie magazines. Etta had expressed her opinions on this to my Grandpa many times: *'Movie stars might as well be prostitutes or slaves for what little freedoms they have.'*

"My Grandpa Massey told me that her overzealous embracing of such crap as this irritated him to no end. He contended with it because it became a part of the package that came with the attentions volunteered by Etta Dykes. *'No sooner had the Lindbergh kidnapper/killer been executed than she got on the Hindenburg kick. That's all I could hear when I could get her to herself. She even mimicked the radio announcer:* "It's burst into flames . . . Get out of the way, please, oh my, this is terrible . . . Oh, the humanity and all the passengers." *'She wanted me to congratulate her on her fine dramatic renderin' of the radio announcer's words, and I would, of course, silly fool that I was becomin'. And then we would have our little diversion, and I'd be on my way.*

'Thank God, this Hindenburg thing didn't last too long, but then if I am to be damned to Hell, Amelia Earhart disappeared somewhere over the Pacific Ocean. If I remember, that happened in the summer of 1937, and she talked about it off and on until she died. I've thanked God a thousand and one days that she never got interested in Wallis Simpson and that mousey little King of England that she whored around with. Etta would have exhausted me to the bone if she got interested in that. Why, they even went over to Germany to see Hitler, and Etta paid it no never-mind. I've never been able to fathom why one silly thing caught her eye and another went by her without one little remark on her part. Womenfolk are funny that way.'

"Grandpa, over the course of the following years up to the beginning of America's involvement in World War II, continued to rendezvous with Etta Dykes. Their routine became almost predictable to them. It had not aroused undue attention from any of the neighbors, and likely Clayton Dykes could have cared the less if, indeed, he had known. The location of the Dykes' house, the approaching road ending at a cul-de-sac at the front of the home, provided a degree of security with the massive trees that bordered the road. Neighbors, too far away to observe the comings and goings, paid little attention to a mail truck which came by every weekday at its usual and predictable time. Had there been another vehicle, the neighbors might have taken note.

"Grandpa chuckled when he told me what all he had learned

about Amelia Earhart. *'Hell! I learned what her middle name was and I learned that she was born in Kansas. I even found out from Etta that she had at least two nicknames which her family used. I think one of them was "Meeley." Even her sister had a nickname— Pidgeon, or Pidge, I forget which. I learned that her family moved to somewhere in Iowa and maybe on to Minnesota. So much crap to listen to just so I could get a little favor every week or so! I look back on all that now and know that Etta could have talked about anything under the sun, and I would have listened—actin' interested like. What a fool we each had to be! It might've been easier if we had just got it on like animals and then go our separate ways until next time. It's easy to look back; it's hard to look forward; and now I don't even think about lookin' at all. I'm too damned old to care! Or to look!'*

"Grandpa often reminisced about other topics which entered their relationship. The Amelia Earhart interest on Etta's part, though consuming at times, began to fade away in the late summer of 1939 when Nazi Germany invaded Poland; and then the following year France fell to the Nazis. *'Etta was shocked when she read of the fall of Poland that the Nazis had accomplished in just a few days. She was ecstatic when she learned what the German word "blitzkrieg" meant, but when France fell to the Nazis the followin' year, she became solemn. She had looked at me in the silly girlish manner that she often affected and had asked me:* "You won't go to war, will you Elbridge?" *I told her, God, woman! I'm too old to fight all them young'ns. And America don't plan to go to war. We're peace-lovin' men over here. Out of the blue comes Pearl Harbor, a place nobody in their right mind had heard of, and before you could count to ten—war, war, war! That Roosevelt bastard had it planned all along. Etta would wring her hands and want to talk about everything under the sun when we got together.*

Over and over I had to tell her we didn't have much time. We had to get on with it, and she would agree and in the middle of our little set-to she'd start talkin' about Norway or Finland or Denmark or somebody's son who had been on Pearl Harbor and was lost on December 7. And she worried about the Jews over in Europe. What we ended up getting' out of our little weekly ritual boiled down to nothin' more than a physical release, but like trapped fools we kept on keepin' on. It's a hundred wonders we didn't get caught more than once, but we never did even get caught once—fools in fools' clothin'!'

"One of the most ironic things that Grandpa ever brought up during our many conversations was his revelation that Etta and Clayton Dykes had invited Grandma and him to a Christmas-type supper at their home about a week before Christmas. Grandpa could remember that it was December, 1941, because Pearl Harbor was fresh on his mind, and America had already stepped into the war a week or so before.

"Etta had done the whole affair up right: she had mailed an invitation to Grandma and Grandpa. The invitation had noted the exact date, the Saturday before Christmas, and the time (6:00 PM, he recalled); and Grandma and Grandpa had, for no obvious reason, thought that there would be other neighbors in attendance. Were they ever wrong! Grandma Massey had formally accepted the invitation by return mail. It turned out that they were the only guests!

"Grandpa told me it was a bit hard at times to act *natural* in the presence of Clayton Dykes. He said he had had to guard his every word and had been forced to control his facial expressions when, and if, he looked at Etta or even at Grandma, for that matter. The evening was made a little more comfortable by several generous slugs of Clayton Dykes' good bourbon, but even so, according to

Grandpa, he felt compelled to exercise more caution after his couple of drinks. *'Your Grandma enjoyed herself to the hilt; and she and Etta made plans to work together in the comin' year on charitable causes. Clayton seemed to take all of the conversations at face value and gave little in return,'* Grandpa had revealed. *'I was taken aback that Etta and your Grandma hit it off like they appeared to do,'* he had explained to me in afterthought.

"I have to state that I never intentionally initiated these conversations with Grandpa. He would start his reminiscing, and I would be caught up in his storytelling before I could escape from him. Vicariously, I did not wish to escape. One day he started a conversation, and his opening line was: *'My whole bein' changed the day that I learned Etta had died. My whole bein' left me, and I was only part of a man.'* Tears had come to his eyes as he declared that he had become *'only part of a man.'*

"Looking at him, I suddenly realized how fragile he had become both physically and spiritually. I could easily picture myself several decades hence what with the endearing portrait of an old man now before my very own eyes. I viewed myself as a carbon copy of the old gentleman minus the scores of years he had on me. For the briefest instant, an epiphany of sorts in the form of a stunning thought beset me: *'The fruit never falls far from the tree.'* For the oddest of reasons I then laughed aloud at this totally unrelated and equally asinine thought I had just had."

Chapter Twelve

Koskobe Renner:

'And she would call me Mr. Jessup.'

"I made it through the war okay, and Daddy didn't have to go down to the courthouse and look at a list to see if there was a *Renner* on the list, worse yet a *Renner* with the first name *Koskobe.* I don't even know if there was any courthouse list during World War II. I had heard tell of telegrams being sent from the War Department about soldiers suffering injury or death on some faraway battlefield.

"My little brother, Bob, got called up near the end of the war, and he also got through it without a scratch. He was a scrappy and gung-ho little shit, so different from me and almost a twin version of our Daddy. Everybody said I was a copy of Daddy, but I could see so much of Daddy in my little brother.

"Anna, my sister, got a job at the San Jacinto Ordnance facility near Houston, and she always felt that she had contributed to the war effort as best she could. I never did quite understand what she did at the Ordnance, but I think it had to do with weapons storage or something like that. Her job classification did require some degree of a security clearance, so it must have had some importance attached to it. Neighbors' tongues started wagging when government men come nosing around in Walkamile asking a bunch of loaded questions about Anna. These same tongue-waggers thought Anna was in trouble, but, of course, she wasn't. They were just checking her out for a security clearance. After the war, Anna would never elaborate on her war work other than to tell people when they asked that she had worked at *The Ordnance,* as she called it with obvious affection.

"Mama died during the war, and we all got compassion leaves, and Anna was able to get a few days off from her job. Daddy was as lost as could be, like a baby lamb that had strayed from its mother, when he came to the full realization that he no longer had a helpmate like Mama. Almost overnight he became a different person both in his physical appearance and in his mental attitudes.

"I think all of us kids had not appreciated the things that Mama had done for us all. At Mama's wake we talked with considerable appreciation and affection about these things: her Monday washings which consumed her from dawn to dusk, her Tuesday ironing that saw her standing at the ironing board for hours on end, her Wednesday cleaning of the house from one end to the other, her Thursday set aside for the multitude of outside chores (raking, hoeing the garden, working in the flower beds, cleaning out the chicken coops, horse and mule stalls, etc.), her Friday baking for the weekend and part of the next week, her Saturday preparations for the Sunday dinners that we had taken for granted over the years. All of these duties were conducted without Mama having any sort of electrical appliance to aid her. It would be many years later before we got electricity.

"The rules and the general atmosphere of our home changed on Sundays. On Sunday Mama went to church, often without Daddy, and us kids were forced to tag along dressed in our Sunday best: Anna in a starched print dress, a matching bow in her hair and a white lacy handkerchief in her hand; I was expected to wear my only suit coat and a white shirt that was beginning to feel too tight around my neck, and poor Bob ended up with hand-me-downs. Anna once jokingly told him that he looked like a little tramp all dressed up with no train to catch! He cried for a long time and then told on her. Mama was not too happy when any one of us tattled on the other.

"Our quartet was a common sight as we headed out by foot or by wagon to the Walkamile Christian Church. We all laughed when Anna reminded us that us three kids would pray for rain so that we wouldn't have to go to church. I recalled that our prayers didn't seem to get answered much because I remembered more times going to church than not! I also recall that the church benches were hard as rocks, and we were expected to be quiet and reverent during the long, long services. Our sore butts and our boredom on Sunday mornings—these things we never got used to while growing up.

"The awful reality and finality of Mama's passing hit us like a ton of bricks as we watched the coffin being lowered into the ground. Emotionally shattered, Anna, Bob and me tried to hug Daddy, but he was so strung out with grief that he was unable to put his arms around us. He either lacked the will to do so or he was so overcome with his own grief that he could not be a part of our own grieving process. He just stood at graveside trying to cry, stiff as cured lumber. Regardless, we held on to him like he was the only thing we had left in this world. In fact, he was. Changed by the loss of his other half, our Daddy was still our fortress against the things that life could throw at us.

"When I had to return to my Army base in Louisiana and when Anna had to leave for Houston, that left our little Bob with Daddy. Bob had not been called up yet, but he knew that it would be no time until this happened. Both Anna and me still considered Bob as our *'little Bob'*, and this seemed to piss him off at times. As Anna and me left the next day, we made sure to hold on to Daddy and Bob one last time. We needed this comforting as much as they did. Our world and our reality at that moment seemed a million miles away from Walkamile, and in that instant neither one of us wanted to depart. Both of us could easily have willed ourselves to stay there, to never leave a place that was so much a part of us and Mama for that matter. The Army base in Louisiana and Anna's job at the Ordnance paled in importance to our need to stay until, of necessity, we were forced to let go. I can still recall this one thing as one of the most painful heart-breaking times in my life, and I'm sure if she was asked, Anna would say the same.

"The neighbors could not have been more supportive to us while we were home. Etta and Clayton Dykes were much too generous; Leah Philbin and Ruth came to pay their respects, and they both seemed shell-shocked when they looked at Mama in her coffin. The Masseys come by, and Elbridge Massey promised me and Anna a ride to the bus station if we needed one—*'Just you let me know which day,'* he said to us. Alicia Woodman's family surprised us with a visit, and we found her mother not near as weird as Alicia. Doctor Goldman and his wife, Miriam, drove up near the end of the wake, and Doctor Goldman left some pills with Daddy, telling him to take one and rest. Mrs. Goldman smiled the whole time they was there as if she was happy—she was a beautiful woman who had a faraway look in her eyes. I think that she smiled at us in an attempt to let us know that she cared for us. Perhaps it was her way of coping with the thought and reality of death.

"Old Jessup come near the end of the wake and walked up to the back of our house. He had removed his hat, and he held it nervously in his hands as he stood on the back door stoop. I'll not soon forget what he said about Mama when we asked him to come in. He said, *'She was one fine lady who always spoke to me when she saw me.*

And she would call me Mr. Jessup and she would tell me to stop by her house next week when the pole beans would be ready for pickin' and she'd give me a big mess. Yep, she was one fine lady.'

"I personally saw to it that Old Jessup got a steaming cup of coffee and a piece of Mrs. Massey's red velvet cake before he departed from us without any fanfare. I also saw to it that he sat at our dining table with me while he ate the cake and drank the coffee. He had quietly told me, *'It would please me mightily if I didn't have to go in the front room and look at Mrs. Renner. I want to remember her like the last time I saw her.'* I had held his left hand and with a squeeze had let him know that was all right. I had the strangest thought as we sat at the table: I was able to recognize that Old Jessup owned a certain nobility and grace that I would only hope to have in my later years. That thought, and his presence, was comforting to me. Daddy, in his own way, had a streak of calmness in him which give him a manliness that I mightily admired.

"Daddy died in 1950. Doctor Goldman said it was heart trouble, and I know the doctor was right to a point. It was heart trouble—a broken heart. Daddy never recovered from losing Mama. The gnawing void in his life was much too large for him to fill up again. He slowly become a shadow of his former self. He told me once that *'A man can only fall in love once. When that love is gone, there won't be another one, no matter how hard a man might try to find a second love.'* Over the years I doubted his words of wisdom, but in a way I think he was right. I loved Mama as much as he did, and I couldn't imagine another woman coming into our lives and replacing her. The Mama I knew, and the loving soul mate Daddy knew, both was irreplaceable in our hearts."

❧

Chapter Thirteen

Anastasia Woodman:

'Never approach a bull from the front . . .'

"My Aunt Alicia had an abiding interest in the history of our community. When she had graduated from Rice Institute, she pursued advanced studies at Harvard and, within a short time, she earned two advanced degrees. Scholarships, fellowships and grants had continued to come her way, and it seemed to the members of her family that all she did was to attend school on a year-round basis. When she came home to Walkamile (the rarest of demanding circumstances such as Grandmother's death, or a wedding of someone to whom she had been close to in prior years), people called her Dr. Woodman. She paid little attention to this nominal designation for the simple reason she was called this every day by her collegiate intimates at Harvard. It had, in a sense, become a second nature occurrence to her. I always sensed deep in my heart that she would have loved for everyone to call her just by her first name.

"Proud of her roots, Aunt Alicia went to great length to uncover the history of Walkamile from the time it was established in 1830 (or earlier) to the time she had departed for Rice Institute. She would regale her friends of academe at Harvard with tidbits of information such as: *'Walkamile is located on an elbow of the*

Trinity River about seventy-five miles northeast of present-day Houston. It was founded about 1830, so some of the old-timers have recorded in diaries, and became in time a pivotal point on the Liberty-to-Nacogdoches Road and stage line.' Her friends would smile at her personal merriment and enthusiasm as she began her story. No one dared remark that their own histories stretched back to the early 1600s in this Massachusetts area, though in their private thoughts they all wished to laugh aloud and call attention to this fact.

"Aunt Alicia always desired that these selfsame academicians would ask her how the community received its unusual name, but they never did. So . . . she introduced the subject herself. *'One might wonder how a small farming community such as Walkamile was thusly named, ne'cest-pa? Oral histories provide interesting, and often eclectic, versions of how the community got its unusual name. Indeed! Foremost among these was the tale that if one walked a mile from where the river boats disgorged their passengers and freight as they docked at high water, one would be in the very middle of the community of Walkamile—ergo Walkamile! A small, fully functional hotel and several boarding houses would greet the weary travelers and/or steamboat employees.'* Aunt Alicia, when relating this segment of her historical exposition, would pause for theatrical effect and continue in a tone of near-confidentiality: *'It is told that there were other diversions which many of the locals chose to ignore. But I shall allow those matters to lie dormant for the moment. Ahem! The lurid details of these establishments have perished with the wilting scourge of time.'*

"I have been an attendant victim of my Aunt Alicia's historical prattling on several occasions, but I must confess that each time she narrated her drawn-out tale, I savored it as much, or more, than I had the time before. She would continue, as was her wont, by lighting afresh another Pall Mall cigarette. Holding it so with great flair, she would think for a few seconds and her voice would grow more serious: *'In the early days the community flourished what with the steamboat activity and the thriving sawmills as well as the agricultural activities in the rich blackness of the river land. Cotton on the black gumbo, corn and hay on the sandy rises, were major crops. Though commercial records are not available in extant form, it is thought that Walkamile was a significant partner and contributor to the shipping of cotton via the Trinity River to the Port of Galveston. Some Virginians and Carolinians, who resettled to the area especially after the Yankees destroyed our way of life, attempted to grow a broad leaf tobacco strain with little success.'* If her cigarette had gone out with her inattention to it during her talk, she would light another one—and the reportage would continue unabated.

"When Aunt Alicia mentioned *Yankees*, everyone within earshot hoped to High Heaven that she would not get on her *War-Between-the-States* high horse. That tale, unto itself, could easily consume several hours, and near the end of it she would be frothing at the proverbial bits. We, who were listening politely to her, hoped against hope that she would relate anecdotes rather than the *Yankee* tales.

"And she would on most occasions: *'In those days of steamboats and river crafts local lore tells of young boys who climbed to the highest point of The Red Clay Cliffs, just north of Walkamile, to watch for river boat traffic. Seeing an unscheduled steamboat or other river boat approaching from either direction, the boys would race to the center of Walkamile to announce the imminent arrival. Local businesses used the boys' announcements to prepare for the extra work necessary for such an event. And, I might add, the announcements gave the ladies time to gussy up a bit.'* Aunt Alicia always paused, hoping to draw the obligatory chuckle from one or two in her audience who recognized her double entendre when she had purposefully stressed the word *ladies*.

"Whether or not she received the chuckle, she would continue on a serious note: *'Many narratives tell of several suicides at The Red Clay Cliffs, but none of these has been substantiated from a historical standpoint. If you could view The Red Clay Cliffs from the proper perspective, then some credibility in these suicide tales would be plausible.'*

"Aunt Alicia had delved into disasters which affected Walkamile to one degree or the other. The most interesting one was the Yellow Fever Epidemic in a nearby community called Cincinnati. *'Yellow fever outbreaks in the 1850s had a deleterious effect on the general economy in Southeast Texas, but Walkamile was largely spared. Cincinnati, a prosperous town in an area slightly west of Walkamile, was wiped out by one such outbreak. There are conflicting historical evidences that the residents either died or were able to relocate before becoming victims of the outbreak. Walkamile, not affected, continued to thrive until the early 1870s when a railroad, which connected Houston and Dallas, bypassed Walkamile approximately twenty miles to the north and west.*

'Walkamile old-timers recall that in its heyday their fine little community boasted of two doctors (one who could pull teeth), a wagon master, two cotton gins, a stonemason of Italian heritage, two blacksmith shops and a tannery. If prompted, the old-timers would own up to the fact that there was one legitimate saloon and several more that operated sub rosa. These self-same old-timers would then laugh and add: "And they even had a post office, a real one, which depended totally on the reliability of the stagecoach line and the incoming river crafts. And we are told there was a tribe of

Indians across the river, peaceful ones, thank God!"

'My research over the years has noted other beneficial additions to the community. After Texas joined the Union in 1846 (a sad, sad mistake!), a full-line grocery store came to the community as well as a farrier and two blacksmiths—and a dry-goods store operated by a Jewish family from Atlanta, Georgia. And even a professional saddle maker set up shop. Available records tell us he was an artisan of the first degree.

'On the southern edge of the community a shy, untalkative old fellow who appeared from nowhere one day started cultivating honeybees. It was thought he was Polish by descent, but no one knew for sure. He had a way with bees, being able to go into the woods and capture a hive of wild bees with minimal, if not magical, effort. Local lore intimates that he did not use a smoking technique as was customary in the handling of bees. It was told that his presence permeated an unwashed body stench so malodorous that the bees succumbed to his every demand. Regardless, he produced a honey product that became a much-in-demand item from as far away as Galveston. Prithee, my dear listener: Would you have partaken of his honey?' Again my Aunt Alicia would pause dramatically unless at least some of the listeners responded with nervous, if not embarrassed, laughter.

"My Aunt Alicia once wrote me from her apartment in Cambridge about a cocktail party she had attended at which were several Negroes in attendance. I've kept her short letter all these years and treasure it so. It read:

> *'My dearest, dearest Anastasia,*
> *I am at home today after having lectured for four*
> *ungodly hours on a subject so boring that it would*
> *put a sleep-deprived person in a permanent*
> *slumber. My Dear—I make my sustenance doing this.*
> *I was invited last evening by a faculty member to a*

*cocktail party at his residence. There were three
Negroes in attendance at the professor's party.
Anastasia, I must tell you, they spoke the King's
English with such smooth grace that my Southerness
paled in its pitiful delivery. I felt that I belonged to
a 'race without consonants' as Willa Cather once
wrote. And they were from Africa of all places!
And they did not wear loin cloths and have bleached
bones twisted in their hair!*

*Absolutely no more news. I just had to relate to you
my novel introduction to real live, educated Nigras!*

Darling, be well and happy as, indeed, I am.

Ciao! A.W. . . . . . .

*P.S. And my thought for the day: Never approach a
bull from the front, or a horse from the rear—or a
fool from any direction!'*

"Each time I read this cherished letter I pray to God that Aunt Alicia had not dominated the cocktail party with her Walkamile Tale or her even more considerable Yankee Narrative. Surely she did not. If she had, I'm positive those polished Negroes went back to the hinterlands of Africa and told amazing stories of this wonderfully wacky woman with a strange accent who told riveting tales of Yankees and Rebels and battles described in the goriest of details."

Chapter Fourteen

Patrick A. Goldman:

'I could have been a man!'

"My father, Adler Goldman, was away at university when one of the more tragic events occurred in Walkamile—the sudden and unexpected death of Etta Dykes. He had returned home for a mid-term break from his studies to find the small community in a whirling tizzy of gossip and quite open statements of opinion as to the cause of Etta Dykes' demise. Wherever he went within the confines of the community, he overheard many conversations in which he personally chose not to engage. Remarks such as: *'You know he did it, and if he didn't do it he could afford to have it done!' 'Somethin's fishy all right. A healthy woman so good at heart, don't ups and die all by herself!' 'You know, it could be some of them Gypsies from that circus that pitched itself over at Romayor!' 'Can't figure out why he'd want to git rid of her—she was his money tree! Hey! Maybe that's the reason he wanted to git rid of her! How dumb can I be?'* The fact that he was the son of the doctor who had visited the scene of Etta Dykes' last moments was a bit ironic in itself. Perhaps the remarks he overheard were made for his benefit or made in the vein of a hopeful venue that he, as the doctor's son, might offer added insight into what really occurred at the Dykes' residence. My father would not have been as gullible to enter into rash speculation of this sort.

"My father told me that he tried to talk to Grandpa about Etta Dykes' death, but Grandpa, a doctor to the core and a tight-lipped one to boot about personal medical situations, had told him to *'put the quietus on such talk'* and that had ended his inquiry. My father did learn that Grandpa, the County Sheriff (with no deputies accompanying him) and Clayton Dykes with one his flunkies had arranged for Etta Dykes' body to be removed from the Dykes' residence.

"It was only a short time, so my father learned, before her corpse was on its way to Houston where, the very next day, she was cremated. Formal obituary notices with engraved printing and black borders appeared on the same day of her cremation in all the local business establishments. The fact that this event occurred so quickly brought on more talk within the community, according to my father. He heard further remarks: *'Very well planned, I would say!' 'The blood didn't even have time to dry! Why, the printer's ink dried quicker!'* Rumors spread around the county like wind-blown leaves on an early autumn day: *'It was murder!'* one group contended. *'But who did it?'* another group rebutted with a question of their own. *'It had to be suicide sure as certain,'* came from some residents who only knew Etta Dykes by name.

"Returning to his studies at university, my father informed me that he never broached the subject of Etta Dykes' death again with Grandpa. Over the years, however, more spurious rumors piled on the rumors already foisted about, and Etta Dykes' untimely demise became a much-discussed topic of conversation among many of the residents of Walkamile. It eventually became a legend unto itself of sorts.

"Some in the community noted that Clayton Dykes began to lead a life, not with a pace as frenetic as before, but one that sequestered him in a tighter circle of trustworthy acquaintances and associates. He had few, if any, real friends, though he still wielded considerable influence in the surrounding area, mainly because of his financial standing. He was now an even richer man than he was before Etta Dykes' death. Gossip of this type tended to leak from more reliable sources than does the speculative prattling of neighbors, especially in a small, tight-knit community.

"Etta Dykes last will and testament had withstood the probate process. With his power and influence, Clayton Dykes, according to my father, was able to maintain an enclosing atmosphere of secrecy as to the contents of the will and its ultimate disposition. It had always been an acknowledged fact that Clayton Dykes had the County Judge and the entire Courthouse in his pockets. Any leaks would have to come from the loose tongues of attorneys and their employees, not the purchased politicians.

"I had spent a long weekend with my Grandpa a couple of years after Grandma had died. I had hoped that I could draw him out of the funk that he seemed to be in of late. He had given up drinking about the time that Grandma became ill. He no longer practiced medicine, but he was always in demand when anxious mothers had questions about why Little Susie or Dear Little Jeb wouldn't do such-and-such. It seemed that he could never escape from the demands of his profession, try though he might. People would drive up to his home, ring the doorbell, knock loudly on the door and shout his name: *'Dr. Goldman, I know you're in there! I need you bad! I need you bad!'* And Grandpa would go to the door, not reluctantly, and again he would be entrapped in his old world of seeing to the medical needs of his old patients—ignoring his own needs both physical and mental. He had told me once long ago that this was what doctors do, like it or no.

"Fortunate for both of us, no intruders had broken our pleasant environment's peace when we arose late on that Saturday morning. Old Jessup, as faithful a friend and attendant as could be desired, had appeared early, right on an ingrained schedule. He had seen to Grandpa's *'ablutions'* as he called the bathing process for Grandpa. He had then prepared Grandpa's breakfast and mine, and I had made coffee, and Grandpa suggested that we have the coffee on the screened-in back porch.

'There'll be a breeze there,' he had said. *'Your grandmother, my dear Miriam, and I used to sit there on the rare morning when I had a bit of freedom from my duties. Wasn't often, but when it happened it was a true escape for me. Your grandmother, when she was clearheaded, was a most delightful companion, but there were many days when she would just sit and stare out to a point beyond the yard fence. It was as though there was something out there that she was searching for—but I never gained any knowledge that she ever found whatever it was.'*

"Old Jessup brought out a tray with two cups, sugar and cream, and a Thermos of coffee. He bid us his leave with his customary remark, *'Anything else, my Good Doctor?'* When Grandpa shook his head in the negative, Old Jessup departed through the back door.

"As we sipped our coffee, Grandpa placed his coffee cup in its saucer, sniffed the air and remarked, *'I smell gas. Do you?'* I had thought a bit earlier when I was percolating the coffee on the gas stove that the flame had burned a bit too yellow, indicating air in the gas line.

"I nodded to Grandpa in agreement that I did smell gas. He continued: *'I'll call the gas company Monday. Son, life is strange in so many ways. Each time I turn on the gas on the stove or one of my space heaters, I recall an event that happened long ago—Etta Dykes' death. She was Clayton Dykes' wife. You know, I'm sure*

Adler has told you, that Clayton married her for her land and money. She was a good woman—did a lot of good works for those less fortunate than she. There was always talk, of course, about her and Massey, the postal route driver. Maybe it was true, maybe it wasn't. I can't say one way or the other. And for what it's worth, I don't care one whistle.

    'But the gas smell brings me back to the day that the Sheriff— who was it back then?—Earl—Earl—damn it to Hell I can't recall his last name! Bruntlett! It was Earl Bruntlett who found me on a call and told me he needed me to go with him to the Dykes' place. Etta was dead. She had been murdered, so he said. Son, I was never surprised a bit as to what could happen in our community. We were a small gathering as far as population is concerned, so I guess it would be no different if we lived in New York City. New York City is no different than we are here. It's a bunching of communities connected to each other, block by block or grid by grid I guess you could say, and everybody brags about living in a big city. They actually live in a small community within a big city. That's all.'

"Grandpa had paused, realizing that he had strayed from his topic of conversation. *'What was I telling you, son?'* he asked me. I smiled at him, and told him that he was relating the events surrounding Etta Dykes' death. I hoped against hope that he would continue. For purely personal reasons, I longed to know what happened at the Dykes' home on that day. I suppose I was wishing to find something that perhaps, after knowing, I would have been better off not knowing.

    'Yes, yes! The gas! I left my car wherever I was and went with Bruntlett to the Dykes' home. Bruntlett and I didn't talk at all as we drove the short distance. Being a sensible person, I felt a bit uneasy at the oddness of what was occurring. Why a sheriff in an official capacity would go to the trouble of looking me up while I was on a

call and asking me to go with him to the scene of a crime—not unusual—but not something that comes up often. I was not a coroner, but as a doctor I could tell a lot of what had gone on at the scene of a crime just from purely medical reasoning.

'Well, we arrived at the Dykes' Place. Clayton and one of his hired hands were outside appearing for all intents and purposes to be waiting on us. We got out of the Sheriff's car and approached the two. Clayton greeted me cordially as I could expect under the circumstances, and he seemed to nod knowingly to the Sheriff. The Sheriff suggested that we go inside right away. Clayton was as calm as any gentleman farmer could be who might be greeting expected guests. I found this odd. The hired hand was a different matter. His eyes seemed flinty, and he kept looking about in a very nervous and uneasy fashion. He clearly was not comfortable in his skin. I found this a bit disturbing.'

"Grandpa picked up his coffee cup, took a sip and discovered it had gone cold on him. *'Nothing worse than a cold cup of coffee unless it's a cold floor in the middle of the night when you're getting up to pee. It's a time like this when I crave the contents of a bottle. But that would be personal suicide for me. Son, what I'm about to tell you now, I've only told one other person—my dear Miriam. Your papa tried to get me to talk about Etta Dykes' death, but I never would. It was too dangerous and foolhardy back then to even think about sharing what I knew with anyone other than Miriam. I even lost some sleep on worrying that Miriam might talk too much to someone while she was under the happy influence. I've never breathed a word of any of this to Old Jessup.*

'That day, when we all went out to the Dykes' place, the Sheriff told me in no uncertain terms to leave Old Jessup at home. Etta Dykes, to cut to the unvarnished truth, had been savagely murdered. She had been tied to her bed, her arms behind her, her

legs tied with rope and then splayed apart and tied to the foot posters of the bed, left and right. Her mouth had been taped with some sort of industrial strength tape. She was nude, but she had not been sexually violated as far as I could tell. All the shades in her bedroom had been pulled down, the windows had been closed tightly, the electricity had been cut off at the switchbox, and the gas had apparently been turned on in her bedroom's space heater.

'For whatever reasons, Clayton Dykes informed the Sheriff that he had found Etta in the condition as I have noted to you when he returned from a business engagement at the Courthouse. He had summoned his field hand, Travis Mangum, to come to his aid, and they had managed to turn off the gas and raise the windows to rid the house of dangerous gas fumes. They had left the electrical circuit box untouched until they were sure that a sudden spark would not cause an explosion. Whoever had accomplished this heinous act had done a bang-up job from a premeditative standpoint. For this person or persons to approach the Dykes' residence in broad daylight with ropes, tape, and whatever else they had felt was necessary in the carrying out of this act—Etta Dykes would have had to know them. They surely had used a plausible ruse to convince her that Clayton had wanted them to do some work on the residence while he was away. This work, of course, would require rope and tape and access to the interior of the house. I find this scenario terribly far-fetched.' Grandpa made a double fist with both of his hands as if to relieve some of the inner tensions he must have been feeling as he relived that day.

"I could think of little to say to my Grandpa. I did ask him finally why he was telling me this. *'On that day, son, I discarded all the values—moral, ethical, whatever—that exist in a decent man. I went along with the ebb and flow that could have carried us all out to sea. If I had been honorable to the very spirit of which I was constituted, I would have walked away from that scene and called in higher powers—Texas Rangers, anyone of higher authority—and there would have been closure to Etta Dykes' horrific death. But no! I went with the ebb and flow because I was afraid for my life and for the life of my dear Miriam and Adler. I've lived with the shame of my inaction for all these years. I even accompanied Clayton and the Sheriff to Houston the next day and participated in another series of charades.*

'The very afternoon of my first involvement with this unholy mess, I went with Clayton and the Sheriff to the County Judge's office, and I swore to the powers that be that Etta Dykes had taken her own life. Each step of the way I just seemed to dig my personal Hell deeper and deeper. I've thanked God over and over that Old Jessup was not allowed to go with us that day. If he had, he would've become the victim of one of those Nigger lynchings that happens around here out in the country. Thank God again, they had sense enough to tell me to see that he stayed home. He would have seen through the smoke and mirrors they all were using to hide the murder of a fine woman in our community. And he would have become another victim in short order. I am convinced of that.'

"Grandpa and I sat in a vacuumed silence for a long time. I pulled my chair nearer to his own chair and looked him straightway in the eyes. *'What else, Grandpa, could you have done?'* My voice was more resolute than I expected it could be as I looked into his eyes.

"His hollow reply stunned me with its ringing but agonizing clarity. *'I could have been a man, son. I could have been a man!'* He then burst into a deep, visceral bawling. At that moment of self-accusation, Grandpa began the sharing of his long weekend with me that became much longer—much too long for the two of us. To this day, I can hear the resounding end of his conversation with me: *'I could have been a man!'* Those six hollow words will never leave my memory bank." ☙

☙

Chapter Fifteen

William Beatty Heart:

> '*. . . only your Grandpa's second love.*'

"They left for Hardin, Texas, early one Monday morning as the edge of the sky turned rosy and the mists rose slowly to their oblivion—my Great Grandpa, Brother Billy Heart, and Brother Andrew Cole. Brother Cole was still weak from the unexplained illness he had suffered during the Walkamile brush arbor revival. His complexion looked washed out in the early morning sunlight, and his movements seemed tentative at best. He had blamed his gimpy walk on staying in bed for several days. For this reason, he had asked my great grandpa to drive. My great grandpa, isolated as he was on the farm, had not had the privilege of learning to drive an automobile.

"My great grandpa had been around automobiles a bit, but he had never been afforded an opportunity to drive one. He sensed, however, that there couldn't be much of nothing to it. He'd seen many young men driving the roads in and around Walkamile, and they seemed to be having fun doing it. If it looked easy, then it had to be easy. *'Just sit up front and guide it down the road. Why, any fool can do that!'* he had considered.

"They headed out east on a dirt road after Brother Cole showed him how to start the car. At first, my great grandpa was able to hold the steering wheel in a steady position. The gas pedal didn't seem to be a problem, but the foot clutch was a complete mystery to him. They met no other vehicles on the road at first, so my great grandpa drove down the middle of the road with a degree of comfort in what he was doing. Then the road became hilly, and my great grandpa was forced to shift gears. When he tried, there would come forth a mighty scraping sound, and the old jalopy would lurch and sputter and almost stop in the process. *'Dang, fellow! Don't you know nothin'?'* Brother Cole would yell. *'I thought you told me you could drive! Hell! You couldn't drive a jackass and it don't require no shiftin'!'* Brother Cole added. As if they were not having enough trouble, they were in for more excitement as the road became steeper. The climbing was laborious, and the old jalopy stopped dead in its tracks at the crest of a red clay hill. The radiator cap was hissing like a bouncing water kettle on a too-hot wood stove!

"Great Grandpa jumped out of the front seat to get away from the increasing hissing, and as he did so the jalopy started rolling slowly down the hill. Brother Cole yelled: *'God damn you to Hell, Heart! You're 'bout to git me kilt!'* With these words uttered in total frustration, Brother Cole, no longer tentative in his movements, somehow transported himself over to the driver's position behind the steering wheel and managed to apply both the brake on the foot pedal and the pull-brake mechanism. The old jalopy, with a mechanically overpowering intent of its own, finally rolled into a dried-out bar ditch and hissed to a chugging stop. *'Heart! Git your ass over here and git that bucket and git some water. It'll take us a passel of Mondays to git to Hardin at the rate we've made so far. You ain't worth one shine in a bottle of Shinola! And don't take that radiator cap off right away or it'll burn you to Hell and back and then blow up in your silly-ass face!'* he yelled at Billy Heart, as he found an empty bucket in the back seat.

"My Grandpa, Daniel, Brother Billy Heart's only son,

entertained me with stories like this one while I was growing up. I'm certain that he embellished his narratives to make the stories more appealing because some of the incidents he relates are more than hard to believe. His version of what happened to my great grandpa after he arrived in Hardin for the brush arbor revival borders on fiction. But I'll let his voice tell it as I heard it from him many times. My voice and choice of words wouldn't do justice to the tale.

'It's needless to say that Brother Andrew Cole got well quickly after the steep hill episode. He got rid of his gimpy legs quick. In fact, he drove the rest of the way to Hardin. They arrived late that Monday evening and located where Brother Corliss Weatherby and his family lived. Brother Weatherby was the pastor of the Jesus Saves Apostolic Church. He and his wife, Sarah, lived in a small shot gun house painted white less than a hundred yards from the church. The only touch of class to the little house was dark green shutters around each window that seemed to make the white paint look whiter. Brother Weatherby and his wife were taken by surprise when two preachers arrived. They had expected only one. They had farmed out their fifteen year-old daughter, Jolene, to obliging neighbors for the duration of the brush arbor revival. Brother Cole would stay in her bedroom in her absence. He would be near to the Church should he need a respite to pray and await the Lord's giving of Scripture to him for his next sermon. Brother Cole had told the Weatherbys that he always waited for the Lord to provide him with the necessary divine inspiration. When it did not come, he told them, he had to prostrate himself in prayer for a long period of time. It would be a true blessing to be able to walk to a quiet sanctuary and find inspiration.

'Brother Weatherby arranged for Brother Billy Heart to stay with one of his parishioner's family about a mile away. Brother

Cole would be put up at the parsonage as had been previously planned. Brother Billy Heart had fully realized his dream of escaping from the rigors of farm life, but he had not anticipated the amount of work which would come his way in this brush arbor revival way of life. He had his awakening the next morning, a Tuesday, even though he had been forewarned of their intentions to pick him up early that morning. He had been inclined to think that preachers sleep late.

'Brothers Weatherby and Cole had yanked him out of comfort's bed at the parishioner's house at an early hour. They were heading out at first light to the edge of town to size up a site for the brush arbor revival. On Brother Weatherby's truck there were shovels, saws, axes, water jugs and almost any other tool a poor farm boy could imagine. Brother Billy Heart, in his wildest dreams, had jumped from one frying pan into another frying pan that seemed much larger and far more demanding. The only decent thing that Brothers Weatherby and Cole did was to tarry for a decent interval and have a cup of coffee with the parishioner while Brother Billy Heart gulped down a biscuit and a fried chunk of ham. Then they were off. So much for preachers sleeping late. Brother Billy Heart saw a Big Ben clock on a dresser as they left. It read 6:23 AM.'

"My Grandpa would roar with laughter when he had safely taken the three preachers to a brush arbor work site with his storytelling. *'This is just the start of the story, my boy. Both Brother Cole and your own Great Grandpa couldn't seem to avoid trouble. It goes without saying that the construction of the brush arbor took several days of felling trees, making rough-hewn benches, gathering dry pine straw for the floor, hundreds of fresh green boughs for the roof and seeing to it that the area around the arbor was cleared. The brush arbor revival didn't start up until the following Thursday night.*

'First rattle out of the box though on a Saturday afternoon, Brother Cole is caught taking a mid-afternoon nap with Sister Weatherby at the parsonage, and the Good Brother Weatherby runs Brother Cole off with a Hellfire-and-Brimstone cussing. He then looks up your Great Grandpa over to the parishioner's house and asks him to come stay at the parsonage and finish the revival. Your Great Grandpa obliges, finishes out the brush arbor revival, passes the hat as much as possible, and meets a young lady who was to be an instrumental force in his life, though he could not have anticipated these chains of that circumstance. She was your Great Grandma, and she taught your Great Grandpa how to read and write and do ciphers. Your Great Grandpa, in one of his more mellow moods after he learned to read and write attributed your Great Grandma's appearance on the scene to a Bible verse which he paraphrased often: The Lord works in mysterious ways, his wonders to perform.*

'You might be wondering, as you should, if your Great Grandpa ever learned to drive an automobile after his traumatic experience on the trip to Hardin. Yes, he did, but when he was at home in Walkamile, he always rode a horse. He treasured one in particular—Felicity. Felicity became a family member more esteemed than a blood relative. I've heard stories of your Great Grandpa going miles out of his way when he was on the revival circuit to get Washington State apples for Felicity. She preferred them greatly over New York State apples or the little bitter ones we always tried to cultivate in Walkamile. One Christmas your Great Grandpa had a bushel of the Washington apples shipped to Walkamile just for Felicity. Kids in the community were lucky to see one or two apples at Christmas, and here was a horse eating high off the hog. I can't tell you how many years Felicity was a part of the picture, but she grew old and gray along with your Great Grandpa. They became inseparable. He brushed her religiously* *sometimes twice a day; he checked her teeth as if he was a dentist; he made sure her hooves were in excellent shape at all times; he prepared her stall in the cold winter months so that she would stay warm; he would have installed her in his bedroom if he could have figured out a way to do it. He treated her like the Queen of Sheba, and she responded with an affection that I can't describe in the proper words. Your Great Grandma, in her lilting laughter, would tell anyone who would listen that she was only your Great Grandpa's second love. 'Felicity is his one and only love,' she would state with magnanimity."*

~

Chapter Sixteen

Harrison Dykes:

'It's not that the mountains are so high . . .'

"You know for sure that you can't put something over on a smart woman if she sets her mind to finding out a secret. That was my biggest discovery when Anastasia Woodman contacted me on behalf of her aunt, Alicia Woodman. I had been the best kept secret in Southeast Texas for many, many years until Ms. Alicia Woodman got to prying around and found that I was the son of Clayton Dykes by an unnamed woman. How she found me out is not a point of contention, but all things of this nature do, at a point in time, reach either a contentious state or some form of resolution or truce. As I said—a smart woman can find out any secret. And so she did. And I met Anastasia for the very first time.

"The gnawing bone tossed out by this Anastasia was that Ms. Alicia Woodman wanted me to *'illuminate a heretofore dark secret'* (as the niece Anastasia had phrased it to me when she first contacted me). I'm not at all inclined to think that something of which you know little can be illuminated. That would be similar to a duck hunter exposed to the wintry dampness and cold of a duck blind for hours on end trying to light a cigarette with a water-soaked match. Or worse yet, when you fart you hurriedly reach for a box of matches and find not a one of them will strike! The duck hunter will do without a much-needed smoke, and the farter will helplessly smell his own noxious fumes. *'Illuminate'*, Ms. Anastasia requested. I don't think so.

"My Daddy indeed was Clayton Dykes, but I was not the offspring of Daddy and Etta Dykes as best as I could fathom. Far from that—I was likely an unwelcome outcome of one of his dalliances over in Romayor, just across the creek from Walkamile. Maybe, maybe not. I don't know to this day who my Mother was or is, and when Clayton Dykes died, I was flabbergasted when a battery of over-aggressive lawyers contacted me.

"I had heard of Clayton Dykes before the events of this one strange day; I had known that he owned thousands of acres in the county just west of us, but my name wasn't even Harrison Dykes at that time. I could have had little insight into the possibilities of something so remote as being the son of such a man. I had gone through my first twenty-one years under the name of Vance Lakey, and I had been raised by an elderly woman I believed all those years to be my Grandma. Her name was Nora Lakey. Supposedly, I was an only child abandoned by her oldest son, Roger Lakey. I loved her as if she had been my mother, and I certainly didn't spend a lot of time asking her questions which she wouldn't, or couldn't, answer. Kids growing up usually accept the status quo though they may, at times, ponder why one family appears to have more than they do. Other than that, kids are not overly curious along these lines.

"One day, as the lore goes, Roger Lakey simply disappeared, leaving me in the care of his mother. His wife had died during childbirth. Naturally, being a tiny infant of an indeterminate age, I could not have remembered any of this. I have no idea if any of this has any basis of truth in it or if it is a part and parcel of the rumor mill which usually operates overtime when something of this nature occurs in a small community.

"I've never bothered to challenge my "Grandma" Lakey. That would serve only to place her in an untenable and uncomfortable position.

"Likely a shaky foundation of a truth exists somewhere, but one is led to wonder since the lawyers handling Clayton Dykes' estate swarmed all over me from the very outset. They came from Houston and Beaumont and Huntsville to the west. And they swarmed about Nora Lakey with a fervor and unbridled enthusiasm that bordered on crossing an imaginary line of common sense and respect for an old lady. And I loved that old lady; she was my "Grandma" come Hell or High Water; she had raised me, and as far as I was concerned she had done a pretty good job of it considering what she had to work with. Whatever the truth and whether it came out in dribs and drabs or in sheer volumes of prior discussions—I would protect my "Grandma." Looking back on all of this now, I should have been more aware of the reasons "Grandma" and I moved to Houston with very little commotion attached to our relocation.

"My "Grandma" Nora Lakey had always seemed to have a sufficiency of means to see that I received a proper education while attending the Cleveland public schools. I lived closer to the Walkamile School than I did to the schools I attended in Cleveland. But arcane school districting regulations prevented me from attending classes at Walkamile. So for all those years of schooling, I was bussed to Cleveland, twenty or more miles away.

"Grandma" didn't work at a regular job, but she did maintain a considerable garden from which she often sold fresh vegetables and melons during season. She had jokingly called her involvement in gardening *'truck farming without a truck';* and "Grandma" kept a well-ordered house and saw to it that my clothes were always in the finest condition. I was happy to be Vance Lakey. I was happy to live with my "Grandma." Oddly, under the circumstances of our existence, "Grandma" always came up with money when it was needed—not to an excess, of course. But she seemed always to have ample funds. Usually, if I hadn't behaved like an out-and-out prick for a day or two, "Grandma" always shelled out for the things that I felt were important to me. When I reached eighteen, my request for wheels was kyboshed by "Grandma" Johnny-on-the-spot. She informed me in words that required no translation that if I wanted a car I'd have to work for it. End of that story!

"Upon Clayton Dykes' death our lives changed dramatically. With a suddenness that was both unsettling and welcomed in a way, "Grandma" Lakey became a woman of some means with a promised inheritance from the Estate of Clayton Dykes. She had kept this knowledge to herself over the years as she saw to my proper upbringing. And I, a real nobody, who would not have known Clayton Dykes if he had walked in our front yard, with the same degree of suddenness became a very rich young man at twenty-one years of age. Clayton Dykes, so we were informed, had rewritten his Last Will and Testament after the death of his wife, Etta Dykes, and I was the sole beneficiary other than the specific assignment he had made to my "Grandma" Lakey. He had even gone to a great deal of trouble to set up an irrevocable trust fund to ensure that I would be financially secure for the rest of my normal expected lifespan. That meant, so the lawyers explained, that I couldn't spend it all at one time. In addition, he had arranged with the greatest attention to detail to have the vast acreages of the estate managed by a trustworthy panel of businessmen (a consortium was the word in the will) with whom he had conducted business over the years. Too, "Grandma" would be taken care of for the rest of her life as he had spelled out in an assignment.

"All of this was done with the most diligent care and secrecy on his part and on the parts of those who would be involved in the implementation of his wishes upon his death. How Ms. Alicia Woodman could ever discover who I was would remain her own secret. Since she apparently had learned so much about me, my "Grandma", and my inheritance, I may as well share with her what little I have learned over the ensuing years (which is next to nothing as far as I'm concerned).

"I had been assured that none of the details of Clayton Dykes' wishes would be a matter of public record—even the adoption papers for *'Harrison Dykes'* which presented themselves with a timeliness that would normally have raised eyebrows. All the ducks had been lined up with a precision that must have cost Clayton Dykes a pretty penny. But, as I soon discovered, Clayton Dykes had a lot of pretty pennies to spend. He had had an astute business sense and an innate flair for making money. But, as the lawyers reminded me, when he had first come to the table, he had had little to offer to his marriage other than a charm which must have swept Etta Dykes off her feet.

"I learned mostly by outright questions to the lawyers that the Etta (Harris) Dykes and Clayton Dykes union had not been a happy one. Without any room for error or disguised misjudgment, several of the lawyers shared tidbits of gossip that had made the circuit in Walkamile. These items had been presented to me at my urging, and once they realized there would be no recriminations from me an effusive outflow began. *'It was a widely-known fact that your father was a womanizer to the nth degree. There were no bounds to his extra-curricular activities apart from his marriage. He could be devastatingly charming to any female, and once they succumbed to this charm, they were apt to be one of his victims, perhaps unwillingly and unwittingly,'* one lawyer offhandedly proposed . . . *'No need to embellish the gossip at all. There are elements of scuttlebutt abroad about some of his physical characteristics to* *which none of us should ascribe any merit—if you pick up on my* *drift at all.'* I had not the slightest idea what his overblown remark meant, neither did I bother to ask because that would only have inflated his already pompous ego.

"Another lawyer, so long in the tooth that he probably didn't give a damn what anybody thought of him, had added further insight to the couple's relationship: *'Rumors had spread all over* *the community at a point in time that Etta Dykes was carrying on* *with some man who she carelessly saw maybe once a week. No one* *would dare to name that man, but everybody knew who he was. No* *one would name him specifically at that time because he would* *have lost his job. I imagine Clayton knew who he was, but he* *probably didn't care. I won't say his name because I have some* *inside information from an old lawsuit that could come back to* *haunt me.'* He made his remarks in words that seemed at first to hiss as he spoke, as if what he were saying was something we all should accept as vile and contemptible.

"And even another lawyer had put in his unsolicited two bits worth: *'Harrison, there're lots of other tales out there, but I can see* *no reason to add them to what you've heard. If true, the tales are a* *shame; if false, the tales are still a shame, and a black mark on* *your Daddy. You don't need any more spurious chattering from us.'* And that had ended my foray into the obviously seamy world of my Daddy. I feel much as my lawyers do: there would be little to gain in ferreting out what may or may not be even a modicum of truth. That's why I won't share any gossipy treacle with Ms. Woodman.

"Over the years, when I had been presented with what I thought was a problem that could not be solved on the spot, I had somehow harkened back to a saying that my "Grandma" Lakey had spoken on many occasions: *'It's not that the mountains are so high; it's that the valleys are so deep.'* I had never appreciated the profound nature of her oft-used statement when she was faced with a dilemma. Now I do! And now that my secret is obviously abroad upon the land, I'd give a pretty penny to discover who coined those statements. Ms. Alicia Woodman is so clever—maybe she'll know who first said those remarkable words. In the interim, I plan to be happy. My "Grandma" and I moved to Houston from Romayor with as much discretion and as little to-do as possible.

"Grandma" still calls herself Nora Lakey, and rightly so, and I am called Harrison Dykes with no soul that I know of in this big city knowing the difference. I'm presently working on my Masters at the University of Houston. I don't work. Why should I? But I need the business background that a good education affords. At the moment, I don't plan discussing the *'dark secret'* which Anastasia and Alicia Woodman have unearthed. If I am a product of Clayton Dykes and an unknown woman (which obviously I am), then I should not boast of my ancestry. My ancestry occurred as the result of the accidental feat of another. I am not special because of my ancestry; I am special because of who I am.

"When I first started considering the female Woodman's requests, I had felt obliged in a way of sharing some of the details of my sudden good fortune. Now I think that I will not. They'll have to opine and speculate and guess if they wish to get at the whole truth. And if they should discover the truth, wherever it is, they may wish that they had not opened up the proverbial can of worms. Personally, I don't share their enthusiasm at this point in time.

"Do I plan to return to Walkamile? Will my "Grandma" Lakey continue to reside in Houston or return to Romayor? I would think not. The chapters of our lives there are closed. Each of us, in our own way—mine in a blissful ignorance and "Grandma" Lakey's in a strict compliance with a pact made long ago—paid certain dues as we met certain obligations. Again, mine were unwitting; "Grandma Lakey's were of a willing nature, I would hope. I plan to ask her one day what was the hold, ironclad so it seems, that Clayton Dykes had over her. Did she know something that she herself could use as a guaranty or as a sure-fire bargaining chip? I can fathom no plausible connection between the two individuals. I would not think that their paths would have crossed and crisscrossed too many times over the years. Perhaps I would be better off not knowing. What's the old saying about leaving a stone unturned?"

Chapter Seventeen

Micah Abraham Jessup:

'Your Grandpa is as fit as a broken fiddle.'

"Abraham Jessup, my Grandpa, became ill quite suddenly. As a child I thought Grandpa would live forever, but now that I was a grown-up and having finished my university studies I knew better. When I received the telephone call from my mother, I sensed that Grandpa's demise was imminent because her voice spoke more than volumes about her concern. My mother could never disguise her true feelings, try though she might. So . . . I flew home, prepared for the inevitable, but within a microcosm of my own spirit I sent little praise offerings to God and greedily asked God to let the old saint live many more years. I could not envision my world with him not a major part of it.

"The plane trip from Atlanta to Houston was delayed by one of those weather anomalies which springs up out west and sweeps across the country. It always seems that Texas is assaulted first by fierce blue-black clouds, winds of inestimable force, thunder, lightning, hail and then a washed-out calm that belies the savagery of what has just occurred. This condition was what greeted me when my plane landed two hours late in Houston. I grabbed my overstuffed bag from the overhead bin and raced toward the rental car kiosks near the Baggage Claim area. The car rental took a bit longer than I had anticipated, the clerk giving me a more than cursory inspection. The thought entered my head that the clerk might have been taken aback by the fact that a Negro was renting a car. She eyed me continuously and then carefully checked my Georgia Driver's License front and back and performed the same assiduous inspection on my American Express Credit Card. Finally, after waiting for a rental bus outside, I was off to a nearby lot of rental cars. The clerk's last remark had stung me a bit: *'Drive careful! You know you're in Texas!'* Her admonition, as loaded as it could potentially be, could have been innocent. I had grown accustomed to double meanings in many aspects of my life.

"Within an hour I was home. Home! Home! Home! Walkamile showed evidence of the bad weather which had roared through the area several hours earlier. But it was home even in its strewn debris, its fallen trees, and many downed power lines. My mother's place had been spared most of this, and the electricity had not gone off. Mother was at the front door when I drove up. *'God! How can you ever leave a place like home?'* I whispered to myself. There was an unreality to my being back. To me the world of Walkamile was comparable to a parallel universe especially after my settling in my comfort zone in Atlanta. From the red clay of Georgia to this sandy loam of Texas . . . the transition to home environs occurred as if all the pine trees whispering in the wind were speaking to me: *'Welcome home, Prodigal Son.'*

"My mother and I hugged a long time, and then I placed my travel bag inside the front door and asked, *'How's Grandpa?'* I could not be diverted from the true purpose of my visit home.

"Before my mother could answer, a strong, silky voice called out from the front bedroom, *'Your Grandpa is as fit as a broken fiddle, thank you very much!'* Then I heard his rolling laughter.

'Oh, God!' I thought, *'I've missed that voice so much!'*

'And I flew all the way from Atlanta to be insulted by someone who is allegedly a very sick man. I personally think you're a con artist of the first degree, old man.' I had entered the bedroom and as I finished my verbal sally with Grandpa, tears were streaming from my eyes and his. I bent over the bed and half-lifted his upper body into my arms. It felt as if I was holding a pillow case filled with brittle bones. There was a jolting pulse of an eternity passing by as I held him, and we both remained quiet despite the obvious bodily ebb and flow of a pure and unadulterated love for each other.

"My mother finally broke the silence: *'Micah, pull up that chair and sit down. You and Grandpa can visit if he feels up to it, and I'll get you both a cup of tea—five minutes at least! Mavis—you remember Mavis Murray—she brought over some orange-flavored herbal tea.'* Grandpa distorted his face on purpose when he heard about the herbal tea. Then he stuck his tongue out. We both laughed at the same time.

"After Grandpa's initial excitement at my coming home he was never as vibrant in the coming days. He lay, propped up on two oversized pillows, and stared at me or whoever was sitting with him. He ate what was spooned for him without protest: chicken broth, ice cream, pureed vegetables, and even oatmeal which he had shunned when he was well, calling it *'baby's mush.'*

"We turned on his radio and hoped that the music and endless chitchat of the announcers would enliven his spirit. And Doctor Goldman, who had retired long ago from an active practice, came to see him twice each day. Those two were a sight to behold: Grandpa, ancient and quite ill, and Doctor Goldman, ancient and lost as a waif, both in a world that had by now passed them by. For me, the sight of them was uplifting, but in one of my weaker moments I had to will myself to suppress tears. They were passé in a sense. And worse yet, the overweening atmosphere from which they were sprung was now disappearing before my eyes. I was suddenly saddened with an immediacy that I had not felt as my plane landed in Houston.

"My mother told me over supper the first night that I was home that the relationship between Doctor Goldman and my Grandpa was a bond that neither she nor I could ever fully understand. *'The slave thing that some of our kind is so hung up on now don't hold much water as far as I'm concerned. Why, they calls us white niggers! Them two are brothers. Grandpa's not his slave or flunky. Grandpa's his friend. And Doctor Goldman? Why, he thinks of Grandpa as a third arm. Doctor Goldman wouldn't be able to turn a corner if it wasn't for Grandpa. Oh, yes! It do look like Grandpa waits on Doctor Goldman from mornin' to night, but the Good Doctor Goldman waits on other peoples from mornin' to night, so he's a slave, too! Micah, you don't think I'm wrong, do you?'*

"I had put down my fork and reached across the table and took my mother's hand in mine. *'Mother, these pork chops are divine. Have you been talking to God about your cooking lately?'* This was one of our private jokes. My mother had used remarks when she discussed her recipes with others about praying to God that her cake wouldn't fall or that her yeast rolls would rise properly. I loved to tweak her every chance I got.

'You stinker! You didn't answer me! I can't be serious around you for one minute!' she protested. *'You—you have to be your Daddy made over in the flesh. Oh, Isaac could tease me just so!'*

"When she spoke of Daddy, an empty look came to her eyes and an old pain seemed to be revisited. I released her hands. *'Mother, you are always right. I'll add only one thing to what you said and that's the following—we are all slaves one way or the other.'*

"Grandpa lapsed into a deep sleep the next afternoon. He

breathed deeply and desperately as if holding on to a connection which neither he nor any of us could see or pretend to understand. I sat by his bed during the long nighttime hours, and my mother and women from the community, black and white alike, shared the daytime duties. Grandpa had so many friends and acquaintances wanting to help that my mother had to turn down many offers of help. There were a number of young white men from outlying areas of the county who stopped in after their day jobs and proposed to do chores and errands for my mother. Their remarks to my mother touched her heartstrings and made her proud: *'Grandpa Jessup helped my Daddy out one day, and Daddy never forgot it. Said you could always depend on Old Jessup.'* Or *'Grandpa Jessup stood up to a bully once when that bully was tryin' to pick a fight with me. He told the bully to tuck his tail between his legs and go on home and next time he showed his face to be a real man. He had told me then that a bully was nothin' but a liverless coward scared of his own shadow! I thanked him mightily. I was a scrawny little kid then, but I don't forget kindnesses.'*

"Doctor Goldman still came twice each day, and it seemed to me that he aged incrementally with each visit. He examined my Grandpa with his stethoscope, held his right arm and listened to the pulse, and then he would pat Grandpa's hand with a lingering attention which did not go unnoticed to anyone in the room. About the third or fourth day after I had returned home I had begun my evening shift sitting with Grandpa when Doctor Goldman arrived. He performed his cursory examination and then took a seat near my chair. I could sense, by his prolonging of putting the stethoscope away, that he wished to talk.

"Then he began: *'Micah, my son, I feel compelled to tell you that you should consider yourself one of the luckiest young men in the world at this very moment in time. You came into this world black, and that in itself stacks the odds against you from the minute you are born. Your Daddy died much too young, but you have been blessed to have a fine and courageous mother. She saw to it that you finished all the grades you could here in Walkamile, and I bet my last nickel that she made you study. Then, if I remember the old chain of events, your mother and this dear old soul lying here* (he pointed to Grandpa) *would not let you stop your education after eight grades. Your mother sent you off to Houston to a fine school there, and your aunt—what was her given name?'* He paused and awaited my answer.

"I answered him clearly: *'My Aunt Audie.'*

"Doctor Goldman allowed the name to sink in almost as if he were tasting the two syllables of her name, and then he continued: *'Audie. Aunt Audie! I remember meeting her. When she visited here in Walkamile, she always fixed us up a big pot of chicken and dumplings—to die for! Your good aunt saw to it that you finished high school. And then you were on your way because you applied yourself, and your mother and this dear soul* (again he pointed to the bed where Grandpa lay) *and your Aunt Audie pushed you when you needed pushing. Then college, and now you're a long way off making a good living. Where is it you live?'*

"I got up from my chair and turned on a small table lamp. *'Atlanta, and I teach some college classes there, but I miss Walkamile and my family so much. This old place never really leaves your heart. It's always home.'*

"The lamp cast splinters of light and a shadowed glow across the room. Doctor Goldman looked directly at me, and the lamp's light reflected against the lenses of his glasses. He stared at me for a moment and then almost whispered his final remarks to me: *'Micah, I love Abraham—like a brother. I never had a brother in real life. Your Grandpa was a man's man. I look back now and regret a thousand times over that I was not able to become even half the man he was.'* Doctor Goldman picked up his bag, looked about the room as if he had misplaced something, and then in a weariful, shamble-footed walk he departed. In that one split second I saw an old, old man and sensed deeply within me how the face of my own mortality might one day appear unto me.

"I sat speechless after he left. I was awestruck that for the first time in my life I had heard a white man call my Grandpa by his real first name: *Abraham!* My teetering emotions had been swept away by an outgoing rip tide. I said another one of my silent prayers: *'God, I hope you allowed Grandpa the honor of hearing the Good Doctor call him by his first name. It would please him so!'"*

Chapter Eighteen

Charity Chambers:

'... his boyish glee was so pure.'

"We received official word that my Uncle Stace was to be released on April 2nd. My mother and I had visited him at least twice a year during the ten-year period he was a resident of the mental institution in Austin. During our early visits we became so depressed that it's a true wonder that either of us ever returned—but we did. We'd make the long bus trip to Austin, stay overnight in a cheap boardinghouse and get up the next morning and catch a taxicab out to the institution. We'd stay as long as we could, but we both felt wretched from the moment we arrived until the time we got back home after the long bus trip.

"The things we could bring Uncle Stace were very restrictive. My mother had eventually decided that we all would be better off mailing packages to Uncle Stace. If he never received them, that was the luck of the draw in my mother's eyes. She could rest at night, she proclaimed, knowing that her intentions were in the right place in her heart. When we did visit Uncle Stace, we'd ask him about such-and-such item that we had mailed him, and he would stare blankly at us. Whether he had received the item, or whether he fully understood our question was a point up for debate. Each of these exchanges with him tore at our hearts in ways I can never describe to someone who hasn't experienced such things.

"Over the ten-year period we both watched Uncle Stace transform from the broken individual we had seen being driven off in the Sheriff's car to a frighteningly quiet man who looked blankly at the world around him. What he saw was known only to him, but it would not have been difficult to paint the picture of what came into his limited view. He saw metal bars on all sides of him seven days each week; he saw cold, impersonal concrete everywhere he looked; he saw large keys jangling from the waists of insensitive guards who likely viewed him as a mere piece of discarded humanity; he saw dim lighting in places that needed bright lights; and he saw stark lighting where dim lights would have brought a semblance of comfort to him; he saw other tortured souls who either stared at the same things he did or who ranted, raved and screamed at ghosts of the past either imaginary or real; and he saw himself, the ultimate torture, as he might have been; he saw Matthew Chambers' being floating within his view with the tractor plow embedded in his chest; and he saw the grim specter of death as it callously erased the slightest smile on Matthew's face after Dr. Goldman had given Matthew the shot to do away with his pain. And as all of these specters streaked across his plane of vision with a predictable constancy, he withdrew to a world where he thought he could balance what he saw and heard into at least a muted reality. But he failed. At his own recognition that he was helpless against all about him, Stace Wellborn ceased speaking.

"And surely Uncle Stace heard the muted cries of Joshua Philbin as he was being tossed into the hole in the ground on that rainy day—the thud and the splash of water and the finality all screaming out in non-unison. And he could recall the odors of the supper he had shared with the Philbins that same evening after he and Jeremiah Philbin had filled up the hole at the cemetery with the viscous red mud: fried squirrel that was served on a big stone platter, the heads of the squirrels showing their sharp teeth as if in protest and denial of their impending death; the beans floating in grease that seemed to move in eddying patterns; the cornbread which gave off the rancid smell of ham drippings; the coffee, too strong to appreciate on an empty stomach. All of this: the food, the combined odors, the atmosphere, the meaningless chatter of the three Philbins made his heart and soul come up empty. And the crowning insult to his already fragile integrity: the Philbins talked and laughed about Joshua's death—how he had gasped for a final breath, how he had finally turned a light shade of bluish-gray, and how his death rattle sounded like water gurgling down a little stream.

"Uncle Stace was brought to us on the prescribed day. We had been briefed on both his physical and mental conditions, and we were troubled by the fact that he no longer spoke to anyone. We speculated on how we would be able to communicate with him. My mother and I had fixed up a special bedroom for him. We had taken great care that he would have clothes in the small wardrobe that would fit him, but we waited until he was settled in before we all went in to Walkamile to buy him some decent brogans. It was not a trip I care to remember. Uncle Stace was so out of his element that he became, within a matter of minutes, a quaking bundle of flesh. We were forced to return home immediately before his actions created an unexplainable scene in the store. Uncle Stace was a fish out of water; in his role as a free man, now he had been terribly miscast in a role that he no longer knew how to play. A sad, sad man, he was genuinely out of his element.

"Uncle Stace and I went for long walks in the early April warmth. He stopped to look at, and feel, and smell every weed, plant and bush that we saw. Once he broke off the tiny stems of a pepper plant and slid the seeded portion through his teeth. I did the same. He then smiled broadly as if he were recalling a time long ago when he had done this same act as a boy. When the pepper began to sting a bit in his mouth, he laughed with the joy that a young lad might exhibit. His gaiety was uninhibited to the maximum as if he were having the time of his life. I could have cried upon realizing that his boyish glee was so pure that I could have sworn that I was looking at the face of a five-year old.

"Trees of all kinds were like a balm to his bruised and tortured spirit. He reveled in the greens and golds which slashed through the woods. He touched the emerald velvet mosses as if they were prized gems. He stood for minutes on end and listened to the swishing noises as the gentle wind, really no more than a light breeze, made its way through the pine needles on the massive pine trees. His eyes glowed with a splendid, new-found wonder, his face creased into a look of fulfilled and recognized peace, and he threw his head back and then closed his eyes. It was as if he were hearing God's own angels playing their golden harps especially for him. As quickly as he had allowed himself to be engulfed in the reverie of the pine trees, he as quickly returned to the real world around us. Watching him, as I did, I felt a persistent urge to reach out to him and ask him to speak my name or just any word that would come to him. Something inside of me held me back, however. The doctors at the institution had told us that Uncle Stace would speak when he was capable of throwing off the demons that were assaulting his very being. No sooner than that time, they had stressed.

"One morning a bumblebee stung him on his left hand. He had been about to pick a dandelion when the bee struck. He wished only to hold the dandelion's blow-ball, wispy and insubstantial, near his mouth and blow it into smithereens of tiny white parachutes. His hand turned red from the sting almost instantly and began to puff up. Without any forethought, Uncle Stace bent over and yanked a plant up by its roots. He stripped a handful of green leaves from the plant and crushed them into a wadding, then placed the wadding in his mouth and chewed for only a few seconds. He next took the chewed-up leaves from his mouth and placed them over the bee sting and held them tightly for several minutes with his cupped right hand. He did not allow me to take part in this at all, and he gave all the evident clues that he wanted no sympathy on my part. The beauty of my knowing this was that he communicated all of this with his eyes. He had not said a word since he had returned home. Spoken words did not appear to be one of his requirements for communication. Regardless, the red puffy area on his hand was absent when he removed the chewed-up leaves. There was no look of wonderment on his face after this simple procedure. Stored somewhere in his memory bank was this peculiar knowledge which he had learned from someone many years before.

"Uncle Stace absolutely adored the blue-bodied and green-bodied dragonflies that appeared in the mid-morning hours and in the low afternoon light near sunset. He would try mightily to have one light upon one of his fingers and, if successful, he would stare fixedly at the glassy panes of their wings as if each one was a new-found wonder. The iridescence I saw in their coloration reminded me of the stained-glass windows I had noted in several churches. In a fashion they were like flying rainbows.

"We owned an outdoor cat that we had named Pesky, and she had little to do with any of us other than to accept our food offerings if she were so inclined. Skittish to the point of not allowing anyone to touch her, she had taken up residence in a storage shed at the back of our house. My mother and I had made limited attempts to bond with Pesky, but each time either of us approached her she would scamper off. Finally, we both gave up.

"Pesky gave birth to a litter of three kittens two or three months after Stace had been returned to us. When the kittens were about three weeks old, according to our calculations which we had based on her behavior, Pesky did something that my mother and I could not believe: she dutifully carried each kitten from the storage shed to where Stace was sitting in a chair under our lone chinaberry tree. More amazing was that she basically presented each of the kittens, one at a time, to him and left the first kitten in his care until she could bring the second one and then the third one to him.

"We watched as Stace took the little balls of fur from Pesky and gingerly held them close to his chest. He stroked each one of them with his big hands with a gentleness that moved both my mother and me to tears. Pesky had hopped up in his lap by the time he had picked up the second and third kitten and was demanding her full share of attention from him!

"It is difficult for me to describe the electricity of this scene, but some intangible forces compelled me to believe that these three little creatures, their mother and my Uncle Stace were in direct communication with each other and somehow were in complete harmony with their individually known universe. Of course, not a word was said unless you might think that the accepting meows from the kittens were words in their common language. I will not forget the spine-tingling sensation that overcame me as I watched. It was a natural and flawless thing of beauty. Our tears were a confirming recognition of this beauty. Pesky and the kittens had bonded with Uncle Stace on their terms—not his.

"Another occasion I've not forgotten: one day when Stace was sitting quietly on our front porch in an area shaded by a honeysuckle vine, I observed another interaction which is difficult to describe. Several monarch butterflies, elegantly regal in their makeup and coloration, were hovering about and floating near to the abundant flowers on the vine. It appeared to me that they were in an obvious competition with a magnificent silver-spotted skipper and a flawlessly artistic duskywing which seemed to slice through the air with velvety maneuvers. Stace had suddenly become very still as he sat nearby—in fact, he sat stiffly in the chair. First, one butterfly flew over to where he sat and lit on his left shoulder; then another, and another. After the exodus from the vine the monarchs seemed to preen and primp on Uncle Stace's shoulders, flaunting their pristine magnificence for several minutes. Then as abruptly as they had chosen his shoulders as their base, they departed and flew away from the porch and the vine, carried by a gentle updraft of a westerly breeze. The silver-spotted skipper and the duskywing lingered for mere seconds before making their own exits. The look on Uncle Stace's face was one of total wonderment as he accepted the unprompted choices made by the butterflies. A thousand words from Uncle Stace could not have painted a better picture for me as I watched discretely from our living room. His face expressed all facets of the wordless encounter: from their initial acceptance of his broad shoulder as a preening site to their sudden leave-taking.

"My mother accepted her brother as he was. She made no attempts to get him to talk. Her theory, as good as any I suppose and in agreement with the doctors' admonitions, was that he would talk whenever he was good and ready. *'What he has closed off in his mind and in his spirit is none of our business. It could be that that's his way to cope in this world that now scares the bijesus out of him. You and me? We can't know what bugaboos are after him. We just need to love him and act interested in him at all times. We can never allow him to think that we are goin' to abandon him. That's all we can do. Beneath all of what you see is still your Uncle Stace and my brother Stace.'*

"Uncle Stace lived with us after he came home from the mental institution for seven years before he died. My mother found him dead in bed one morning. She came to our kitchen where I was fixing breakfast and took me in her arms. She wasn't crying as she spoke to me in a soft voice, *'Your uncle's dead! And my only brother is gone.'* My mother and I went to his bedroom, I with a dreaded reluctance. What I saw provided me with a solace I could never have dreamed of: Uncle Stace lay on his back, and he had a smile of peace on his face. What I saw at that moment was the Uncle Stace I had once known when he was in fine fettle. I wanted to speak to him and tell him how much I loved him, and I felt that he would surely rise up from the bed and speak to me. Instead, my mother and I stood there for a long, long time in a tight embrace, crying our hearts out."

Chapter Nineteen

Mavis Murray:

'You've just took a long, restful sleep.'

"I never married. I think you'll know why before long if you keep on reading this. My inner psyche, damaged beyond repair, would not let go of some wound-up mechanism which, if it had become unwound, would have released me from a bushel of doubts I had carried within my heart since I was seven years old. I became a good student in school, trying as best I could to put aside certain concerns I had about my origin and my trying relationship with both my grandmother and my mother. I could not, even if I tried harder than should be expected from any ordinary child, wholly accept Adrian, my supposed "father." There was a link missing from the chain when it came to this matter. That missing link would not let me connect to him. Under the best of circumstances I might have succeeded, but my circumstances shied away from anything that could be considered a norm. Normalcy had flown out the window when Adrian came on the scene.

"My mother played at the game of marriage. *'Ad'*, as she called him at all times, was a celebrity for a short time when the County Judge had deemed him to be a war hero. That appellation faded rather quickly for reasons I could not comprehend. But my Mother would not speak of that matter at all when I was in their presence.

In fact, evasiveness and verbal wordplay seemed to rise up instantaneously if I should suddenly interrupt their secretive conversations.

"I did overhear my mother and Ad discussing why he had been turned down for a government stipend relating to his prisoner-of-war status. Then, within a matter of weeks, I had overheard a heated exchange between my Mother and Ad which ended with nasty remarks and a slammed screen door: *'I can't figure out why you don't get your lazy ass out of this house and get a job like the rest of the soldier boys that come home from the war! Did you let them Krauts cut out your nuts?'* Then the screen door slamming and Ad striding out in an exaggerated gait in the direction of the feed lot at the back of our house—that's how I remembered that scene. The language, foul and not understood by me, repelled me and my naïve sensitivities.

"I was fourteen or fifteen, I think, just going into my first year of high school when the worst possible thing I could have ever imagined happened. My mother and grandmother had departed for Huntsville, about forty or so miles away, early one morning. School had been out for several weeks, and I had been allowed to be lazy for a change. They had invited me to go with them, but I begged off. God! I wish I had gone. That's looking back, and that won't profit anybody a bit to engage in that.

"I was in my room reading a favorite movie magazine. As I reached over to turn on my bedside lamp, I sensed a *presence* in my room, and before I looked up from my magazine, I heard Ad's voice, husky and unnatural in tone. It brought shivers to me—it was not like his voice at all. I can never forget what I heard: *'You and me, we got to quit bein' like we are to each other. You and me—we need to get to know each other like a daddy and his girl should. It ain't healthy for any of us to be actin' like we do. No, girl!'*

"I looked up and dropped the magazine on my bed. What I saw in his face was so frightening to me that I could not even attempt to scream. My throat was dry, and I could barely breathe in and out. My lips felt parched. For a fleeting moment my eyes seemed to open but became frozen in a locked position. The picture I am trying to paint is one that can never be painted with his exact look fully captured. His face bore a look of pure evil! His eyes, now dark and menacing, sagged and drooped, and his lips quivered. He rubbed himself in his front with one hand and took off his belt with his other.

"Then I leaned back against the headboard of my bed, my body stiffening but my arms and legs shaking as if I were freezing to death on this, a warm day. He spoke again, his voice a lower sound, almost the growl of a cornered beast: *'You and me, I got somethin' for my little girl. It'll make her like me a lot. It might even make her love me.'* He then walked toward my bed, hopping on one foot as he yanked off his khakis, one leg at a time.

"God is good to victims in a way, I believe. I cannot recall one concrete thing after I heard his words *'love me.'* My physical body and my mental defenses must have kicked in to spare me from remembering the assault which occurred. I had no real concept of time, but it seemed that the violations of my body and spirit were endless.

"It was dark when my mother and my grandmother got home. Their wafting voices came to me like surreal music on the early evening air, and I could not force myself from my bed, though I desperately wanted to flee to them or at least run toward the sound of their voices. I could see my body on the bed, my disheveled hair, my torn dress, and uncountable large red spots staining both my bed linen and my ravaged underwear, and I was floating above all of this in an ethereal paradise so pleasant that I did not wish to leave it.

"The thrust of a remark that Ad had tossed at me as he received his apparent satisfaction came forth with a brutality that plunged me back to my own painful reality. He had hissed as he departed: *'You, girl, you mention this to your Mama or your Grandma and I'll go straight to the law and tell them what they did to your Grandpa— they smothered him, they did!'*

"Doctor Goldman was sitting by my bedside when I awakened. I recognized him immediately but it was as if I was again floating above the bed. My bedside lamp had been turned off, but another light cast its shadows from an adjoining room. I could not feel anything, and I had no concept of what time it might be. In the warmth of my drug-induced cocoon I was surprised that I had awareness sufficient to recognize Doctor Goldman. Perhaps he really wasn't sitting at my bedside. Perhaps it wasn't Doctor Goldman sitting there—perhaps it wasn't Doctor Goldman sitting there . . . and I seemed to hear the echo of my subconscious thought processes.

"My mother was asleep in a chair behind the doctor. I knew that it was my mother. I recognized her, but I could not force myself to speak. *'You've just took a long, restful sleep,'* I heard my mother say. *'The Good Doctor gave you something to make you rest.'* Her voice seemed to travel to my ears in wave-like motions. Perhaps she really wasn't in my room at all. Perhaps she wasn't in my room at all—and the maddening echoes continued!

"I still could not speak to the doctor or to my mother, but I wanted to tell them that Grandpa Philbin had been smothered to death. Deep, deep inside me I had a clawing feeling that they were going to do the same with me. *'Why can't I talk out loud?'* I asked myself, but the words would not form on my lips. *'Why would they do that to Grandpa Philbin? Why?'* I asked over and over, but the forced words betrayed me as they fell back within my dry throat. Over and over they reverberated, reaching the wall only a few feet away and then somehow being flung back by an unknown and unseen force.

"When I could no longer try to ask questions, I screamed in what seemed to be an unending shriek for help. I had never known my Grandpa, but in a flashing illumination I thought I saw a man's face. It was laughing at me! I had no spirit of resolve to challenge the laughing face. I wanted so much to close my eyes and never wake up again.

'Doctor, can't you give her something?' Now I heard my grandmother talking. She sounded ethereal as her voice slowly faded to nothingness. I couldn't make out if her voice was real or not. Was she in the room? The thought was dull and heavy on my mind as I tried to consider it. Over and over I pondered the thought. Over and over.

'I'll give her one more of these, and then I'll have to go. Just keep her quiet, and she'll eventually be all right. It may take a long, long time though.' I felt a needle prick my arm, and I immediately slept but heard unrecognizable voices: Doctor Goldman's authoritarian words, Grandpa Philbin's gasping, Ad's slurring talk, and my own dry-throated screaming into the vastness of a night, asking for help. There was none, but I slept."

⮂

Chapter Twenty

Koskobe Renner:

'Koskobe, can you do it?'

"Even after my Daddy died in 1950, his carpentry/construction business continued to flourish. Anna had agreed to run the bookkeeping part as well as to supervise the office duties, and my brother Bob and me did the legwork behind the purchasing of materials, house and/or business floor plans, and finally the behind-the-scenes involvement in the construction projects themselves. On rare occasions we had to meet with architects who were asked by builders to oversee our construction. Neither Bob nor me cared one whit when this happened. We ended up doing it our way, even though we listened politely as college-trained professionals argued over some crappy thing that didn't amount to a hill of beans as far as we was concerned. But that's the workaday world, plain and simple.

"It turns out that Daddy had been a masterful teacher, teaching us the ropes down to the everyday nitty-gritty of this extremely competitive business. He had started out as a carpenter himself and over the years had honed his reputation as a competent and honest worker. This solid reputation led to his entry into the broader construction field. His word was all anyone needed, and he accepted a handshake from a customer as a bond of trust.

"We built our continuing business on his reputation and with some simplicity just carried it forward into our own work. Right after the war there had been a bit of a lull in business, and our workload fell off a lot, but when this great country of ours got itself involved in another war—well, things seemed to pick up again. Daddy had said a hundred times over that despite the untold negatives, war always brought on profit. Of course, that didn't mean he was a war-monger who wanted war just for the sake of his own interests. No way! After all, my Daddy had named me *Koskobe* for a reason.

"We somehow survived the 60s. I remember that time as a time of turbulence. You couldn't turn on a radio or a television without hearing something about *flower children, dope, sex and free love, and 'Nam.'* The young people, during that drawn-out decade, thought only of themselves and spurned everything that was considered *establishment.* In a way, I suppose me, Anna and Bob was establishment. We was trying to build our business so that something would be left when we made our final exit. Then we reached the 70s and all hell broke loose with the Watergate mess. Right after Tricky Dick bid his farewell, I recall that we was just floating along with ordinary construction jobs—really nothing to boast about—but we all was making a honest living.

"That's about the time when I was contacted by Alicia Woodman, Ph.D., all the way from Harvard University, that is in the early to middle 1970s. Dr. Woodman had been in the same grade as Daddy from the first grade through the twelfth. Daddy said Alicia Woodman had more brains than the law allows. Her contact came first in the form of a telephone call from Dr. Woodman herself. Then followed a lengthy letter, typewritten and all, in which she outlined her dreams for a special facility in Walkamile. Her outline of her dream plan was almost too much for us to believe, too good to be true, especially when a small-time outfit like ours was handed such a plum job.

"She must have thought a whole lot of my Daddy to seek out what had once been his small business to handle her *'grandiose'* plans. She had used that word in her letter, and Anna looked it up for me—and I had chuckled at her blustering so. She knew for sure that Daddy had died in 1950 because she had made a respectable contribution to a local charity in his memory. And she had made a point of mentioning *dear Arppra'* several times in her letter. In a way, I guess she had a bit of respect for me and Bob, too, or she wouldn't have bothered with us from the git-go.

"It seems that Dr. Woodman had been awarded an open-ended grant from a prestigious think tank consortium. It appeared, on the surface, that she would have a 100% free hand in disposing of the value of the grant on any project which would enhance the cultural improvement of a community smaller than 10,000 residents. Walkamile easily qualified, as she pointed out in her letter.

"The federal government would underwrite the future maintenance of the facility, and various sponsoring organizations all over the country would endow the funding for administrators and teachers/mentors in all areas of the facility's daily operations. Everything, according to her proposal letter, appeared to be wrapped up in a neat, if not air-tight, package. All we needed to do was to submit our own proposal of construction costs in a binding contract form. Easier said than done! That meant lawyers and accountants and God-only-knows-who-else. But we'd be fools of folly to let something like this slide by us.

"What Dr. Woodman had in mind was the construction of a viable youth center which would offer summer classroom facilities for history, art, music, and remedial tutoring in the language arts, science and mathematics. The facility would also offer a *'potpourri'* (Anna found this in a French dictionary for me) of athletic equipment: a regulation gymnasium, swimming pool, shower facilities for both boys and girls, gymnastic equipment, a regulation tennis court (I didn't know a soul who played tennis), a complete commercially-rated kitchen and other venues unheard of even in the best of public and private high schools in the area.

"As her proposal stated: *'No expense is to be spared so that Walkamile shall have a state-of-the-art facility of which we all shall be selfishly and inordinately proud.'* Her proposal ended with what Anna called a *'quixotic question'* handwritten in ink in her own hand: *'Koskobe, can you do it? If you're anything like your father, Arppra, I know you can, and I have full confidence in you and Anna and Bob.'*

"We—Anna, me and Bob and all of our other employees—took the bait; and Anna and me began a series of meetings with lawyers, accountants and even an architect out of Beaumont. All of this took several weeks, and during that period of time, Dr. Woodman called me two or three times each week, remembering something else which she wished to *'unload on me'* as she would laughingly phrase it. It may sound a bit odd for me to admit it, but I actually looked forward to her calls, finding her off-the-wall humor would uplift me if I happened to be down-in-the-dumps. And she never talked down to me—not even once.

"During one telephone call, Dr. Woodman brought up the subject of audio-visual equipment for the classroom settings; another time she spelled out her interest in an intercom system (*'Every school up here has this system.'*); and even once she skated close to the edge of her own modesty when she had to broach the subject of differences between the boys' and girls' bathroom equipment. I may have sent her over the modesty's edge when I assured her that Walkamile had advanced a little beyond the two-holer stage when it came to toilets. Irregardless, there was a long, long silence on the other end of the telephone. Whether the silence was a rebuke of my attempted humor or whether she had had to gather her wits before continuing—I'll never know. In only a moment she was rattling on just as before with all the confidence of someone who knows that they have the upper hand when it comes to brain power. I sure wasn't in her league in that department.

"When all the paperwork and all the legalities finally got ironed out to everyone's satisfaction, Dr. Woodman foisted one more surprise on me in a personal letter she wrote: *'I have made it clear—crystal clear to the powers-that-be in Walkamile—that it is my most serious wish that the facility be made available to the sizeable Negro population in the Walkamile community and surrounding area, always on an equal basis. There is no plausible reason on earth that the Negro children not have an opportunity— mind you—to use the facilities on every day of every week. It's a pity, pity—don't get me started on that subject—that we all cannot forget the black and white thing of skin color and get on with all of us being true Americans. Sharing is what this great country is about.'*

"The letter continued: *'A firm schedule will be established from Day One so that there will never be any future misunderstanding regarding this matter. They have their unique cultural events— Emancipation Day (or Juneteenth, as they call it)—and there will be other special events that will present themselves that are uniquely theirs. I am sure that cultural events surrounding their celebration of what we know Up East as Black History Month—in February—will require extensive use of these facilities. This time of honoring their cultural heritage already has almost fifty years behind it. Such things relating to their heritage as African-Americans should be encouraged in that they are laudable.'*

"I was glad that this matter would not be in my bailiwick. Leave that to the big boys and the political blowhards who always appeared at any event which would produce results to their advantage—and get them votes.

"With all the *T's* crossed and the *I's* dotted, the groundbreaking ceremony was a limited and simple affair. Dr. Woodman flew in from Boston, made a short speech which praised the efforts of many of the local citizens, and, with a sense of dramatic dignity, took a shovel long used by my Daddy and shoveled the first earth from the building site. As several cameras clicked, she added a closing remark: *'This wonderful and future edifice, which I now christen the Walkamile Cultural Center, belongs to all of us. My dear friends of Walkamile, remember that each time you take advantage of the activities and planned programs here, you are contributing to the cultural elevation of our fine community. So now I bid adieu to you all for a very brief time—all of you, my friends.'* There was resounding applause as she handed the shovel to one of my workmen.

"It took a year for the Walkamile Cultural Center to stand before us completed. The Grand Opening Ceremony was scheduled for September 27-28, 1975, a two-day affair covering an entire Saturday and Sunday. Anna had fretted for weeks about the dress she would wear and how she would have her hair done. Bob and me—well, we had to make a trip to Kerr's Department Store in Huntsville to see if they could roust each of us a suit to wear at the Grand Opening. Bob asked me if Kerr's was still in business. I didn't know for sure. Regardless, without a doubt we could now afford several new suits bought from any store in the area. Dr. Woodman had brought a golden egg to us on a silver platter."

Chapter Twenty-One

Anastasia Woodman:

'. . . Johnny-on-the-spot with the grass turning brown.'

"I always felt *minimal* while in the presence of my Aunt Alicia. I knew she possessed an intelligence so far above and beyond me that it took incredible effort on her part to come down to my level. But she did, for she was always an integral part of our family whether in Massachusetts or visiting us in Walkamile. I often wondered if she did this by means contrived in her own mind as a step-by-step process or whether all of it was a mapped-out but subconscious undertaking on her part. The final how of the situation was of no great concern to me. In the end she and I communicated easily with each other. I viewed her in the light of a combination mother, aunt and an older sister, though at times she could individualize herself and be just one facet of these three to me.

"We often shared secrets with each other like little giggling girls. There was never any doubt in either of us that one would betray the other. What was said in private was sacrosanct; what was uttered in public was often preplanned so that the remarks would sally forth as off-the-cuff and terribly clever *bon mots*. We thrived on these hilarities (not in the faces of the recipients of our rehearsed rejoinders in all instances) but in our private moments. I fondly recall one incident in which Aunt Alicia rose to the occasion when she was able to deliver a well-timed zinger with such aplomb that I had remained speechless when the combined thrust and impact of her delivery had hit their mark. She had been superb on that particular evening.

"A member of the Walkamile City Council (he's deceased now, so I won't mention his name) had the reputation of being an outrageous flirt of the first order. It was not beyond his limitless arrogance to think that every woman in Walkamile, in fact in the whole county, would willingly acquiesce to his increasingly aggressive flirtations. Aunt Alicia and I had heard of one such flirtation device that he had used on several women, much to their immediate embarrassment. His *modus operandi* was one characterized by an unmitigated gall.

"He would, as we were told by close friends, approach an unsuspecting woman in a public venue and whisper in such a manner that he could always be heard: *'Gosh, lady! If I weren't such an honorable gentleman, I'd tell you that I'd love to get in your pants!'* The victim, knowing that everyone within earshot had overheard his arrogant remark, would wish to die a thousand deaths *Johnny-on-the-spot with the grass turning brown.* No suitable grouping of words would come to their quivering lips with an immediacy, and they would be left standing or sitting where they were and looking quite foolish in the aftermath, especially with their inaction. In almost all situations, the victimized woman would not allow that any of this had really occurred, hesitant to tell a husband or a boyfriend lest a serious altercation arise at a later time.

"Aunt Alicia had come home to Walkamile for an extended stay one summer. She and I would pass our time with many 'What if?' scenarios over our morning cups of coffee or involve ourselves with such silliness over a cup of tea in the afternoon. This particular City

Councilman's name came up during one of these sessions, and the game was on. One of us, either Aunt Alicia or I, would get the City Councilman's goat to such an extent that he would likely never try such a gambit as *'I'd love to get in your pants'* for the rest of his life. We knew, in time, that one of us unwittingly would be cast into an environment in which this fellow would insinuate himself upon either of us as one of his chosen victims. His pursuit was relentless, so many of our friends had warned us. We had to make plans for such an occurrence. And so we did—diligently and with *'malice aforethought'* as Aunt Alicia so aptly put it as her eyes sparkled with magnificent mischief.

"We had both been invited to a fund-raising Spaghetti Supper which would benefit a crippled children's facility sponsored by the national Elks. The event was held at the local high school's cafeteria. Of course, all of the City Council members, the Mayor, the Fire Chief, the Police Chief, the various ministers of all the Walkamile churches and just your usual, everyday citizen would be in attendance to support the fund-raising. Aunt Alicia and I arrived at the prescribed time, bought our *'spaghetti ticket'* as the young receptionist called it, and then we got in line to be served. By the luck of the draw we had to pass by a long table at which were seated the various City Council members and other prominent citizenry.

"Well, you guessed it. There he was! The City Councilman (I shall not name him out of respect for the fact that he is now dead) was seated about halfway down the long table. When he spotted Aunt Alicia and me, his face broke out in a big smile. He could not contain himself when he realized that he would be able to speak to Dr. Alicia Woodman who was visiting from Massachusetts. True to form, he made the most critical error in his life with his arrogant and ill-timed proposal.

"In a loud voice filled with melodramatic overtones, he looked straightway at Aunt Alicia as she was being served and said (so that everyone at the table could hear him): *'My dear Doctor Woodman, if I were not such an honorable Southern gentleman, I would tell you in no uncertain terms that I would love to get in your pants.'* The loud talking, the clanking noises as food was being served, the shuffling of nearby feet, the intimate chattering and laughter of a table of women—all of these came to a massive and hasty silence deadened by shock.

"Without missing a beat, as if she were a maestro in command of a large orchestra, Aunt Alicia looked straight into the eyes of the City Councilman. Standing stiffly erect though without a hint of arrogance, she responded in a voice crystal clear so that everyone nearby could hear: *'My dear fellow! If I were not a true Southern lady, I would throw my plate of spaghetti in your ugly face. Being that I am, I only wish to inform you that there is no room in my pants for you because one asshole already resides there and it desires no company, especially yours!'*

"It took only a matter of seconds for the entire coterie of prominent men at the table to stand and applaud boisterously. The City Councilman in question made a hurried exit from the table, and we did not see him for the remainder of the evening. The loud talking resumed; the spaghetti servers began to serve the lined-up patrons as if nothing had occurred; the noise of shuffling feet and the pleasant chatter and laughter of women were once again heard.

"When Aunt Alicia and I got home that evening, we sat in the kitchen and laughed until Aunt Alicia called out helplessly: *'Anastasia! I have peed my pants because I've laughed so much!'* She then asked me, *'Do you think he'll ever have the courage to run for public office again in this lifetime? We could campaign either for him or against him, you and I. Can't you see us carrying signs as we walk around the courthouse square? Let me think! Our* *signs could read **Vote for the Uninvited Asshole** if we're for him and dear, we'll have to come up with a placard or billboard sign if we oppose him. I've run out of ideas and also of laughter. What a day we've had! We must tell Murt for I know he will enjoy every little word of this episodic event.'*

"When Aunt Alicia enrolled at Rice Institute right out of high school, she was only sixteen, I think. Dr. Goldman had somehow arranged for her to board with a professor of English and his wife on Sunset, a street very close to the school. She had told me a number of anecdotes of her life as a college student during her first year. *'Darling, I was as green as a gourd when it came to the many niceties and social graces that confronted me in the academic setting. This was not my dear Mother's fault at all. Living as we did in little rural Walkamile automatically sets limits as to our breadth of experiences in the social aspects of life. When I initially realized my own limitations, I made up my mind then and there to watch the more experienced persons—and I began to mimic their behaviors. All in all, I became a quite competent actress. Who on God's Earth had ever been forced to use a finger bowl? I observed the protocol and then followed the inane ritual to the letter of the law. A totally impractical exercise in good manners, it became a bit of a game to me. And darling, suddenly I was one of them—as phony as the first day of the Summer Solstice is long.'*

"Aunt Alicia's studies at Rice Institute encompassed a range of courses catering to her love of the *'-ologies'* as she referred to them with unbridled affection. At Harvard, where she pursued her Masters, she specialized in Psychology and wrote a thesis entitled *When Small Town America Meets Big City America.* The head of the Psychology Department praised her work as *'brilliant—on a plane twice removed from the extraordinary.'* Her Ph.D at Harvard was awarded her after she sliced through the heads of several

Liberal Arts professors during her oral examination. Her subject matter had been *Our Personal Culture: What We Cannot Know About Ourselves.* Aunt Alicia once told me that getting the Ph.D. was like the time when she was a child and had fallen off the old log at Menard Creek—easy, nothing to it, so she had said.

"On other occasions, you would not guess in a thousand years that Aunt Alicia was anything more than an ordinary country girl. One day, when she had come home for a Thanksgiving break, she and I were walking in nearby woods. The hint of autumn was pervasive in the air—dust on the horizon, leaves of brilliant reds and yellows and golds strewn about on the path—and we discovered a dried grapevine which had once been attached to a small tree. *'Muscadine! Aren't these the grapes that would blister your lips if you ate too many of them? Child, let me tell you. When I was much younger, we felt compelled to mimic the screen actors who looked so elegant smoking their long cigarettes in almost every scene in a movie. Of course, our hides would have been tanned royally if we had dared to smoke real cigarettes and come home with smoke odors in our hair and clothing. So . . . we smoked grapevines! And dear, we burned the bijesus out of our lips! Blisters, either from the lit vine or from what was in the vine in the first place. What memories!'*

"There are hundreds of other fascinating episodes I could relate about Aunt Alicia. And I bet that she could tell you an equal amount of stories about me. But she wouldn't if I asked her not to do so. She's that kind of aunt; she's that kind of friend. And now you all know why I might, at times, feel *minimal* in her presence. I shouldn't though, and my Daddy Murt, her brother, never did. We were all comfortable in our own skins around each other. That's what families are all about."

&

Chapter Twenty-Two

Patrick A. Goldman:

'Mrs. Snobby Bitch is in the E.R.'

"My Grandpa lost both his physical and mental grip on the everyday mundane things which make up the basic elements of a life. At first, the physical part presented itself in a noticeable fashion: shuffling feet, a pronounced limp—sliding one foot and stepping heavily on the other, hands shaking when attempting to sign his name to a check or to a document, and other small behavioral actions to which the average young person pays no heed at all. Deep was the hurt for those who loved him and saw the inexorable toll on his body and on his once-proud bearing.

"Worse yet, the mental lapses, at first ignored by my father and me, became more tangible and could not be overlooked by us. While either of us was in his presence we noted that Grandpa would not always turn off a gas jet on the kitchen stove in a timely manner, allowing pots and pans to burn; dirty dishes would pile up in the sink willy-nilly and he seemed not to be bothered by them. His prevailing attitude was one of very poor logic—that the dishes would clean themselves and somehow find their way to their proper place in the china cabinet.

"Once fastidious to a fault, Grandpa became sloppy in his dress, and it was not unusual to see him wearing a food-stained shirt for days on end. Of course, these things became a matter of course after Old Jessup had died. And Grandpa abhorred shaving each morning. *'Where in God's Name am I going that I need to shave?'* he would argue.

"Dad and I arranged for a part-time housekeeper, Mrs. Myrtle Froman, to check in on Grandpa every morning around eight o'clock. Faithful to the terms of our agreed arrangement, Mrs. Froman lasted little more than a week. Grandpa yelled at us: *'I don't want to be molly-coddled by some woman. Breakfast in bed, my dear God! And I don't want to get naked in front of her and then have her bathe me in a tub. Can't a man have any privacy around here? I'd rather go dirty. And while I'm dirty I can eat a bowl of cereal, thank you very much, just as well as I could if I were sparkling clean.'*

"Oh! How we longed for Old Jessup! He could talk Grandpa into doing anything, and there would have been no raised voices and no arguments of any consequence. He had manhandled Grandpa those many years when Grandpa would get rip-roaring drunk and would not allow anyone else within ten feet of him. Old Jessup and Grandpa existed in a climate of détente in which their constant give-and-take ameliorated any sore points and avoided those elements which might have caused friction.

"My own Grandma, even on one of her good days, could do absolutely nothing with Grandpa. I think I might know now why she sipped her paregoric and skirted the pharmaceutical rules with her pain medications. Grandpa was, and could be, a royal pain-in-the-ass. He and Grandma must have adopted a mythical peace treaty early in their marriage because neither of the two ever seemed to cross an imaginary line into the other's emotional territory.

"Dad and I checked around in the Negro community to

determine if we could find a reliable young black man who had a sufficiency of diplomatic skills to handle someone like Grandpa. Grandpa had many, many friends in the Rogersville neighborhood where most of the blacks lived. There were no takers. Quite a few young black women were qualified to do this type of work, but we knew from the experience with Mrs. Froman that bringing in a black female would send Grandpa up a tree in a flash. We were hoisted on our own petard, I suppose, or on Grandpa's as I reminded my father.

"Or were we? I was teaching school in Huntsville, and my classes would end on the last Friday in May. My Dad finally conceded to my offer of staying with Grandpa over the summer. Not being married at the time, I could arrange for my landlady in Huntsville to watch over my apartment during the summer. I would have to pay the rent, but I would be able to hang on to it. And I would become Grandpa's around-the-clock companion or his *valet du jour* as he had once called Old Jessup.

"When we told Grandpa of our intentions, I initially thought he would bust his gut, but he said little of nothing. I think, deep down in his heart of hearts, he realized that he truly needed help. He smiled at me the first day I was in attendance and quipped: *'If you paint your face black, I might think of you as Old Jessup; but . . .* (and he paused dramatically as if he were a seasoned stage actor) *you're not in his league at all.'* We laughed at the same time, and I knew that we would get along reasonably well. I dreaded the thought of our first confrontation, however, when and if it came. I hoped it would never come.

"His deterioration was hardly gradual. Each day I saw marked changes in him, almost perverse, and my heart hurt to observe them. I treated him with exaggerated kindness which very often pissed him off, but we would end up laughing at my attempts both to badger him into doing something or into not doing something. I reminded him constantly that I was not Old Jessup.

"Each morning he anticipated my arrival in his bedroom (I slept in a small room just off his bedroom) though he would not have admitted it in a thousand years. I often made a production in awakening him even though I knew for a fact that he had lain there awake while I had been brewing the morning coffee.

"A typical scene might go something like this: 'Good morning! Is there a Doctor in the house?' No response. Silence. 'Paging Dr. Goldman! Dr. Goldman! Dr. Goldman, you are wanted in the Emergency Room. Mrs. Snobby Bitch has been admitted to the ER and she is in great pain. She cannot fart!' My use of the word *'fart'* would cause Grandpa to become unglued. He hated the word—all four letters of it—as he had expressed to Dad and me a hundred times.

"Grandpa would rise up slowly from the bed and stare at me in a poorly disguised countenance of disgust. *'Where's the coffee?'* he would inquire, making no mention of my use of the hated word.

"I can't bring it to you until you take care of Mrs. Snobby Bitch in the ER,' I would rejoin, and he would toss anything he could get his hands on at me from his bed. And, of course, we would both join in our communal laughter. And our day would begin on that note.

"I've not forgotten those three months. In retrospect, I treasure those few weeks in which I formed a bond with the old fellow, even if the bond proved to be tentative during some of the rough times. When Grandpa began to fail to the extent that he remained in bed a large portion of the day and night, I began to go through his personal papers to arrange them in a semblance of order for the lawyers, accountants and others who would be involved in the probate of his estate. He was not aware that I was doing this, even though I was only one room removed from his bedroom. I was thankful that he never suspected that I was engaging in such an activity.

"One afternoon in early July, I came across innumerable newspaper clippings, medical notes and other papers relating to Clayton Dykes and his death when he apparently had lost control of his truck and had smashed into a huge tree at the side of a road. I had forgotten that Weldon Froman, a 16-year old kid (the son of Mrs. Myrtle Froman) had survived the wreck. The newspaper article I happened to read first had made mention of this fact. Some of the medical papers included a *Weldon Froman* as a patient of my Grandpa. I wondered at this inclusion.

"I could help but wonder why Grandpa would have taken such an acute interest in Clayton Dykes' death. And also in Weldon Froman. Rightfully so, I did recall Grandpa's almost confessional talk with me about the day he went to the Dykes' home when Etta Dykes had supposedly committed suicide. I've not forgotten his chilling remark to me after I had asked him: *'What else, Grandpa, could you have done?'* He had answered: *'I could have been a man.'*

"Intrinsically, I felt that what I was doing—insinuating myself into Grandpa's personal papers, into a part of his life which he had not shared with me or possibly anyone—was one stage of rape. What I was doing was a flagrant and unsolicited action as regards Grandpa's privacy. If he were well and discovered that I was entering into something like I was doing now, he would have disowned me hook-line-and-sinker and would have thrown me overboard to boot! On the other hand, my actions now might, in the very near future, protect his privacy.

"At Grandpa's death, my father, whom I knew to be the executor of Grandpa's will, would move in and start tossing things out to High Heaven. He was not a keeper of *'things'*; and what I now had in my possession regarding Grandpa's interest in Clayton Dykes, and Weldon Froman for that matter, if left in place, would be lost. Knowing this, I gathered all the related materials, placed them in a large manila envelope and locked them away in my suitcase. I would take the time later to read these materials to determine if I could find any clue as to my Grandpa's inveterate interest in the two. I felt no sense of shame or guilt as I did this. Grandpa would never know of my betrayal if, indeed, it could be called that."

Chapter Twenty-Three

William Beatty Heart:

'I could smell work a mile away.'

"My Grandpa Daniel often told a funny tale about his daddy who was known always to him as Brother Billy Heart. In his nasal voice infused with the twang of our part of Texas, he regaled me with the antics and actions of my Great Grandpa. He would begin: *'Don't know if you know it or not, but my Daddy couldn't read, write or cipher at all. I don't know for certain why he weren't schooled as a child—maybe he had to work in the fields back then—lots of young'uns did. It was a hardscrabble life twice over for many of the families settlin' in and around here. A hard livin', that's what it was. Now my Daddy—I know this for a fact—he had a bit of a lazy streak in him that run from his head to his toes. He told me one time that he was a lazy soul growin' up and he'd right for sure do almost anything to be as far away from the smell of work as he could. He'd laugh at me when he told me this and he'd always say: 'Why, I'd let work catch me if it could for I darst not try to catch it. I could smell work a mile away.*

' I know for a ironclad fact sure shootin' that my Daddy went to a revival when he was a young man—eighteen, so I heard—and got religion on purpose so that the work on the farm wouldn't catch up to him. As for me, I don't cotton too much to this approach to

getting' my own religion—'cause it all sounds like he could rightly be called a real-live hypocrite. But that was his doin' and if he thought that one day he could stand up and face his Maker with a clear conscience, then "hoecake" as Grandma used to say when she approved of somethin'.

"My Grandpa Daniel dipped snuff. He swore by Red Rooster and said carelessly that anybody that dipped Levi Garrett had to be a bit daft. It would be his usual procedure to pause, tap his little tin snuff can (he used Grandma's little Levi Garrett cans which I've always found funny), open the can carefully and take a sufficient dip to replenish the glob what was already between his lower teeth and lips in the lower portion of his mouth. I was always fascinated with the almost mechanical nature of this act. Without a doubt it was a practiced art—he'd done it enough to be able to do it in the dark. Quite often he would give me an empty snuff tin which he had very carefully cleaned with soap and water. I would open it and take in the pungent smell that the tobacco had left. If I could, without getting into too much trouble in the kitchen, I would fill the little tin with sugar and cocoa—and I would have my own tin of snuff. I owe the condition of what teeth I have left today to this childish play!

"Grandpa would continue with his story, not bothered at all by the ritualistic interruption: *'Now, my Mama—she's the one he met at the brush arbor revival in Hardin—she used to say that your Great Grandpa had his arrows set on her and no one else. I doubt that some 'cause he told me that there was many handsome girls on his revival circuit showing off in front of him and settin' their own aim at him. He laughed a lot when he spoke of this 'cause he said he got a great entertainment out of bein' chased by all the young belles. He also said that most of 'em were a silly lot, thinkin' that bein' a preacher's wife would be a bed of roses with excitin' travel.*

'When your Great Grandpa went off to Hardin after that first

brush arbor meetin', he did seem to remember a lively young lady who attended the revival every night. He had found out somehow that she was a teacher in a little community near Hardin—but nothin' more than that. The revival preacher he went off to Hardin with—I hear—got his little pink ass in trouble over in Hardin with the preacher's pretty wife and got run off by the preacher! Your Grandpa was invited to take over the brush arbor revival and was invited to stay at the parsonage—and as they say in some of the movie pictures—the rest is history.'

"Finishing his tale, Grandpa related how my Great Grandpa stopped off in Hardin on his way back home after several revivals on the road, one in Batson he said, another in Rye, one in Schwab City and the last one in Knight—sort of in the middle of nowhere. He proposed to the preacher in Hardin that he might should do a follow-up brush arbor meeting with the souls that had been saved when Brother Cole and him did the first one. The local preacher agreed, and that's when my Great Grandpa set out to win over the pretty young schoolteacher I would never know but who would, of a fact, become my Great Grandma.

"Family lore tells me that Great Grandpa just up and showed up at the young woman's school one day. It was located two or three miles out in the country in a tiny farming community. She was the teacher for all eight grades housed in one large room. In the days to follow, Great Grandpa would manage to arrive at the school just when the school's dinner bell rang out. It wouldn't surprise me if he didn't linger in the nearby woods and wait for the dinner bell to sound.

"Now, totally insinuated into the life of the school, he would always make himself handy by drawing water for the classroom, chopping wood for the big black stove at the front of the classroom and producing kindling which he had already chopped into usable pieces. He had even served one or more times as monitor for the boys when they took their toilet break, going to the three-holer behind the little school. The eleven students in the class, seven girls and four boys, accepted him as one of their own after a week or two of his regular visits. At the insistence of their teacher, they politely addressed him as Mr. Heart and responded with *'No sir. Yes sir. Thank you, sir.'* when he asked them questions or said something complimentary to them.

"My Great Grandpa apparently felt at ease among the students. He watched them as they recited their lessons: the alphabet, the multiplication tables, the exciting spelling bees, the fascinating geography lessons, the handwriting exercises. But, most of all, he watched Miss Elinor Hatchett. Our family lore passes down tales of her beauty: she was willowy with blonde hair which was upswept and wrapped into a bun at the back of her neck. Her eyes were a blue, piercing so I've been told, and they seemed to dart all around taking in every aspect of her surroundings. She seemed always to wear dark blue dresses which accentuated her eyes.

"It is told that her students believed that she had eyes in the back of her head because, when writing something on the blackboard at the front of the room, she would single out one of the students and tell that student to *'Sit up straight, Mary Lou!'* or another *'No whispering, Jonathan!'*

"My Great Grandpa's easiness in the classroom came to an abrupt halt one late autumn day when Miss Hatchett asked him to assist her with writing something on the blackboard. In a state of absolute panic, my Great Grandpa did the proverbial quick-step and remembered something he had to get done that very moment back in Hardin. My Great Grandpa could neither read, write nor do ciphers. Family stories have been passed down that highlight this happening as the moment that Miss Hatchett's heart was won over by the brush arbor revivalist who had accepted Jesus Christ only for the purpose of escaping the hard work of farm life. That he could neither read, write nor cipher were not problems to this enterprising young woman. She could fix these three things.

"These same stories tell that their courtship was more of *'lessons after school'* than it was of the typical spooning of those days. In three years my Great Grandpa, Brother Billy Heart, and my Great Grandma, Miss Elinor Hatchett, were married in Huntsville, Texas. They ate a wedding lunch at a local hotel. It is told that my Great Grandma gave him two first grade reading primers and two writing tablets along with several No. 2 cedar pencils as her wedding presents. It is not recorded what Great Grandpa gave her in return. He had managed to come up with sufficient greenbacks from the offering hats to purchase Grandma a simple gold band. The jeweler had insisted for an extra $2.00 that *'Jet aime'* be engraved inside the gold band. My Great Grandpa had told my Great Grandma that he thought it meant *'eternally'* which was good enough for him. *'That's exactly what that little Jew told me,'* he had claimed.

"Great Grandma's wedding band was handed down upon her death to their oldest (and only) daughter, Hannah. From that point on the ring was passed on each generation to an oldest daughter. It wasn't until my Aunt Bethany Colbert got hold of the ring many generations later that the truth of the matter regarding the engraving came to light. She had accepted the story of the engraving on the ring at face value, believing the very romantic association behind the so-called history of the ring as to the jeweler and the engraving. Unfortunately, her daughter, Elizabeth, went off to college and took a minor in French. That's when the truth came out. I doubt if Aunt Bethany or any of the others before had given any token thought to the two strange little words engraved inside the ring. And it goes without saying that they surely didn't discuss whether the two words were French or Latin or whatever.

"It takes my Aunt Bethany to tell the story: *'Elizabeth, my daughter, went to Baylor over in Waco to get her degree, and she decided to become a teacher. She chose French as her minor—which we all thought was a silly choice and would do her just about as much good as learning Pig Latin. We could only recall knowing one Frenchie in all of our lives, and he was a coonass Cajun from over in Lafayette, probably running from the law.*

'After about a year of instruction in the French language, Elizabeth stunned us all with her outrageous claim. She was home one holiday, and she sprung her discovery on us all. She asked to see my wedding band. Well, I took it off and handed it to her. She was going to get it when I died for sure. She examined the engraving on the inside very, very carefully and handed it back to me.'

"I always hoped that Aunt Bethany would not stop in the middle of the story, but she always did for whatever reasons. She finally started again: *'Elizabeth looked me straight in the eye and told me that the engraving did not mean "eternally" as Brother Billy Heart had avowed to Miss Elinor Hatchett. She reminded me, as if I should have known this all along, that "eternally" in French is "eternellement." Well, any fool can see that what's engraved inside the ring don't even come close. Elizabeth had then added that the "Jet aime" engraved inside the ring was most likely a bastardized spelling of the French for "I love you"—'Je vous aime' would be the proper French she reminded us all, as if we should have known this from the outset. Quite frankly, none of us really cared one way or the other. But the ring was a part of our family history from the very day that Brother Billy Heart had bought it.'*

"So—the mystery of the ring's engraving was solved if the family could depend on Elizabeth's opinion. Looking back on the scene in the jewelry store (as I can only imagine it might have been) my Great Grandpa Billy Heart would have tarred and feathered the Jew jeweler had he realized that he had been conned out of $2.00 or, worse yet, taken for a fool over some French wording. But, on the other hand, the Heart family had received inestimable value from the ring's worth over the many years— engraving be damned!"

Chapter Twenty-Four

Micah Abraham Jessup:

'You will sit with family today.'

"I had returned to Atlanta after my one-week visit home. The faculty associates and students who had learned of my Grandpa's illness came forward with their heartfelt remarks which I found uplifting as I reentered my world of academe. Far back in my mind, however, I could hear the silky voice of my Grandpa as he greeted me when I arrived in Walkamile for my visit. Too many things, once simple and unheeded, now called attention to a most precious gift that I would soon be without. Trying to steer clear of these things was not only impossible, it was improbable in my daily existence. I saw Grandpa everywhere I went. In all my waking moments I thought of him; when I slept fitfully I dreamed of him.

"On a rare occasion, when I quizzed the students on a topic's theme, I would be temporarily taken aback when one of my male students would respond to my question. The timbre of the student's voice, silky yet electric in its tone, would hearken me back to my Grandpa's voice. Odd, I thought, that something I had paid no attention to just several weeks ago had now become a signal and flashpoint to my own response system, causing me to relive moments of just a few weeks earlier. I found this a bit unnerving but tried not to show my discomfort.

"I fervently wished that I could call my mother daily to check on Grandpa. She had no telephone, and that fact alone ended my yearning to hear a voice from home, even if that voice brought no reassuring news. My days at school passed slowly by, and my evenings at my apartment passed more slowly. I tried very hard to maintain my own standards of professionalism in class, but I could see chinks in my own armor. Then in the middle of my first afternoon class on a Monday afternoon a secretary from the President's office came to my classroom and requested that I step outside of the class for a moment. Her news, delivered as carefully and gently as was humanly possible, almost physically felled me. She had quietly said: *'Micah, your Grandfather has died.'*

"No tears. No tears at all. I stood there and then leaned against the classroom door which I had closed earlier. Fleeting thoughts of what I should do arrived and departed in a succession which I could not assimilate. Then I heard the secretary's soft voice, distant, coming to me through an enveloping mist of tears in her eyes. *'The President wishes to see you when you have regained your composure. Don't worry about your class. I'll see to it that they are informed of your circumstances, and I'll dismiss them for the remainder of the period.'* She took both of my hands in hers, looked me straight in the eyes and said, *'I hope you believe me when I tell you that I do understand. Grandpas are special people. I know. I lost mine last October.'*

"Again . . . the journey from Atlanta to Houston. A different car rental, a different clerk who paid absolutely no attention to the fact that I was a Negro from Georgia renting a car. On the surface it appeared that she could have given a tinker's damn whether I was a Negro renting a car from her company or a rhinoceros standing there requesting a family sedan.

"The drive home, slightly more than an hour, was absent

pleasurable moments. Unlike my prior trip home when a storm had swept through the area, I noted little that brought forth comfort or balm to my stricken heart. The roadside looked drab; the drainage ditches were overgrown with weeds; Highway 59 stretched northward ahead of me like an endless ribbon of asphalt going nowhere. When in the past I had crossed the Trinity River Bridge I had always felt an exhilarating upswing in my mood, knowing full well that I was almost home. On this day—nothing. Nothing except the thought that the home to which I was coming no longer housed the dearest friend a young man could claim.

"Two days later Grandpa's funeral was held at the Dunbar Fellowship Church at ten o'clock on a bright spring morning. The Church, which normally seated 120, filled to capacity by 9:15. Church brethren and able-bodied young men, black and white, began to haul in deck chairs, card table chairs, and other appropriate chairs and placed them outside on either side of the church's entrance. When they had finished just before the service's start time of ten o'clock, one estimate was rendered that said there were an equal number of seats outside as there were inside.

"Some enterprising soul somehow set up a loud speaker system and placed it outside the church's front door. Surprisingly, with all the hullabaloo preceding the service, the Reverend Gordon Leeward initiated the celebration of Abraham Jessup exactly at ten o'clock, One parishioner had been heard to remark to another: *'Now that Brother Leeward—he'll give you your money's worth. That's for sure!'*

"My mother, my Aunt Audie and her family members from Houston, and I sat in the family section provided at the front of the church. When Doctor Goldman arrived near the start of the service with his grandson, Patrick, my Aunt Audie got up from her seat and approached them before they could be seated. Her words to them broke all the barriers that may have existed, imagined or real. She spoke with warm conviction: *'You will sit with family today. You and your grandson are family. Now that's that! No protesting.'* She held on to Doctor Goldman's left arm and steered him along with Patrick's assistance to the family section. My mother stood, and Doctor Goldman, unstable on his feet and teetering, held her in an embrace with no words spoken. He then did the same to me before Patrick seated him next to my mother and Aunt Audie.

"The booming voice of Brother Leeward a few minutes later put an end to the idle chatter which always goes on at a funeral: *'Please stand as we recite the 23rd Psalm as the onset of our celebration of the humble life of our dear friend, Abraham Jessup.'*

"The words of the Psalm began: *'The Lord is my Shepherd . . .'* and I remember very little else that transpired in the next several hours. To my consciousness now, as I look back, comes the realization that we all were home again. Scores of friends, neighbors black and white, some of my classmates from Wheatley High School, and even from my college days came by. The extra tables set up in the kitchen, dining room and on the front porch were loaded with a feast that would do honor to royalty.

"When the last person had departed and the final vestiges of the day had been erased from our normally serene home, my mother, my Aunt Audie and I truly felt the jolt of reality which further accented our loss. The departure of so many people left us trapped in a void so distressing to our psyches that we may as well have rubbed our fingernails on a blackboard. The sound would not have alarmed us or brought us out of our stunning recognition of reality. My Grandpa had touched our lives in uncountable ways for so many years that we, in our grief-stricken time, had not yet learned to accept his loss. The thought of *'Time heals all wounds'* gave us not one degree of comfort as we, especially my mother and me, started our lives all over again. This moment, frozen in time as it were, would only be the harbinger of many more days, weeks and months of missing the old fellow we all loved so."

Chapter Twenty-Five

Mrs. Myrtle Froman:

'Dear God, open a door for me.'

"I was pleasantly surprised to hear from Anastasia Woodman about our family history relatin' to the Walkamile community. Our family was what you might call a late-comer family to the community. We had no real history in the community other than the fact that my son, Weldon, was ridin' with Clayton Dykes the day he lost control of his truck and smashed into that tree—killin' hisself out and out. Thank God, merciful God, that Weldon survived with what Doctor Goldman called minor injuries.

"I didn't plan to answer Anastasia except maybe give her our full names and birthdays and where we was born and who died when. That was plenty enough, I thought, and besides that too much nosiness on somebody else's part was right persnickety. Our neighbors didn't need to know our goings-on. Not at all! That was family business. All of this did get me to thinkin' 'bout what had happened to us since we moved into Walkamile.

"Doctor Goldman had been called to the scene of the wreck two or three miles out of Walkamile and had attended first to Clayton Dykes, but, findin' him dead on the scene, he then turned his attention to my son, Weldon. Weldon looked a sight accordin' to the Doctor. I guess the flippin' of the truck up in the air several times before it hit the tree must have took its toll on him. He was one lucky young'un though. He had bruises all over him, all of them not seen real good until the next day when his blood had had time to come to the top and bruise up a bit. And for some reason he had real trouble walkin' for three or four days. He told me his behind was so sore that he couldn't hardly stand it. Course he wouldn't let me look at it, you know, him bein' a boy of sixteen and all. I laugh a bit when I think of that 'cause he don't realize that I cleaned his butt for two or three years when he was a young'un. But kids? Funny critters they can be at times and bashful to the hilt when it comes to their private parts. Especially at sixteen! Like they got somethin' that nobody ever did see, I'd say.

"Doctor Goldman, along with that nigger of his (can't even remember his actual name), took Weldon to his office and give him a good goin' over before he let him go to me. I got to his office just as he was clearin' up his lookin' Weldon over. He told me that I should bathe the scrapes and scratches that Weldon couldn't reach all by himself ever day with soap and water. *'Apply hydrogen peroxide to them after you cleanse them with soap and water, then pat them dry with sanitary cotton balls. Weldon'll come around in no time and be as good as new.'* The Doctor didn't mention Weldon's behind to me at all, but he did say that Weldon might have an uncomfortable time getting' about and around for a few days. *'I almost booked him in the hospital for X-rays, but I decided at the last instant that X-rays wouldn't pick up anything I don't already know. Just as well to leave well enough alone,'* he had said at the end.

"Things went along okay for awhile, but Weldon changed a whole lot before my very eyes. At first I think he was so happy to be alive after seein' what death is all about in the form of Clayton Dykes layin' out on the grass deader than a door nail. But he pulled back from hisself and growed quiet—so quiet that I got worried that he mighta been hurt in the head in the wreck and it were just now comin' to bear bad on his mind. I tried to talk to him, you know private-like, but a mama can't talk none to a son who don't want to talk. And sixteen years old! What a troublin' age for a child—one day a child, the next day they think like a grown-up man—and not a bit clear either—I know. Lord, I know. This switchin' back and forth can drive a mama off her beams. A child one day, a man the next and then God knows what!

"I begged Weldon to talk to me 'bout what was botherin' him, but he would yell at me and tell me to stir my own peas. I hadn't brought him up to be mean like that to me. It weren't him at all. Not by a long shot. He was always kind to me specially after his Daddy died when he was thirteen. I don't think he ever rightly got over that. But his school work fell by the wayside and teachers wrote me notes tellin' me to come talk to them. I did, and they all seemed interested in Weldon and wanted him to do better. But one after the other told me he weren't doin' his lessons in class and never turned in homework assignments. Two or three of his teachers said he acted like his head was in the clouds half the time. It troubled them, they said, but all said the same thing: *'Not a whole lot we can do for him if we don't know what it is that's troubling him. We're here to help, Mrs. Froman. Weldon, like all the other pupils, is very special to us.'*

"One teacher gave me a word that I'd been tryin' to come up with myself. She said, *'Mrs. Froman, Weldon is withdrawing into a shell. I'm so afraid that something has occurred in his life recently that may have triggered his non-responsiveness to his usual environment and his accustomed interests. Whether it's the loss of his father or something else that you and I have not discovered may be the answer to his behavioral tendencies lately.'*

"For me, the teacher's words sounded high-falutin', but they did have a deep meaning. *'Withdrawin'* was the word that got to me. It was what I had been tryin' to come up with for weeks. Somethin' had happened to Weldon, and he weren't tellin' nobody. He was tryin' to live with whatever it was and was tryin' to solve his own problems without any help from any other soul. He was still a child! He couldn't handle all of this by hisself. I needed a way to reach him, and I prayed to God ever night: *'Dear God, open a door for me. I'm a ignorant woman, not havin' much book sense, but I know down in my heart that my son Weldon is grievin' mightily and he don't know how to ask for help or who to go to in his tribulation. Open a door for me, Lord. Open a door! If You open a door for me, Lord, maybe I can open a window for him. That's fair enough, Lord.'*

"I prayed this prayer ever night for weeks on end. I didn't even have to think about it to say the words. They just come to me one by one and I say them in my dull, ignorant way. But God listens, I know. He hears the rich, the poor, the ignorant like me and even the smart ones that is been to colleges. In His time, whenever He is ready, when His time is right, He will open a door for me. I always have faith—lots of it, lots of it.

"The door opened one Saturday mornin' when I was cleanin' up Weldon's room. I was strippin' his bed to wash the sheets when my homemade mattress pad came undone at the bottom edge. I thought to myself I might as well wash that too while I'm at it when I saw something green that looked like it was all rolled up. Lookin' closer, I saw that it was money—a real wad of it. Pickin' it up, I could see that it was a pile of money! I unrolled it and counted the bills—five $20 dollar bills and six $5 bills.

"I was out and out flabbergasted. Ain't no way, I thought, that my son could have that much money. We was 'bout as poor as church mouses, and I didn't have no more than twenty dollars to my name in my purse, try as I might to save for a rainy day. Weldon and me made it okay with the piddlin' jobs I had workin' for different ones here and there, and Weldon would pick up a dollar here and there doin' odd job work for Clayton Dykes or a neighbor who needed a bit of help now and then. But $130! Lord alive! He couldn't make that in three years of summer work and I'd know 'bout what work he was doin' and how much he was makin'. Somethin' troublin' was goin' on in Weldon's life.

"The Lord had opened the door for me, but I didn't have one inklin' if I had wanted this door opened or not. Didn't we all when we was young'uns hear a fairy tale about a little girl who opened up a box? I remember some of that, but I think that girl regretted that she had ever opened up the box. I felt the same way. Lord alive! What would I do? I said another whispered prayer to the Lord: *'Okay, Lord. I thank You for answerin' my prayer, but I need guidance now, Lord. Tell me where to go and what to do next.'*

"I decided to put the $130 in a safe place, wash the sheets and mattress pad, put 'em back on the bed and let nature take its course. If Weldon would be upset by the money missin', then so be it. He would come to me, and maybe we could talk and get to the bottom of what was botherin' him to death. Maybe, I thought, but no guarantees.

"Weldon come home late that day from parts unknown. He would disappear for long hours durin' the day and just pop back in the house like nothin' in the world had happened. This bothered me to no end, but he paid no attention to me when I told him that he was all I had in this world. Today though he would not pop back in and find that nothin' had happened. Somethin' had happened whilst he were gone. In less than five minutes the *'shit hit the fan'* like my dear departed husband used to say. Thank God, I was ready for it all 'cause I had the upper hand—the money—but he had the key to the secret where the money come from in the first place." ❧

Chapter Twenty-Six

Charity Chambers:

'. . . but don't let it take you out to sea!'

"After Uncle Stace died, my mother and I plodded on in a sort of movable haze—dreading the emptiness of the early mornings almost as much as we did the soft evenings when we tended to reminisce about a life which might have been. The mornings were especially hard on us—very hard. When Uncle Stace had been with us during his two separate stays, we both subconsciously pooled and concentrated our efforts toward his well-being. Our own ease and comfort were always secondary.

"After his release from the mental institution our guidelines in handling his needs were fairly consistent each day. His breakfast had to be prepared; one of us had to see to it that he washed up before coming to the breakfast table; one of us would always sit with him at breakfast and carry on with him in a one-sided chatter. We both felt this was important to him in so many ways—offering him trust in us and the feeling that he was a very important part of our family. Our bantering was always performed with happy subjects: the antics of a cat or dog, a raccoon we had seen in the nearby woods, a mockingbird chasing a squirrel, or some totally silly thing that my Mother or me had done the day before. We never, absolutely never, talked about serious things or problems we might be having in our own daily lives. These things simply did not exist in the ambient world we were attempting to create for him.

"My mother worked at the school cafeteria three days each week and on those mornings she departed long before Uncle Stace or I had awakened; I had to assume the full responsibility of seeing to Uncle Stace's welfare. We had all but given up on any efforts to keep the farm duties we had engaged in when Daddy was alive. My mother had to leave very, very early in order to be at the school on time.

"In a fashion, remote but somehow instilled in his thought processes, Uncle Stace's awareness provided him subtle clues as to when these particular mornings would come about. How he knew was beyond me, but he did. He possessed no outward or identifying sense of Monday-Wednesday-Friday or for any other day of the week for that matter. He seemed to like my idle chatter, one-sided though it was. I must confess that it was a bit mindless, but it seemed to appeal to him on a level that I could never understand.

"He especially loved to hear our stories about animals, tame or wild. If the animal I talked of was a wild one, I always gave it a funny name: Fuzzy Wuzzy, Loonie the Coon, Whistler the Mockingbird, and so forth, each of these in its own time bringing a chuckle from Uncle Stace. Our fun was harmless and was not meant to degrade him in any sense of the word. And I hoped against hope that some silly word would awaken something in Uncle Stace so that he would again talk to us. The Lord only knew what might trigger a response from him—not my Mother or me. We had tried innumerable approaches without results. We had both prayed that one of our actions—just one—might be the golden key which would unlock that part of his brain which somehow was suppressing his ability to talk.

"I also did silly but thoughtful little things for him: if flowers were blooming in our yard I would pick one even before the sun had come up, neaten it up a bit by stripping off any ugly leaves, trim the stem with scissors and place it on his plate with his food. When he seated himself at the table (with my urging), the first thing he would do was pick up the flower and turn it around and around in his hand, carefully examining each aspect of it. Then he would smell it. In many cases the flower would have no fragrance, and Uncle Stace would look at me, puzzled. If a flower perchance had fragrance, he would hold it to his nose for an extended amount of time, breathing in the deliciousness of the scent. Then he would smile at me and begin to eat his breakfast robotically after placing the flower in one of his pockets. The flowers that had no fragrance—he left on his plate. I found this odd, to say the least, but I'm sure in his mind his act had a distinct and meaningful purpose.

"I've never regretted the amount of time that I gave to Uncle Stace. Oh, I'm sure that I must have missed out on many things in the community, but, all in all, family is so important to me. Family comes first, and the other stuff comes if you can work it in. My mother and I never felt that we had been deprived of anything. I would have liked to go to college, but that fanciful dream was out of the question. My mother just didn't have that kind of money. We'd have been okay with that if Daddy had lived. He and my mother were a real team, and I know they would have worked out something for me so that I could have gone to college. Maybe things work out the way they're supposed to, but when they do there's a lot of associated pain with the results. *'Go with the flow,'* my Daddy used to say. But then he would add, with one of his appealing laughs, *'But don't let it take you out to sea!'*

"Somewhere deep in my heart of hearts I can never erase the sight of Daddy under the tractor. At times I wish that I had not seen what I did, but on the other hand, if I had not gone to the field where Daddy was, I would have destroyed my very being with a guilt trip for the rest of my life. My mother, I know, feels the same way. Of course, we both can still see Daddy lying there. When Doctor Goldman told us that Daddy never felt any pain after the initial shock of the accident, my mother and I were comforted to a degree, though I think we doubted his words at that time.

"The Doctor's words have stayed with me over the years: *'Our Great God was a marvelous Creator when He designed the human body. Your beloved Matthew went into a state of shock within seconds after the accident'*. I can't imagine in my numbed state how on Earth I could have remembered the Doctor's words. I had stood there at the accident site in the field for so long that my body, my heart, my soul and my eyes and ears had left me—like being there and not being there, if you can know what I mean. My arms and legs had grown stiffly numb, yet I felt at times that I was above the scene looking at the goings-on as if they were not really happening. And I was only a kid of a kid!

"Now that Uncle Stace is gone and Mother and I no longer have the awesome, time-consuming responsibility of providing care for him twenty-four hours each day, I hope to work little jobs as I can get them and save up enough money so I can go to business school in Houston. There's always an advertisement in the Houston paper listing the many fields I could pursue if I could get my business school diploma. All of it sounds so exciting to me. This'll have to wait a while until I can save up the money. I don't want my mother to know about this because she has it hard enough as it is.

"Oh! How our lives have changed since losing Daddy and Uncle Stace! But I can dream! The business school is on Caroline Street in Houston. Even that address sounds exciting. I know I could rent a room near the business school and take the city bus to school and back. And I could work at a part-time job to help with the expenses. And I could eat my meals in one of those cafeterias they have down there. I've heard that the business school helps needy students get jobs, especially if the students have completed one year of school-work. Right now, all of this is a pipe dream for me.

"Several weeks ago I saw a little advertisement in the *Huntsville Item* about a part-time job at Renner's Construction Company. It sounded interesting mainly because the job was in Walkamile. I telephoned the number listed in the paper and made an appointment for an interview the next day at 2:00 PM. I was told to ask for Anna Renner when I showed up for the interview.

"I don't think I've ever met Anna Renner before. Verity, my mother, may know her. She has two brothers that I know about—Koskobe, the one with the really funny name, and Bob, a younger brother. They both showed up to help when Daddy died in the tractor accident. I remember seeing them there, but that's about all I recall about them. I know they're carpenters.

"Much to my surprise the next day at the interview I discovered that I actually like Anna Renner. She was all business, which I had expected, but she came across as warm and friendly and down-to-earth. She described the job in simple terms: lots of paperwork, mostly filing, writing up the monthly statements for those who have credit accounts, going to the bank and post office, some sweeping and dusting as necessary, answering the telephone (this horrified me!) as needed—and four hours of work each day, Monday through Friday. I could not have been happier with this description except for the telephone part.

"Anna Renner told me that she had two more interviews the next day and that she would contact me one way or the other. She then suggested that we take a tour of the building so that I could get a feel for the nature of their work. We passed by an office that had a name on the door: *K. Renner. 'That's my brother's office—Koskobe Renner. He's President of our construction company.'* There was no one in the office.

"Down the hall we heard talking followed by the clicking sound of a telephone being returned to the cradle. A short, well-formed man possibly in his late 30s or early 40s rose from the desk and walked toward us. *'Bob, I would like you to meet Charity Chambers. You remember Matthew and Verity Chambers, of course. Charity is their daughter, and she's interviewing for the job I advertised. Charity, this is Bob Renner, our baby brother.'*

"A faked look of pain came to Bob Renner's face as he spoke: *'Charity, good to meet you. Hope you can start in thirty minutes. I'm so far behind with my paperwork, but Anna says it's all my fault.'* He extended his hand in greeting and then remarked: *'On my way out, Anna. Gotta run!'* and off he raced, almost a blur as he departed.

"Anna laughed. *'That's our little brother, Bob. Pay him no mind. He's always behind and always in a hurry.'* She then made an aside remark to no one in particular: *'He needs a good wife to get him organized. Enough said!'*

"The next evening about six o'clock a strange car stopped outside our house. At first I didn't recognize the person exiting the car. But it was Anna Renner! She knocked on our front door, and I heard her ask, *'Is this where Charity Chambers lives?'*

"I went to the door, my heart all aflutter—knowing that she would offer me the job. I opened the door and asked her to come in, but she declined by saying, *'I can't, dear. Sometimes I feel like I'm Bob. Busy, busy! But I wanted to let you know that the job is yours hands down. You may start tomorrow—eight o'clock sharp.'*

"My first real job! I couldn't wait to tell my Mother when she got home. Maybe I could still have my dream of going to business school in Houston. A second advantage to having a job now was that a big time gap that had consumed both my mother and me would be filled by my new job's responsibilities. In a way it was a solace that I would be up and about and busy during a time period which I had devoted almost exclusively to Uncle Stace over the years past. I would never forget him, however, I couldn't. You don't spend a lot of your time nurturing somebody and then just forget them when they are gone. I would always hold his gentle heart in my own and treasure all those unspoken moments that had transpired between us. I long for his smile, and I yearn again for that understood silence between us. Oh, I miss him so!"

Chapter Twenty-Seven

Robert E. Massey:

'. . . to the raw meat and unpeeled potatoes.'

"Anastasia Woodman contacted me, asking if I could possibly assist her with a project which her aunt Alicia had foisted upon her in preparation of the open house for the cultural center. Before responding positively to her request, I told her that I'd be happy to help out any way I could—if I could. I knew my answer was fence-sitting, but I didn't want to get involved in something that I would not be able to do well and something that would take too much of my personal time. This comes across as a bit selfish on my part, but I've learned in a small community like Walkamile not to bite off more than you can chew—trite though that might sound. Sometimes you have to learn to say *'No.'*

"Anastasia said she had a letter from her Aunt Alicia which outlined in great detail the exact things she wished to accomplish. *'I'll bring the letter by your workplace and you can look it over and make your decision. Will tomorrow be okay for me to come by?'* She had asked. I agreed and temporarily forgot about the matter.

"The next day, about ten o'clock in the morning, Anastasia dropped in at the Walkamile Post Office where I worked as a clerk. She politely stood in line, and when I called out *'Next!'* she came forward. I was a bit taken aback by her appearance. She was beautiful! Over the years I had paid little attention to her, thinking of her only as a gangly teenager with ugly braces on her teeth and stringy hair that reached in all directions. Now she was a striking young lady, poised and secure in her bearing. I couldn't say the same for her Aunt Alicia—far from it.

"She spoke first: *'Robert, I'll not take up too much of your time because you're on the job and there are two people waiting to be served. This is Aunt Alicia's letter.'* She handed me a rather thick envelope with her name and address written in an exaggerated hand. *'You'll like reading Aunt Alicia's letter. She doesn't seem to miss a beat up there in Massachusetts. Let me know if you can help out or not. I'd appreciate it so much. I know for certain that Aunt Alicia will appreciate any help you can give us.'* And then she was gone.

"Around noon, I took my lunch break, going outside to the back of the Post Office where a concrete picnic table had been placed under a large sweet gum tree. I took the envelope with me, deciding to read the letter as I ate my lunch. As I slowly munched on my ham and fried egg sandwich, I began to read Alicia Woodman's letter. The letter read:

Harvard Prison (I jest!)

Dearest Anastasia,
Perish the thought that I should be forced to spend another
day in this most miserable of climates. It has rained,
rained, rained; and I am weary of carrying umbrellas,
satchels and books and papers to be graded from
room to room and then to my apartment. Bitch! Bitch!
And the soup is not even hot! Now I know why the
Colonists held The Boston Tea Party—they were strung
out too much on caffeine and buckets of rain.

I have been thinking long and hard about the grand
opening of the cultural center despite the onerous nature

*of my work here. One must always have in mind that
there are other things in life besides that which puts
bread and meat on one's plate. That is where I suffer
so, fool that I am for so many other causes.*

*It is so vital, I think, that the grand opening be an
event which will arouse the community's interest in
the facility, an occurrence—I should think—that will
impress upon them the beauty of what we have in and
around the community of Walkamile.*

*I have in my possession many historical photographs
submitted to me by the loyal residents of Walkamile.
Here at Harvard, I've been able to take certain
advantage of our photographic laboratory's skill to
have many of the old photographs enhanced and
enlarged for presentation purposes. These photographs will be a defining <u>coup de force</u> and will
accelerate the grandiosity of the entire project.
(Anastasia, don't you adore the French? They always
seem to have the most charming essences in their
word choices).*

*Darling, I have rambled so . . . And I must get now to
the raw meat and unpeeled potatoes. I need to ask you
to do something for me; and you know me so well
that you know I would never ask you to do the
impossible. Out of all the delightful old photographs
submitted by our many friends, there was not one—
nay, not one!—of our beloved: <u>The Red Clay Cliffs</u>.
Dearest one—as the French say so eloquently: a
faire pitie!*

*Hasten that I should make the following assumption:
Would it be, pray tell, that The Red Clay Cliffs may,
or may not, have been the site of suicidal jumps in
our early history? My research indicates that there
were stories of such happenings, but I've never
discovered substantive proof of these yarns. No names,
no dates. Another assumption: the area is quite
difficult to reach, especially for the older set, and I
think the only road leading to The Red Clay Cliffs
is overgrown and untended in places. No wonder, as
history has illustrated to me that the youngsters of*

Walkamile expected to be reimbursed by local merchants after having ascended the cliffs to watch for the approach of the river crafts. Those lads were not especial fools. Then, it must be assumed by me, that the reason I received no old photographs is that no brave soul, over the years, has had the inclination to attempt to photograph the cliffs. Is this not so!

Would you be so kind to approach Mr. Robert G. Massey (or is his middle initial "E") and kindly ask him if he would accompany you on some fine weekend to The Red Clay Cliffs so that you can, with your photography skills and your handy Kodak, record some of the beauty of the area? I even think that a picture taken from across the river would be aesthetically pleasing, but that undertaking would require your traversing to the little burg of Goodrich. And it might not work if you did not possess the proper photographic equipment. Oh! Such dilemmas as those that beset us! And long distances separate us!

My dear, drop me a quick line after you've had the opportunity (and pleasure, I'm sure) to talk to Mr. Massey. Be sure to iterate to him that should there be the surprise of any expenses that he shall be recompensed to the penny. And regardless, we shall be in his debt if he should be able to assist us.

My dearest, be well! Now I must assess those papers I have carried around as I have traipsed all over the campus. I had much rather be corresponding with my dearest niece.

FROM: A.W.

"I thought to myself: *'My God! The woman completely entraps you as you read her letter.'* The average person would have written her niece and simply asked her if she could take some pictures of *The Red Clay Cliffs* and send her either the pictures or the negatives, and that would have been that. Not her Aunt Alicia, however! What a trip to read her letter! For a moment, I felt as if I had returned to my boring high school English Literature class where I was forced to read rambling essays by some long-forgotten man who apparently had nothing but time on his hands. At least her letter was engaging in a quirky sort of way.

"I looked at my watch and found it almost time to return to work. To be fair, I'd have to mull over this proposal. It was not an easy or a practical proposition for a person to get near the cliffs; and the road, more so an overgrown lane, was nearly impassable if I could believe the talk of local hunters who had deer stands and a camp near to the cliffs. I'd let Anastasia know of my decision in a day or so. If I agreed to it, I had no idea how I could possibly see to it that she would tag along with a camera, other equipment and maybe even a tripod. How far we could travel in my truck was an unknown.

"Oh well! This didn't have to be an immediate earth-shaking decision on my part. And I didn't think of it as a hike to a picnic spot on a warm summer's day. It wouldn't be a lot of fun for me to waste one whole precious day off. But I was a part of our community, and I should be willing to contribute to its causes. And looking at it another way, maybe I should be flattered that Anastasia's aunt had bothered to have her ask me. And lastly, I would be spending most of a day with a pretty girl—a very pretty girl!"

Chapter Twenty-Eight

Anastasia Woodman:

'Scope out the place.'

"Robert Massey called me the next day during his morning coffee break and agreed to help me with my photography work as outlined in my Aunt Alicia's letter. He volunteered outright to drive his truck as far as was practical. He suggested that perhaps we should set aside one full Saturday to *'scope out the place and set up our plan of action.'* Then, on the following weekend, weather permitting, we could involve ourselves in the real work of photographing the cliffs. His approach sounded plausible to me. I hadn't thought that we could just drive up to a neat little spot and snap pictures at our leisure. There would be a lot more to it than that simplistic view.

"He had proposed: *'I'll pick you up at your house Saturday at eight o'clock sharp. Be sure to wear comfortable duds and sturdy shoes. No need to bring your camera on our first outing. We'll just do some recon work this first time.'*

"Saturday came, and Robert drove up at exactly eight o'clock. I walked to his truck which he had parked in our driveway. He must have been a bit surprised to see me in my favorite old blue jeans, brogans, and a long-sleeved chambray shirt. I had tied my hair back and had not bothered to put on any make-up. I must have looked a sight to him.

"He got out of his truck and opened the passenger door for me. He was attired in what I would have expected: blue jeans, a sloppy shirt and tennis shoes. He also wore what looked to be a baseball style cap. *'What's that you have in the plastic bucket?'* he asked.

"I had made two large sandwiches—smoked ham and cheese—and had managed to include two good-sized apples in the small space afforded by the plastic bucket. *'It's our lunch in case we get hungry. I have some ice in the bottom to keep it from spoiling.'*

"Robert laughed. *'I brought a lunch for us, too. And some drinking water. I'm sure I'd rather have whatever you fixed. Mine's pretty poor pickings.'*

"The original road which had at one time in Walkamile's history led to the base of The Red Clay Cliffs first appeared close to a mile outside Walkamile. Robert slowed his truck as we approached the beginnings of the old road. *'Here we go! Where we'll stop nobody knows, but from the looks of it already I'll bet it'll be sooner than later.'* He had laughed nervously as he spoke in an almost sing-song fashion.

"It seems that we crept along about ten or fifteen miles an hour for a short spell. The road, now really a country lane by today's standards, was covered in pine needles and the usual detritus from small fallen limbs and leaves in various states of decay. Fortunately, there were no large limbs or fallen trees to block our way.

"Robert paid careful attention to his driving, gearing down one moment and then shifting into a second gear the next. I became fascinated with the mottled shadows created by the dense foliage, the undergrowth and small trees and bushes that lined the old path. The sun, peeking through all of this, streaked in filtered luminescence—like daggers of light penetrating and assaulting the thickness of the entire area. If I had been by myself, I would have been afraid of my own shadow (if I could see it), but being with Robert, whom I did not know well at all, provided me with the ability and luxury of being at ease.

"As we progressed, the road became less of a road and more of a pathway—but we were still able to advance slowly. Of a sudden, about fifty yards ahead, we both noticed an oval-shaped clearing highlighted by the streaming sun rays from the east. *'That's a good sign ahead. It might be that the old country lane will clear up a bit and be more open for us. This may be easier than I had thought at first. The cliffs can't be more than a half mile ahead.'* Robert's voice sounded upbeat, and all I could think of to say was not a word exactly but a nod of agreement. His tone of voice betrayed the fact that he was trying very hard to act in a nonchalant manner as if this was something he had done a hundred times.

"We came to the clearing in a few moments and found that our old country lane had turned into what appeared to be a logging road probably engineered many years ago when the lumber companies were after the hardwood trees in the area. From that time on we were able to advance at a pleasant clip, though not speedy by any stretch of our imaginations. Then, almost with the same suddenness that we had found an open and inviting road, we found ourselves (and the truck) at an abrupt but not unexpected ending. The woods ahead in all four quadrants looked like they were begging for someone to view them for the first time in years. They looked impenetrable. The logging road had vanished into the tangled growth of what lay before us.

"I could not determine how on Earth we would be able to find our way near to the cliffs which couldn't be more than a thousand yards ahead of us by an estimation both Robert and I had made a bit earlier.

"Robert spoke first: *'Somewhere in all this mess of ty vines, yaupon bushes and low growth there has to be a trail covered up waiting for our discovery.'*

"I had not uttered more than a dozen words up to this point, but I finally broke my near silence: *'We have to find it or go to Plan B, whatever that is. So . . . it's out of the truck for us both. And be careful—watch out for snakes. I bet you were going to tell me that first thing!'*

"We both piled out of the truck at the same time, each of us looking down at our feet to make sure we weren't stepping out right onto a timber rattlesnake. *'Not just a snake, Anastasia. A big rattler as big around as a small log. This area is famous for them!'* When Robert said this, I knew that he was a teaser at heart, but I still held to my belief that it would pay us to be careful.

"Then came the important question: *'Which way, Callaway?'*

"Robert's response was hardly helpful. *'We have four choices: North, South, East or West. I like North at the moment. And you?'* he questioned me back.

"To continue the humor, I looked in all four directions and replied, *'North it is. By the way, which way is North?'* I couldn't even determine by the sun's rays which way was east—let alone North. All four directions looked the same to me."

❧

Chapter Twenty-Nine

Mrs. Myrtle Froman:

'You don't know the meanin' of torment!'

"I knew, as a mother, that I had to allow Weldon to discover that the $130 was missin' from its hidin' spot under the mattress cover. I couldn't bring up the subject unless I wanted to be tongue-lashed for pryin' into his knittin'. Any mother, if she had any sense, would realize that upfront. My only questions to myself was *'Would he even mention it? Or would he just wait around and let me be the one to mention it?'* The Lord only knows how a child thinks.

"I told Weldon that his supper was on the stove. *'All heated up for you. Put the lids back on the pots when you get some for yourself,'* I reminded him. All I heard was a snarl that could've come from a unhappy dog.

"In a few minutes his shit hissy begun. *'Where is it? Where is it? You stole my money. You stole the money I worked hard for!'* His voice sounded out like he was in doubled-over pain. *'Where is it?'*

"I walked into his bedroom. He had tore off the lightweight spread from his bed; he had yanked off the clean sheets and it looked like he had ripped off the mattress cover. *'All my work for nothin',* I thought to myself.

'I have the money in a safe place—all $130 of it—and I plan to

keep it 'til I find out where you managed to come up with such a amount. Why, workin' as hard as I do—I don't earn no money like that—not even in two weeks of back-breakin' toil.'

"Weldon then flung hisself on his bed, face down, his head braced only by the pillow which he had not throwed off the bed. *'It's my money, Mama, and I earned it fair and square. Oh, Mama! I earned it fair and square, and what I did was real labor.'*

"His voice was so pitiful that I leaned over the bed and started to rub him on his neck. My heart was hurtin' so bad—he was my little boy, the only thing I had left in life since Willard had died. I weren't prepared for what happened next. No mother ever is.

"In a flash—so quick and not thought of by me—Weldon flopped over in his bed and swung at my face with his right fist. His blow landed spat on my upper left cheek and I felt more than real pain. For a little spell I felt like my innards had been ripped out of me, gut by gut; and I lost my balance and fell spraddled out full flush back on my butt to the floor.

"Weldon had never—never—touched me like that before! Oh, there was times when he would tease me by markin' a 'X' on one of my arms with his fingers, and if I didn't rub off the 'X' quick enough, he'd give me a gentle-like tap with a clenched up fist. He said they played that at school but the only time they were supposed to do that was on St. Patrick's Day in March.

"Before I could gain my senses back, I remember Weldon hoppin' up from his bed and steppin' over me like I was trash on the floor. He was cryin' to beat the band. Then I heard this awful crashin' noise in the kitchen—then the kitchen door slammin'. I can't never forget the accusin' words he yelled at me as he run from our house: *'You'll be sorry for what you done! You'll be sorry!'*

"I pushed myself up from the bedroom floor somehow. My face hurt bad, but my heart hurt worser! I couldn't cry and I had a lot to cry about right at that time. When Weldon left, the whole reason for my livin' left with him. Three months had frittered by since he'd been hurt in the accident. Clayton Dykes was dead and gone. I thought Weldon had put all of that behind him. We had talked some about the wreck—dribs and drabs here and there when I thought I could reach him a bit. I told him that Clayton Dykes' death were not his fault. I remember sayin' to him that just because he was ridin' with Clayton Dykes when he were killed didn't make him one bit guilty. Weldon would stare head-on at me and sorta look right through me when I said things like that. He could've been a bloodless ghost for all I felt—I just weren't reachin' him none. He was somewhere in another world where he couldn't or didn't want to be reached.

"The kitchen was a mess. It looked like a summer storm had blowed it apart. The supper I had fixed was on the floor—pots and pans scattered all over the creation, beans and potatoes runnin' in their own likker all over the place, the biscuits turned up every which way but which. When I saw all this, I wanted to cry—and I did. Not for the spilt food—not for the mess I'd have to clean up—not for my hurtin' face where Weldon had slugged me—I cried 'cause I had lost the only creature that I loved.

"I didn't know at that terrible time that I would never see my Weldon again. A week later when they found Weldon's body in the Trinity River, the Sheriff wouldn't let me identify it at all. It had been et up so bad by river creatures that he didn't want to put me through the torment of lookin' at Weldon in that shape. He had been real, real blunt when he told me that, and I had screamed at the Sheriff: *'You think you are protectin' me from torment? Sheriff! You don't know the meanin' of torment!'*

"At that very spot in time, I don't recollect much of nothin', but I do know I heard voices of women—I can't name them there was so many—but I felt gentle hands and I felt cool caresses of washcloths bathin' my face, my neck and my arms. And the lights was soft and I saw Weldon studyin' his school books at the kitchen table. And then I slept for days at a time."

❧

Chapter Thirty

Sheriff Earl Bruntlett:

'. . . things that are best covered up.'

"I've seen lots of things in my long career as Sheriff. Some of them would make you laugh your ass off right off the bat; other things would make a hard-hearted man cry his eyes out, and he wouldn't even be shamed a bit when his buddies told him he had acted like a real sissy. That's how the job of Sheriff is. Laughs one day, tears and sorrow the next. And you don't never know the order they'll come in. Not at all! When you leave to go on a call, it's like the toss of dice. And there are certain things that are best left all covered up—nice and tight—away from the public eye. There's no laughter, no tears, and just about everybody involved would just as soon forget about it for good.

"I first heard from Myrtle Froman the day after her son, Weldon, had left their home, telling her she'd be sorry. She contacted me on a Wednesday. He had left late on a Tuesday evening right around supper time. She had thought that he'd come back home whenever he got over his snit. But he hadn't by Wednesday afternoon.

"She told me everything she knew, sometimes in an order that got to be a tad confusing. But in the end the narrative she give to us made some sense. She had related: *'Sheriff, I didn't have no work on that Tuesday so when Weldon ups and goes off to points*

unknown, I decided to do some washin'. I stripped his bed—sheets,
pillowcase, and mattress pad—and that's when I saw somethin'
mighty suspicious. There were a wad of green under the mattress
pad. I picked it up and found out that it were money: six $5.00 bills
and five $20.00 bills. Lord, Sheriff, I don't make that kind of money
in two weeks! And I know Weldon traipses 'bout the area doin' a
little job here and there, but ain't no way he could bring home that
kind of money.

'When Weldon finally come in from parts unknown late on that
Tuesday evenin', I didn't mention the money to him. I waited on
him to bring up the subject hisself. Well, excuse me, Sheriff, but the
you-know-what hit the fan when he finds his money missin'. There
was a scene—not much at first, but then Weldon ripped off the
sheets, the mattress cover and then he plops hisself down on the bed
face down 'gainst the pillow all the time makin' accusin's at me for
takin' his money. I try—what any mother would do—to solace him,
but he ups and slugs me on my face. It really hurt me and I fell flush
on my backside on the floor. First thing you know he's tearin' off
through the kitchen, knockin' all the food off the stove onto the
floor and that's when he yells at me that I'll be sorry.'

"I felt at the time that there was more to the story than this one
isolated incident, but I wanted Myrtle Froman to volunteer to tell
me so that I wouldn't be leading her in a specific direction. I had to
remember that a young man was missing—probably run off to a
friend's house—and a mother was concerned. This alone was the
basis for my discussion with her. She then started anew with more
information:

'Weldon was a good boy. He suffered a lot when Willard died.
They were a pair if I ever saw one. They did everything together—
huntin', fishin', you name it. And then Clayton Dykes seemed to
come into Weldon's life several months after Willard died. Weldon

was thirteen goin' on fourteen at that time. Mr. Dykes would drive up to our house, get out of his truck and come in our house and talk to us. He always asked my permission for Weldon to do some work for him. And he paid Weldon a right handsome sum for his work. Weldon could make $5.00 for two or three hours of work over at the Dykes' place. And Mr. Dykes would come get him and would see to it that Weldon got a ride back home. It weren't real often but ever week or so Mr. Dykes was able to give him work. I think he had a big heart and felt sorry for Weldon a lot about losin' his Daddy. And I know what Weldon earned from Mr. Dykes has helped us out at Christmas for two Christmases that I can think of right directly.

'I have a real feelin' that the six $5.00 bills was for work that Weldon done for Mr. Dykes over the past two months or so. Now the $20.00 bills—them's a real mystery. I just don't know how he could've got his hands on money like that. The Lord knows, but I don't for a fact. Mr. Dykes never mentioned any work to be done for that kind of money.'

"Myrtle Froman had stopped as if she had told me everything. Then she started to tell about Weldon's problems in school: *'Sheriff, we all know that when a young'un loses his Daddy that he's up for trouble for a parcel of time. That happened to Weldon for a bit, and I thought he got over it as good as could be expected. Mr. Dykes must of helped him a lot, fillin' in as a father so soon after Willard died. But Weldon's schooling suffered some and he struggled and made it through the 7th Grade. Then come the 8th Grade and the 9th Grade and the teachers started askin' me to come in and talk about some problems they was havin'. Weldon was not doin' good in school and they didn't have no reason why. Oh, I talked to all the teachers, and they all said 'bout the same thing: that Weldon was troubled by somethin'. I couldn't help out at all 'cause I didn't know no more than they did. Weldon wouldn't study none, he wouldn't get his schoolwork at home; he'd just ups and disappear when he come from school. Oh, he might grab a bite to eat and then, off he goes!'*

"I asked Myrtle Froman how the death of Clayton Dykes affected Weldon. She paused a long, long time and then spoke with a degree of conviction: *'Like any Mama, I was worried about Weldon bein' damaged by the wreck—I mean in the head—but that didn't happen, I guess. Doctor Goldman tended to him where the wreck happened after he saw that Clayton Dykes was dead. Weldon told me this much. Then Doctor Goldman took him to his own office and doctored his scratches and bruises. Somebody—I don't recall who—come by my house and got me and he drove like all billy hell to Doctor Goldman's office. When I get there, Doctor Goldman's finishin' up with Weldon. That ole nigger is helpin' him. Weldon looks a sight—scratches, grass burns on his skin, and when he gets up off the examinin' table, his walkin' was a sight for sore eyes. He could barely walk straight—sorta walked bow-legged like. The Doctor told me what I needed to do with the scratches and he said Weldon might have trouble walking right for a few days. Oh, and he said somethin' or 'nother 'bout thinkin' bout X-rays but opined that they wouldn't tell him more than he knew already—whatever that meant.'*

"Five days later a fisherman from over at Goodrich found what appeared to be a body of a young male washed up on a sand bar directly across the river from The Red Clay Cliffs. The fleshy parts of the body had been eaten by the denizens of the Trinity River, probably over the seven-day period that Weldon Froman had been missing. I went by Homer Gentry's home (Homer was the Justice of the Peace) and picked him up, and we drove over to the site where the body had been found by Pearliss Clayborn, the fisherman. For a moment I thought Homer was going to faint when we first viewed the corpse, but he finally got ahold of himself and got on with the business of finding out the cause of death. After a cursory examination, he looked at me and said, *'Death by drowning. Must have got caught up in one of them whirlpools right under The Red Clay Cliffs. That place is known for them whirlpools.'*

"The corpse had to be Weldon Froman. No one else had been reported missing, and we had no way to disprove our own findings. I had the body transported back to Walkamile Funerals, and then I drove out to the Froman place. You might recall that I mentioned earlier that some things happen that cause you to laugh your ass off. Well, this was not one of them. I'll never, in a thousand years, forget the agonizing tone of Mrs. Froman's voice when she yelled back at me: *'Sheriff! You don't know the meaning of torment!'* when I told her that we had found her son and that she could not view the body. I've not ever looked upon any countenance that reflected such pain as that etched on Mrs. Froman's face. I can't describe it—I won't even try to."

❧

Chapter Thirty-One

Anastasia Woodman:

'I didn't think raccoons came out in daylight.'

"Robert and I individually poked around the four quadrants of the clearing in a valiant attempt to find what we started to call the *'opening'*. If, and when, we found that, it would free us up to locate the old trail to The Red Clay Cliffs. And we'd be on our way. That was easier said than done.

"The ty vines, the yaupons, the brambles, the low-growing bushes—all seemed to be hiding what we were looking for. Robert had cut us two bamboo-looking poles before we had started, and we were able to push the tip of the pole into the heavy growth. He had jokingly said to me, *'Hope we don't go poking around in a yellow jacket's nest!'* and I thought to myself that's the last thing I wanted to hear. The likelihood of snakes also gave me a fleeting and creepy feeling.

"We struggled for another fifteen minutes or so before Robert yelled out: *'I think the old path is over here on the North side.'* He had parted two small trees with his hands and beyond, about fifty feet or so, he had seen another clearing. *'It looks like it might have been a walking path, God only knows to what,'* he had called to me as I approached him.

"Each of us pushed aside one of the bushy trees and stepped into the darkness of what lay immediately ahead. Indeed, there was a small two-rutted path that looked as if it had not been touched by human or animal form in years. It was not large enough to accommodate a vehicle such as Robert's, but it was a welcomed sight to us. As we entered, the difference was overwhelming in the sense that at one moment we had been in a clearing with bright sunlight shattering the minimal opening in the forested thickness, and now we were engulfed by a scattered darkness interrupted only when an errant ray of sun managed to find its way through the overhead canopy. The sensation was eerie, yet the dimness of our surroundings was quaintly beautiful. I think the two of us felt as if we had made a truly remarkable discovery. The quietude, at first inviting, at times took on an ominous air as I advanced only slightly.

"I stopped for a moment and looked ahead. *'Do we leave our lunch in the truck?'* I called out to Robert, now ten yards or so ahead of me.

"He called back: *'I think so, but I will step back and get the water. Don't think we'd want to be drinking any of this water up here.'* His voice took on a different pitch as he reentered the clearing. It was as though some of his words had been muted by the thick wall of growth.

"Robert carried the water which he had poured into a canvas bag before he left home. I didn't quite know how a canvas bag would hold water, but I chose not to ask what might turn out to be a silly (and feminine) question. Surely it could function as a water container or else I didn't think he would have brought it along for the sole purpose of a joke.

"We each still had our bamboo poles and used them to steady ourselves as we trudged through this almost unbelievable but limited panorama—a smorgasbord of trees, bushes, vines, leaves, and the occasional fallen tree decaying by the path—mushrooms of all sorts growing out of the fallen tree and the ground in what seemed to be a reinstatement of a life form unto itself. God only knows how many of them were poisonous. I did see one stink devil which I poked with my pole, and we both laughed as the brown, snuff-like powder rose up for a few inches and then settled back to the ground. In a way I felt a bit guilty about disturbing what had once been an unusually elegant and misunderstood addition to the forest's floor. It was near to the acme of appropriateness that a stink devil be included in such a scenario as we were now witnessing, bizarre that it was.

"Both Robert and I grew quiet as we continued on the now ill-defined path. We took calculated steps and watched for snakes. The muted coloration created by the dim filtered light would camouflage any snake, and we both had the greatest respect for that fact.

"Robert had said earlier this was a northward direction, but I had no feeling as to the direction in which we were heading. The sun could not be a guide, so repelled it was in the embracing umbrella of denseness overhead. We must have gone a thousand yards or so when we both noticed a significant clearance to our right, eastward so it would seem. It must be that we were approaching one of the bases of The Red Clay Cliffs. Walking another fifty yards or so, before we exited the canopy of trees, we saw the sheer red cliffs in the distance. Coming out into the sunshine, savagely intense, reminded me of when I was a little kid walking out of the Life Theater in Huntsville at mid-afternoon on a bright sunny August day. The sudden blindness was comparable.

"What we saw was a spectacular array of multi-colored strata of clay: bronze, carmine, deep reddish tones, all of these striated with fingers of a white so pure that it dazzled to a complete perfection in the late morning light. The sun, now situated to our right and nearing its zenith of noon, magnified the intensity without detracting from any of the observable beauty. It was a glorious sight, and I tried to think of other shades of red which I knew existed on the cliffs before me. Vermilion, scarlet, magenta, ruby, cardinal, cerise, maroon—all of these, luscious in their own way, were there on the cliff—and I'm sure with God's Palette in hand, mortal man could not paint the scene that stood majestically in front of us.

"Robert lowered the canvas bag into his hands which he held at waist level. *'Need a drink of water?'* he asked me. His question brought me back from my temporary state of reverie.

"I was not about to let him get the best of me. I had no earthly idea how to drink out of one of those canvas bags, but I smartly replied, *'Yes, very much.'* He approached me with the canvas bag held firmly with both of his hands.

"I expected him to bring out a portable tin cup or something, but instead he continued to approach me. *'Lean your head back, and open wide,'* he instructed me. I did exactly as he told me to, and he poured the water down my throat. Fortunately, I managed not to strangle. When I had had enough, I just closed my mouth. He began to laugh and almost yelled out at me in his fit of laughter: *'You're a good sport, and you did it just right. Congratulations!'*

"I had never considered that drinking from a floppy canvas bag would be an art form. We rested for a moment, and then we began our *'scoping out'* as Robert had originally said. It took about two more hours for us to pick out exact sites where I would be able to capture the cliffs to the most prominent effect from the best photographic angle. Robert made notes in a small pad he carried with him, recording the time of day, amount of sun, shadows and anything else that he felt might detract from the photography. When we had finished, we had more than a dozen sites *'scoped out'* for the day we would return to shoot the pictures.

"Though we had, in effect, traveled northward, we had been looking at the southeast side of The Red Clay Cliffs. Robert reminded me of this as we returned to the canopy and finally to the sun-splattered opening in the forest. There were two things that I could not imagine: one, the vastness of this place, especially since we had seen only a portion of the southeast side of the cliffs, and two, how those young lads managed to run from Walkamile in the old days, climb the cliffs and look for river craft, and when sighted, run back to Walkamile and alert the townsfolk. I would mention this to Aunt Alicia when I wrote next. I hardly saw how their action could have been possible.

"I was beginning to get a bit hungry as we neared the opening where the truck had been parked. *'I'm hungry, so hungry that I could eat half of your lunch and half of mine,'* I announced rather flippantly. Robert agreed.

"When we arrived at the truck, we had one big shock. Both the bucket containing my sandwiches and apples iced down, and Robert's container had been broken open, torn apart and strewn all over the clearing. I started laughing when I saw parts of two apples near the edge of the clearing, and I laughed even harder when I saw my plastic bucket halfway up a small tree on another side of the clearing.

"Robert scouted around a bit, found his lunch kit which he casually tossed aside. *'So much for my lunch kit!'* And then we both started laughing at the joke that had been played on us. We had been left without one morsel of food!

"We placed our bamboo poles over to one side, got into the truck and headed back to what we hoped was civilization. We had had a successful day, and Aunt Alicia would be so proud of us once we sent a dozen or so of fabulous pictures to her. All we had to do now was to return and do the photography, perhaps next Saturday.

"Over the roar of the truck's engine, I managed to ask Robert one last question: *'I didn't think raccoons came out in daylight hours and raided for food. I thought they were mostly nocturnal. Are they?'*

"Again Robert started laughing. You know, his laughing was beginning to get on my nerves! In the most serious tone of his voice that I had yet heard, he responded: *'As your Aunt Alicia might say— my dearest Anastasia, those weren't raccoons. Those were bears!'*

"I stared at him for an eternity, and I made up my mind that if he was teasing me again, I wouldn't let on that I knew the difference. I wouldn't ever let him know if I believed him or doubted him or if I was scared. That was the Aunt Alicia part of me coming out. Aunt Alicia had the innate ability to keep someone or something on tenterhooks. It was one of her strengths, and I had inherited some genetic evidence of this very sort. Robert E. Massey would never know whether I believed him or not—not if I had my way."

Chapter Thirty-Two

Patrick A. Goldman:

'Today—I have become a man!'

"In late August, Grandpa died. I had awakened him that morning as I had done all summer long with some silliness which had become our morning ritual. As usual, he had played along with the meaningless insults I had used to wake him up, and he had, with his usual flair, hurled them right back at me. This was our morning war game which, I feel, Grandpa had begun to expect. He seemed to relish our individual ripostes and our snappy and sometimes salty comebacks. Each of us tried mightily to out-sally the other with our verbal assaults. There were never any out-and-out winners of these jousts.

"I had returned to the kitchen to get the coffee when I heard a thudding noise coming from Grandpa's bedroom. I stopped what I was doing and went hurriedly to the bedroom. Grandpa was on the floor at the side of his bed. Quickly I knelt beside him and lifted his head upward. He was not responsive to my actions at all. I checked his pulse (he had taught me this), and he had none that I could detect. I noted a small mirror on the bedside stand. Reaching for it without displacing my hold on Grandpa's head and neck, I held it in front of his mouth. There was no fogging at all. In that one moment

I realized full well that Grandpa was dead. I lifted him carefully and placed him on his bed, and then I called an ambulance.

"The ambulance arrived in what seemed to be mere minutes. The attendants informed me that Grandpa likely had expired the very second he had collapsed and fell from his bed.

"My Dad and I spent the remainder of August and the early days of September settling Grandpa's estate. For the curmudgeon Grandpa had become in his latter days, he had exhibited remarkable abilities to stay on course with his financial and business affairs. My Dad found his personal papers to be in pristine condition and never realized that I had been instrumental in this little bit of scheming. In short order, the lawyers were able to settle the estate. Dad and I were the beneficiaries of the estate, and each of us found ourselves in much better financial shape than we had ever been— especially me, a lowly schoolteacher.

"In the process of going through Grandpa's personal belongings, we found many items which pulled us back to Grandpa's and Grandma's early days at Tulane Medical School. There were certificates of all sorts which lauded Grandpa while he was at the medical school. He had been an outstanding student, as had Grandma in her nursing environs. Looking at these documents, now many years in the past, I could hear Grandpa singing that silly song to Grandma as she cringed in her dormitory: *'She sat by the window and played her guitar, played her guitar, played her guitar'.* Grandpa must have been one card short of a full deck when it came to his rabble-rousing and his *affaires du amour.*

"After Grandpa's funeral (an epic celebration of a true servant's life) I returned to Huntsville and my teaching position. After I settled back in at my apartment, I remembered the newspaper clippings and medical papers on both Clayton Dykes and Weldon Froman. I had left them in my suitcase after unpacking. One evening I took the papers from the suitcase and read all of them through and through, finally falling asleep in my recliner in the wee hours of the next morning. I awakened and looked at a nearby clock: 4:04 AM. I could hardly believe that I must have spent five or six hours going through these papers. And then I was staggered with what I had discovered during my readings. All of it seemed to come back to me in its crushing reality.

"Probably the most shocking part of the medical papers pertaining to Clayton Dykes was a notation made by my Grandpa that a contributory factor in his death had been what appeared to be a *'stab wound of consequence to the lower left neck area.'* Another note indicated that result of death was a combination of *'said wound and subsequent head trauma from impact with windshield.'* There was no mention, anywhere in the papers, that the stab wound occurred as a result of some foreign object either associated with the crash or separate and apart from the truck's impact. There was no mention also that the stab wound was made with a knife or other sharp-pointed device.

"I was stunned as I read these reports. I even re-read them, hoping that I would find some illumination that I had missed during my first reading. I had not, as it turned out. What baffled me was the fact that Grandpa had kept these papers apart from his regular medical records which were maintained at all times in his office. Even I knew this was his protocol.

"My Dad and I had arranged for all of Grandpa's existent medical office records to be stored in a warehouse facility in Huntsville. Dad had found out that certain records had a specific retention period; he therefore chose a simple approach: store all the records. It would be interesting to look at Clayton Dykes' medical records as retained by Grandpa in his own medical office. I wondered if those records, obviously a sham, would shed any light on this enigma.

"The medical records on Weldon Froman painted an alarming picture. In a nutshell, Grandpa's recordation of his examination of Weldon Froman at the scene of the accident and at his medical office delineated some explosive incidents. Apparently, as Grandpa was examining Weldon Froman, he was able to elicit pertinent details from the boy as to what had occurred prior to the truck crash.

"It would appear from the tone of the medical records that the boy talked rather freely. Obviously, the boy was in pain, and I suppose it could be said that he was in a degree of shock from the wreck and its consequences. One segment of the medical report reads: *'Patient informs that deceased (Dykes) had insisted that he wanted to 'fuck' patient (anal sodomy). Patient refused offer for several weeks, instead performing oral fellatio on now deceased (Dykes). Deceased (Dykes) continued to insist re: anal sodomy, made offers to recompense patient, and then forcibly performed this act on unwilling patient the afternoon of crash. Examined patient: minimal tear in anal area; sphincter muscle expanded abnormally. Patient exhibits perturbation and distress as he informs that he stabbed deceased (Dykes) with a sharp object he found in truck's floorboard.'*

"About all I could think of saying was: *'Oh, my God!'* Another thought, random to the point of being remote, hit me as if I had walked straightway into a brick wall. What if Mrs. Froman, who had attended to Grandpa that one week, had run across these papers? Cleaning people and those attending the ill have been known to be *'Nosy Nellies.'* Even I could be categorized as that because I had come across these papers when I was putting Grandpa's business, estate and personal papers in order. Thank God that I had been a *'Nosy Nellie.'*

"When the shock of my discoveries had subsided, I was able to look at this series of events in Grandpa's life objectively. I recalled with clarity that day he had informed me of Etta Dykes' death and the salient issue that he had not stood up and been a man. He had been roped into a subterfuge and had not, in his opinion, the courage to stand up and be counted. His words come to me now: *'I could have been a man.'* Those words are calling out to me now as I consider my own course of action.

"I consider getting my Dad involved. What would that benefit either my Dad or me? I could go to the American Medical Association; I could go to our local District Attorney (not the same county as is Walkamile); I could get a lawyer; I could stir the pot and go to Mrs. Froman who obviously is still grieving over Weldon's death by drowning. Or, in the best interests of all parties involved, I could keep my mouth shut. Which one to choose?

"On the surface it appears Grandpa was willing to overlook the fact that Clayton Dykes, in effect, was murdered. It would appear that if the truck had not crashed into the tree when Clayton Dykes lost control of the vehicle he most probably would have died from the stab wound. It would appear that Grandpa wished, in a revengeful sense, to settle a long-ago score in which he was an unwitting participant in the cover-up of the murder of Etta Dykes. Perhaps, as an end game, Grandpa had considered that his actions in this event would, even in the farthest stretch of his own imagination, provide him an avenue of finally *'being a man.'*

"In my own end game, I chose to do nothing and to tell no one. This would be my life's secret, and I would hold it close to my heart in honor of Grandpa. When Grandpa had faced these particular issues, I think at the end of the day he could have rightfully said: *'Today—I have become a man!'* My inaction will be my gift to him."

☙

❧

Chapter Thirty-Three

Mavis Murray:

'. . . at his banquet of consequences.'

"My mother, Ruth, just pined away when Ad skipped the country after raping me. My relationship with her, tenuous in the best of times, was fraught with too many ghosts of the past—specters in my waking hours that reminded me of that one terrible day when they had gone to Huntsville shopping. And I had stayed at home. Regretfully so.

"Equally, other specters taunted me at night in my restlessness; my grades in school suffered for at least a year. I owned this abiding inner feeling that the girls in my class were looking at me and whispering their catty, vicious remarks into each other's ears: *'Her daddy slept with her! And her own family let him get away with it!'*

"I found that I became tongue-tied if any boy in my class spoke to me. Of course, I wasn't deaf, but I qualified highly for becoming dumb as soon as a boy said one word to me. I don't think though that the boys were as unkind in their treatment of me as the girls seemed to be. I would say on the whole that most of the boys with a grain of intelligence tried very hard to steer clear of me without letting me know that was their intention. They possessed the same information that the girls did, but they chose not to use it in any vengeful fashion. In one way I felt that some of them subconsciously gave me leeway as an umbrella of protection. This was never an overt action on their part, however.

"After one year of a shattered ego and an existence that bordered on just getting through each day and night, I decided one day that whatever I was doing could not be right. I had to change or I would soon destroy what traces of spirit and animation I had left. So . . . saying to Hell with the vicious female classmates in a mental sense, I buckled down and started studying my junior year. My transformation occurred almost overnight. Two six-week terms of outstanding grades in which I made the Honor Roll became the accelerants of better times ahead. In a way, my personal transformation affected those around me. The catty remarks ceased; boys in my classes sought me out to help them with their studies. And, most important of all, I discovered that I could talk to them. I suppose I had emerged from a protective shell which, in truth, had not been a protective shell at all. It had been more like a big rock blocking my cave door.

"Then in the midst of all this self-success, my mother died after giving up all hope when she was diagnosed with lung cancer. When the doctors in Beaumont told her of their opinion, she refused all treatment. She had told them: *'You know, I think I'll just up and go home and die in my own bed.'* I think, quite frankly, that she smoked herself to death. She had taken up the habit years before after she realized that Ad was not the cup of tea she had bargained for. I've always viewed him as the personification of a loser—war hero be damned!

"This hurts me to say this, but during the time my mother was at home doing her dying, I have to admit that I felt little empathy for her. In the back of my mind the haunting words of Ad kept ringing in my ears: *'I'll go direct to the law about what all of them did to your Grandpa—smothered him, they did!'* The horror of those words, the picture of my Grandpa who I had not known, the lingering disbelief that my Grandmother, my mother and Uncle Jeremiah could do such a thing—all of these plus my own fractious relationship with my mother prevented the smallest atom of concern to go out to her in her condition.

"Oh, without a doubt I saw to my mother as would any decent daughter. And my grandmother in her shuffling walk and her nervous existence, behaved as would any mother. She continued looking about her as if those same specters that had taunted me for over a year were after her. Perhaps they were—and rightfully so if she, indeed, had participated in Grandpa's demise.

"The afternoon of the day before my mother died, she seemed to be resting quietly. My grandmother, noting this, decided to go out in the yard to get some fresh air. *'I think I'll do some piddlin' about in the flower beds at the back.'* She had not been gone five minutes when my mother roused from her sleep and asked for a cup of water.

"I went to the kitchen and poured her a cold glass of water from the Frigidaire jar. When I handed the glass to her, she held it in both hands. Then she spoke, her voice husky and weak: *'Mavis, I need to set some things straight or I'll be doomed to the eternity of Hell.'*

"I thought my mother would start talking about our own failed relationship and the aches and pains I must have suffered over the years after the rape episode. What she started to talk about in her weak voice was something entirely different. Momentarily, I realized that my own opinion had been selfish and self-serving. Deep down I felt a stinging guilt for my total disregard of my mother and her own feelings as she approached death. This could have been a sign that some element of empathy had returned to my hardened heart.

"Her voice was whispery as if the words she spoke were only for me: *'Mavis, I know you have a low opinion of Grandma, Jeremiah and me. All these years I see it in your eyes, and I see it in your face when you don't smile when a normal person would smile. I've made you dead inside somehow—most probably by not levelin' with you many years ago. Now I don't have many years left. I don't even have many hours. And Ad deadened you with what he done to you. I can't take none of this here stuff back. It happened—right or wrong—it happened, and I can't change it even if I could roll back the heavens and the earth. Mavis, dear—you know, I ain't called you dear since I can't remember when—there's two sides to ever story. Things is always fifty-fifty when you get down to the brass buckle. People'll say that ain't so, but they don't know nothin'. It's fudgin' on their part. Life is give-and-take; life is fifty-fifty; life ain't fair.'* She tried to take a sip of the cold water, and I had to move closer to help her hold the glass. *'What Papa did to me and Jeremiah and to Mama—terrible things—I reckon he never, never give no thought to what he would have to eat one day at his banquet of consequences.'*

"She continued, after licking her lips. *'What Ad told you that awful day—dear, there's truth in his words. Mama, Jeremiah, and me—we did kill Pa. We smothered him to death after we saw to it that he got drunk as a skunk. We—all of us—had growed to hate him. You might ask me why. I'd have to be truthful and tell you straight that we learned to hate—bad hate—over the years. One day we just woke up out of our beds and said to ourself—enough is enough—and we just up and did it.'* Again, she motioned for another sip of water before continuing. *'It set in a rainy spell like we wasn't used to. It rained for days on end, and the roads was awash with low water. Your Grandma set this up 'cause she believed that no meddlin' officials of the county would be out and about like they was in good weather. Your Grandma did send for old Doctor Goldman when the rains was the worsest. She had a good opinion that he wouldn't come. Didn't matter—your Grandpa was drunk—out of it head to foot. Then when the deed got done, your Grandma had one more good opinion that the Sheriff or the peace officer wouldn't bother to come out. She was right anew. We held the corpse for a day or so, I forget, and we buried him with a real Christian service with old Brother Billy Heart.'*

"What I had heard so far was coming across as so sanitized that I had no idea where it would be leading. I could hear her deep breathing as she talked. I sensed that one way or the other my mother would finish telling me what she had started out to do. Again, selfishly, I said a little silent prayer that Grandma would remain occupied in the flower beds until my mother finished what I had originally thought would be her confessional. As it developed, it was not a confessional. It was the face of truth.

"My mother took a deep breath and asked me: *'Where was I? Oh, I recollect. I ain't told you why we all learned to hate Papa so. Well, I hope to spare you the goriness of it all, but I have to burn your ears a little. My Papa abused Jeremiah from the time he was ten or eleven. Made him do things to him that I can't even describe to you—and he made your Grandma watch the whole thing. Then— I come along—and I come to be the one he does funny things to and he makes me do funny things to him—and he makes your Grandma watch. Jeremiah by this time, he comes old enough to not watch and he runs for the barn or for the woods. Dear, this funny stuff went on and on and on—and one day, out of the blue—we just got enough of it—and we smothered Papa. All of us done the deed.'*

"With her last remark, *'All of us done the deed'*, my mother closed her eyes. She never awakened again, dying the next morning after my Grandmother and I had tried to give her some chicken bouillon for breakfast." ❧

Chapter Thirty-Four

Robert E. Massey:

'We didn't save any food for the bears!'

"The next Saturday arrived—not too soon for me. All week long, behind the counter at the Post Office, I had looked forward to our next trek to The Red Clay Cliffs. The initial thrill of the unanticipated adventures (or misadventures) was largely gone from my mind now that Anastasia and I had made our exploration visit there. At least on the second trip we should be better prepared with what we learned from the first trial run. I had enjoyed Anastasia's company and felt sure I would look forward to being with her once more.

"I smiled as I thought of her Aunt Alicia trying to recall if I was Robert G. or Robert E. Massey. As much of a fuss-budget as she was known to be, her Aunt Alicia was one real stickler for detail. From the first letter she had sent to all the current residents of Walkamile and to all of the former residents she could recall— Anastasia's aunt had worked diligently for over a year to ensure that the Grand Opening of the Walkamile Cultural Center would come off without a hitch. She had bugged, prodded, coaxed, urged and manhandled many of the town's bigwigs about the event to the point that they would do anything she asked of them just to keep her off their backs! That was the skinny about town. How she could pull it off long distance would also rest on Anastasia's local efforts toward promoting the project. Today, Saturday, would be one little rung in her aunt's organizational ladder. And Anastasia and I would be that rung.

"I picked Anastasia up about the same time as I had before. I noticed that she was carrying a metal box which I supposed contained our lunch. A bear would have great difficulty in its breaking-and-entering enterprise with Anastasia's contraption. I jokingly called out to her: *'Robert G. Massey at your service, ma'am; or is it Robert E. Massey at your service, ma'am.'* She pointed at all the equipment she had arranged on her front porch, and I got the subtle message that it needed to be loaded on the truck.

"After we had loaded up everything, Anastasia hopped lithely into my truck, placed the metal container on the floorboard, and responded wittily: *'Which one is it?'* She was dressed similarly as to a week ago, but she had tucked her hair somehow into a red kerchief to good effect.

"As we started off, I answered her: *'I'm afraid it's E for Edward. You may tell your aunt that.'* At that rejoinder, she laughed.

'She does get things muddled up at times,' she said as we left her driveway.

"The trip to the clearing took little time, and we soon found ourselves busily unloading Anastasia's camera equipment: a tripod, oversized camera bag imprinted with the name *'Leica'* on the front side, what appeared to be a folding stool and, of course, the metal container which did, indeed, hold our lunch. The two bamboo poles which we had laid aside at the clearing a week ago remained in place. Again, we would need these as we entered into the dimness of the old pathway. A week in the sun had not harmed them.

"I carried most of the equipment along with our canvas bag of water and still was able to manage the bamboo pole in my right hand. Anastasia was able to take care of the remainder of our equipment.

"We entered the dim canopy from exactly the same spot we had one week prior. It was as if we were stepping into a temporarily abandoned world so distinct from our other world that had possessed at least an obvious reality. Where one week ago we had not known what to expect, this time around we knew exactly what lay ahead. This in no way prevented either one of us from sensing the surreal nature of this place. Though neither of us was afraid of what we might find, each of us took measured steps with the same deliberate caution we had had before. Snakes were not known to suddenly depart from their accustomed territories just because two fools had decided to invade their habitat again.

"We experienced again the feeling of being beneath a huge canopy which could easily have been a giant umbrella made of overhanging branches. I'm sure that another world existed high above us, one in which we could not insinuate ourselves. The sun, as it had done a week before, filtered through the small openings in the canopy and cast mote-filled rays to the floor of the forested area. Shadows seemed to play games with other shadows while the sunlight, frivolous and capricious at odd moments, chose random areas on which to shine. Beneath our feet the decaying leaves, pine needles and the odds and ends of limbs and branches carpeted what may once have been two distinct ruts in the pathway. Despite the eeriness of the place, it was a spectacularly beautiful sight. If Anastasia could capture the essence of the pathway in photographic form, it would be a real coup for our efforts. But we were single-minded and trudged on to The Red Clay Cliffs. That was our primary goal today as her Aunt Alicia had so ordained in her letter.

"In a surprisingly short time we arrived. Again, we experienced the dazzling effect of coming out of a somewhat comforting darkness into a near-radical world of light. And there they were, ahead of us—just as we had left them a week ago. The cliffs looked more beautiful than before with their strident reds and a white that virtually streamed with its purity and loveliness in the morning sun. A sculptor sent by a high-ranking official from a foreign land could not, in any sense of the word, execute the absolute perfection we saw in front of us.

"Neither of us had given any thought of talking to the other, so awestruck were we at the view today. However, Anastasia finally broke our mutual silence: *'Don't you think the sun plays games with us? Look at them! They are more magnificent than I remembered. I hope I can capture them with my humble efforts. I pray that Aunt Alicia will take my inadequacies into consideration when she sees what we shall send her.'*

"The week before we had marked the twelve spots which we had chosen with numbering 1—12, and I had recorded a suggested time for maximum effect in my small notepad. We had agreed, more Anastasia than I, that the timing, the play of the sunlight, estimated distance from the cliff in question and passing clouds would be the final benchmark for her photography. In order, we selected them as I read off the time I had recorded the week before. Looking at my watch each time, I discovered that we were very close to the same time frames.

"Distance in all cases could easily be reckoned in estimated feet, but the sunlight effect and the almost whimsical interruptions by cumulus clouds which tended to create shadowed blights near the cliff's topmost portion were all considered with each number shot. Our efforts progressed without a hitch until we reached Number 12. A large cloud floated over the easternmost cliff, to our right, blocking part of the cliff to be photographed. In an act of desperation, Anastasia elected to take the picture and, as she focused the camera so as to crop the view, she was ecstatic with what she saw. *'I think this may be the best one yet. The effect is one of what I would call a delicate grandeur. I couldn't have planned this at all!'*

"And then our job was over! We stowed our equipment back to its original state and found a shaded area near the base of the cliffs. In the distance to our left we could hear the roar of the Trinity River, muted but pleasing to the ear. In our intense pursuit of taking the pictures neither of us had paid any attention to the sounds made by the river.

"Anastasia opened the metal container which held our lunch, and we sat on two smooth rocks nearby and devoured the tuna fish sandwiches and garden plums even though my watch showed only 10:45. As it turned out, our mission last week had been beneficial to us. It had shortened our planned time by several hours.

"As we started back to the clearing and the truck, Anastasia looked at me with an impish grin on her face and remarked in a tone of voice I could not quite read: *'We may be in trouble. We didn't save any food for the bears!'*

"Amused by her little girl tendency to tweak me when I was least expecting it, I smiled back at her before I said: *'I don't think those bears care for tuna fish and plums. If you had brought salmon croquettes—that might make a difference.'*

"When we reached her home, I helped her take the equipment inside. She accompanied me back to the front porch as I was leaving. I could sense that she wanted to ask me something which she finally did in the same tone of voice that she had used earlier: *'Those were really raccoons, weren't they?'*

"I elected to level with her because I had two things I wanted to say to her. *'Anastasia, you've been one good sport with my constant teasing. I'm sure they were raccoons. They are bandits in the flesh—real opportunists, my daddy always maintained. I've not heard of bears around here at all; maybe over in the Big Thicket area east of her.'* Suddenly, I sort of became tongue-tied as I tried to say the next thing that was on my mind. But I finally managed to get it out: *'Could I see you again, Anastasia? I would like to very much so.'* My question finally came out.

"She replied simply: *'Of course, Robert E. Massey. I'll come to see you Monday to mail these films to Aunt Alicia.'* I think I drove to my house on a set of soft, fluffy white clouds!'

Chapter Thirty-Five

Alicia Woodman, Ph.D.:

'. . . loyal her sons to the last.'

"It would be propitious to my cause, I would think, if I should hold myself to the same rigid standards that I may have inflicted upon the residents of Walkamile—those who grew up with me there, those who have moved away and perhaps even those souls whom I never knew. I had written to all the categories of Walkamilians I just noted a little over one year ago. In my letter I had pre-announced the marvelous news of the cultural center which would be built in Walkamile, and I had gone out on the proverbial limb and had given them an exact date for the Grand Opening of same. Am I an optimist, or what? I would think I'm the latter—a *'what'*. I have always been a *'what'*.

"I realize now that I was over-zealous what with the burgeoning enthusiasm that had gripped me from the onset of the germination of an idea for a cultural center. Foolishly, I asked these selfsame residents to go back into their personal histories and write down those often momentous incidents which had shaped their family's history. So far, to my utter sadness, I've received only handwritten notes in most cases of what I take for a family tree minus the limbs, leaves and the bark! They give me name, age if living, date of birth and death (if they know it), and an occasional marriage record. This is hardly what I had hoped for in my enthusiastic beginning. In a less than subtle way, it is a reproach of the first magnitude.

"For some reason, as I sit here in my office at Harvard and muse—daydream may be a more clarifying appellation—I think of some of the words from one of the ditties sung by the glee club here at Harvard. I believe the title of the song is *'Old Harvard'*, and the partial verse goes like this:

'And like a torch that has burn'd throughout the past,
In thought and in wisdom she shone; loyal her sons unto the last.'

"I sense a loyalty in those citizens of Walkamile in protecting their past from the intrusiveness of someone like me. Oh, I'm positive that my letter may have triggered an urge on their parts to write anecdotal passages of the moments both good and bad in their personal histories. In organizing this fest with my dear niece, Anastasia, I have adopted the attitude that whatever they send to me relevant to their family's individual history, that will have to be a sufficiency for what I intend to do come the Grand Opening. I shall work with what I have—no more, no less. And I shan't create legends to enhance this admirable undertaking, and I shan't create myths to obscure the realities I know and am able in good conscience to reveal.

"This attitude on my part evokes the whispered stories about Leland Stanford and his wife who were dismissed out-of-hand by the then Harvard President, Charles Eliot, sometime in the 1880s when the couple had suggested the establishment of an enormous endowment for the university. The minimal history of Walkamile shall not be besieged with tales of inaccurate historical information. We are what we are—and we shall not embellish ourselves or our personal histories. My dear niece, Anastasia, has brought this point home in a stellar manner in the latest letter I received from her. I shall include at least a part of her letter to elucidate my position:

'*I am troubled by the old legends of young lads in Walkamile climbing The Red Clay Cliffs, watching for the miscellaneous river craft, and then racing back to Walkamile to inform the businessmen that a certain river craft was approaching. After my two treks to the cliffs to take pictures per your request, I cannot, for the life of me, visualize such an occurrence. The distance is too great; the terrain now is near impenetrable (as it most likely was then), and I cannot accept that the cliffs could be scaled handily in sufficient time for an observation to be made. And then the young lads have to rappel themselves down the cliffs and tear back to Walkamile to make their announcements. Why, they would have to be world class athletes to perform such a feat!*'

"While growing up in Walkamile, my family lived next door to Doctor Goldman and his wife, Miriam. As a child, I both envied and hated Mrs. Goldman. She was so strikingly beautiful—I was not. She had glorious red hair—I did not. Her long fingernails were always painted a dark, dark red—darker than blood. My fingernails were bitten off to the quick—and I didn't dare try to paint the god-awful stubs. And Mrs. Goldman wore long dresses that made pleasant swishing noises when she walked—and I wore dresses that never seemed to fit even though my mother spent hours at her sewing machine making alterations to fit my strangely shaped body. And Mrs. Goldman smelled like the early summer gardenias when I got close to her—and I'm sure I smelled like Lifebuoy Soap which my mother insisted was something that could kill all germs anywhere on the body.

"But Mrs. Goldman smiled a lot—and I did not. There was a dreamy quality to her face at all times as if she were contemplating what wondrous event would next happen in her life to bring more smiles to her face. Even as a child, I pictured my own face as too wrinkled. My mother told me I kept my nose in a book too much.

"Mrs. Goldman remained at home a lot. My mother said that was the plight of the doctor's wife. *'Never marry a doctor or a preacher,'* she had admonished me on several occasions.

"What I learned later in life about Miriam Goldman, the smiling woman who possessed this dreamy quality to her face, was that she was happy because she sipped paregoric like you or I might sip a cola on a hot summer's day. And when that lovely effect diminished, she would resort to powerful pain pills to bring her another rewarding feeling. In later years, I have often thought of her: the surface one views does, in no way, reveal the pain and agony that may lie beneath an apparent vision of loveliness. This opinion is brought home to me and is substantiated when I recall the essence that was Miriam Goldman.

"I've never told anyone other than myself that I actually fell in love in the 8th Grade. His name was Arppra Renner, and his name was a palindrome—as were his father's and mother's names. I do believe that he hated his name. Oh, I must admit it was unusual, but it was not a name that could not be dealt with. I knew for a fact that he wished to be called *'Arp'* and his true buddies did call him that. Arppra sat one aisle over from me, the *'R'* students separated from the *'T—Z'* students in which I was included. I know for a fact that I was not a beautiful young lady—horrific horn rimmed glasses and a head too big for my torso—and stringy hair that I could not tame. But I still had feelings, and I still had longings. And at my age and the age of my classmates, I realized that there was more to life than studying—there were boys. And I selfishly aimed my intentions for Arppra. Over the years, when I think of my naïve approach to a drive that is common to all of us, I can only smile and reflect that perhaps I was not the sole person in the class yearning for an

212 ◈ Henry Wyath Gurley

opening that might lead to a full realization of intentions. There had to be other moon-faced girls pining in secret to get to talk to Bobby or to Sam or to Stanley; and there were boys, I am sure, who practiced in front of mirrors at home when no one else was present with a naivety that truly would have been laughable with lines such as: *'Why, Julia, how beautiful you are today in your green dress!'* or worse, *'If I had to take my glasses off, I would still find you just as beautiful!'*

"Arppra paid not a modicum of attention to me. Unfortunately, neither did anyone else in the class. I truly believe the girls despised me because I was smart—too smart at times even for myself. And I had erroneously thought I could have used my intelligence to snare a boy or so in the guise of helping them with their homework. No such luck! One would think I had the measles, mumps or some other infectious disease the way they avoided me. Often, I would smell my wrists to determine if the Lifebuoy Soap smell remained. I would not tell anyone this, but I also discretely lifted my arms and smelled under my arms to see if the Mum was still working to its expected standards!

"As I progressed in school, I started to pick up vibrations that the teachers seemed to dislike me. Not one or two teachers—all of them! I was seldom called on in class though I made outstanding grades in all my classes. There were so many times that I remember that I could have added something to a discussion in a class. No! I had to sit there and keep my mouth shut because I might show up the teacher who had prepared himself/herself only by reading the teacher's instructional material. Nosy to the point of ridicule, I had researched the topics of the lesson and could have expounded for an hour or so if I were called on in class.

"All of my idiosyncrasies paid dividends later in my life—at

Rice and at Harvard. Arcane details came to me in my advanced classes at these institutions, and even I, on some occasions, wondered where in the Hell I had ever learned something so trivial. But dividends continued to come my way. Scholarships, grants, fellowships, summer seminars—all continued to enlighten me and keep me busy in my career and intellectually active in my drive to achieve new goals. I had friends by the score, but not once was I able to have a friendship with a male counterpart that went beyond a platonic stage. So . . . with the intelligence I possessed, I chose (upon realizing this sharpened fact) to concentrate on those elements in my life that would enhance my own inner spirit. I simply buried myself in my work. Harvard's emblazoned motto was *'Veritas'*, and I embarked on a lifetime mission to find *'Veritas.'*

"I had received the long letter from my niece on a Friday. She had sent it and the undeveloped films from the trek she and Robert E. Massey had made to the Red Clay Cliffs (she informed me of Mr. Massey's almost flippant remark about his middle initial). Upon receipt of the film canisters, I had sped across campus to the photography lab and had stood nervously outside the dark room until the irritating red light went off. I almost attacked Shelby Vordner as he opened the door in exiting from the dark room. Shelby was the one person everyone on campus depended on if the word *'f-i-l-m'* was involved. He could perform magic when it came to developing film.

"Shelby insisted that I leave the canisters and *'go tend to your own knitting'* while he performed his magic. I chose not to do so, rather sitting outside the dark room and relishing every word of Anastasia's long letter. As I neared the end of the letter, a smile came to my face, and my heart beat with a renewed vigor, and I suddenly felt warm and flush in certain areas that I had long ago learned to control and to suppress. My dear little niece, Anastasia, had to be in love! Oh, she had not come out with a full-blown weepy declaration, but there were hints scattered throughout her letter that betrayed her. True, I may be her old-maid aunt, but I am smart, and I can read between the lines.

"One part of her letter epitomized the very spark that comes across despite the lack of my hearing her voice, seeing her smile, and noting her familiar mannerisms—on a sheet of stationery which had traveled hundreds of miles across the country. The part was written in Anastasia's swirling, hurry-up style and read:

> *'He almost apologized about his constant teasing;*
> *and then he asked me if he could see me again. I*
> *told him I would see him Monday at the Post Office*
> *when I was to mail the film to you. That Monday*
> *was when he asked me if I would like to go with him*
> *to Galveston one weekend soon. His aunt lives there*
> *and we could stay with her. <u>I am so-o-o excited!</u>'*

"I thought wistfully of the time when I had been the same age as Anastasia was now and how things had seemed far more glorious than they actually were. I was sure that she looked at the stars in the sky mirrored in their icy kingdoms and felt as if she wanted to reach up and touch each one of them. I had felt that way—long ago."

ॐ

Chapter Thirty-Six

Micah Abraham Jessup:

'. . . one of them never-mind things.'

"The trip back to Atlanta after Grandpa's funeral was as bewildering as if I were a small child being sent from home against my wishes. I could look out the plane's window and watch the little white clouds which at times appeared static in their unmoving poses. It could be imagined on my part, if I let my fancy take over my grounded common sense that I might be peering into a pearlized gateway to an unknown realm. Too far fetched for me to accept at a time like this, I dismissed the purely fanciful thought and accepted forthwith that I was flying eastward toward my home—not away from home as I was wont to dream. Now that Walkamile was behind me and the fact that someone I loved too much was dead, I realized full well that I had to get on with the business of living.

"My mother and Aunt Audie would still be there for me—both I knew as fortresses against the perils that any young man faces. But I was on my own. The worrisome thing that I had carried in my heart on both of my trips from Atlanta back to Walkamile and then back to Atlanta twice still remained in my heart. On neither visit had I scrounged up the courage to tell my mother. Far be it from me to announce such a thing to Aunt Audie first. At this point in time when, and if, I opted to broach the very ticklish predicament that I had entangled myself in, my mother would be the first to know.

Grandpa's critical condition during my first visit and his subsequent death had forced me to shelve my own personal situation.

"I knew that my faculty associates and a large number of the students I taught would be supportive once they discovered what I was about. There would be those, I assumed, who would either turn away from me or would ostracize me outright. It was not a clear-cut win-win matter. In the South, especially in communities like the Rogersville section where so many of my black brethren resided— and in Atlanta where I had so far been accepted in apparent good faith at face value—there still existed schisms that separated the white and black enclaves. So far I had not suffered any of the expected indignities of being a black who was living in what might only recently have been deemed a white part of town. I considered that my baptism of fire might soon be coming on both ends of the line.

"I had wanted so much to tell my mother that I had fallen in love with a white woman, a Caucasian. I had wished a thousand times that I could have had the opportunity to talk to Grandpa Jessup. Somewhere within the depths of his love for me I do believe that he would have come forth with that silky voice of his and in one remarkable utterance he would have assuaged my fears. I think he might have said: *'That's one of them never-mind things. Be a man! Your love for your fine woman will carry you through; her love for you will brace you up. Oh, it won't be easy, but life for the sinners that we are will never be easy.'*

"But Grandpa had never said these words to me. I have only put them into a mouth that is now silenced. And I have not approached my mother or my Aunt Audie. The time is not right, and oddly, I am set to wonder if the time ever will be right.

"When I had met Carlene Anthony for the first time quite by accident, I gave no thought as to any future association with her. She lived in the apartment next door to me, and I had seen her come and go on occasion. We had spoken to each other more as a courtesy than anything else, nothing more than a casual hello. I didn't know her name, and I'm sure she didn't know mine. I had seen her name on her mail box Identotaped as *C. Anthony*, and it is quite likely that she had noted my own name on my mail box—*M. A. Jessup.*

"The manner in which we met was certainly less than provocative unless you had been a neighbor with an inquiring mind. I had exited my apartment's front door and was on my way for a few hours of shopping. As I was leaving my own apartment, the door to her apartment opened suddenly, and she burst out as if in a panic. We almost collided. The first words out of her mouth came forth as a mish-mash of excited gibberish: *'There! There! Spewing water! There! Can't get phone! Turn off! Everywhere! All over the place! It's there! Terrible!'*

"When I was finally able to get her to calm down and tell me in broken sentences that the connecting water pipe on her washing machine had come loose, I raced into her apartment without granted permission and managed to shut off the offending faucet. Her washroom, which was "hidden" in a hallway closet, was one big mess, and the excess of water had invaded her living room as well as the little hallway.

"By this time neighbors had gathered, alarmed at the noise and, I'm sure, more curious than Hell would allow at the sight of a white woman running from her apartment yelling in gibberish that could not be understood and then—the *piece de resistance*—a black man coming out of her apartment soaking wet and completely disheveled. Regardless, an apartment maintenance man came by quite by happenstance. Within an hour he had cleaned up the mess.

"As I left, when the maintenance man had things well in hand, Carlene Anthony said to me: *'Thank you, M. A. Jessup.'*

"Without any change in my demeanor, I gave her the finest

elocution I could manage as I replied: *'You're welcome, Ms. C. Anthony.'* With our exchanged repartees over, we both laughed out loud.

"That is how I met Carlene Anthony, and that is how Carlene Anthony met Micah Abraham Jessup. And that was the story that I wished a thousand times over that I had been able to tell my Grandpa Jessup. Too, I would give up a year of my own life if I could have told him how we fell in love, how we both commiserated at the problems which we were sure we would encounter—in Georgia, in Walkamile, in Carlene's own hometown of Ocala, Florida. I would wish that Carlene could have met him and learned to love him as I had done. And I would have wanted him to give his blessings to our planned marriage, and I would have been so honored to have him as my Best Man.

"When Grandpa had encouraged me to study, study, study so that I could get ahead in life and become a free man, he had used an adage that I've not forgotten. He had said to me: *'Wishing does not make it so.'* How true! So I plan to dismiss all this wishful thinking from my mind. The pilot has just announced that we will be landing in twelve minutes. Carlene Anthony will meet me at the gate. I am admirably prepared for the nervous stares which will be directed our way when I hug her and hold on to her for as long as she will allow. She, like my Grandpa Jessup, I love too much."

❧

Chapter Thirty-Seven

Alicia Woodman, Ph.D.:

'What joy in the ride!'

"The first day of reckoning! The momentous days of September 27-28, 1975, are upon us. For me to make a confession upfront might be considered laughable to those who know me intimately. They all think that I have nerves of steel, when, in fact, my nerves are of the most brittle material one could imagine. I am a wreck as I lug my tired body out of bed, but I hear encouraging sounds from the kitchen. And the smell of perked coffee offers encouragement for me to take another step toward the kitchen. The long, boring trip from Boston to Houston the day before has taken its toll on me. I am becoming less of a spring chicken as each day rolls by.

"Murt, my brother, is hustling about in the kitchen, doing, I suppose, what he has done for years. His wife, Evelyn, a lovely, wispy sort of creature (and Anastasia's mother) had died giving birth to Anastasia. Of course, Murt became a surrogate mother along with his expected duties as a father figure to the little princess, Anastasia. Evelyn had told Murt before the child was born that she had always dreamed of having a little princess. To honor her, Murt had named the tiny little girl Anastasia after the Romanov princess who had supposedly been butchered when her father, the Tsar, had been overthrown in Russia.

"I had thought at the time that *Anastasia* was an unhappy choice, but like a good sister to a loving brother who had just lost his wife, I kept my trap shut for once—an amazing feat, I might add. Murt had considered Scarlett as a possible name, but when a friendly neighbor reminded him that Scarlett O'Hara had been a schemer, a devious sister-in-law, and a home-breaker too, he quickly opted out of that name. Scarlett would have been a lovely name in my opinion, but my opinion mattered not.

"By design Murt did not like to speak of Evelyn or to reminisce about the few happy days they had had together. Family and friends alike honored this unspoken wish which Murt somehow conveyed indirectly to everyone. Even Anastasia, as she grew into a lovely young woman, rarely spoke of her mother and definitely not in her father's presence. I found all of this a bit odd because it was my inherent nature to relive those wonderful moments of the past. Even in sadness I somehow found the reanimation of past events invigorating to my spirit and to my sense of family. But I am no fool. I honored Murt's unspoken dictum, but I still held Evelyn in my heart and mind as a piece of a puzzle that was life. Each time I came home, weather permitting, I would see to it that Anastasia and I made a trek to the cemetery. And we would both place flowers on Evelyn's grave, and I would tell her the pleasant anecdotes I could remember which always included Evelyn. I hoped that Anastasia would be able to capture a bit of the essence that was her mother in the little vignettes I shared with her.

"Murt broke my thrall to reverie. *'You're following the trail of the smell of freshly perked coffee. I know this for a fact.'* He rose from the breakfast table and poured me a cup of coffee. He knew by my history that I drank it black.

"Of course, Murt was right on. I had a reputation of not being civilized until I had consumed at least one cup of coffee. Close friends of mine had always remarked snidely: *'Alicia doesn't come alive until she's had at least two cups of java.'* Oh, they were right. I was not a morning person. But ceremonies were scheduled to start at 9:00 AM Johnny-on-the-spot. And, of course, I knew I would be there in fine fettle. I had not worked more than a year to see this project come to fruition only to fall flat on my face at the very moment I had dreamed of for a long, long time. Lights! Camera! Action! Today was the first day of a dream coming true right before my eyes.

"Murt was a wonderful brother. If you had placed a dozen men and a dozen women in a cattle corral and attempted to pair off the brother-sister combinations, you'd never in a million years select Murt and me as brother-sister. Where I rattled off at the mouth excessively and without end, Murt was almost stoic. I do not mean that he never had anything to say. *'Au contraire!'* When he came forth with an utterance, you could take it to the bank and deposit it with great confidence as to its worth and validity. Where I constantly muddled about as if I were lost upon this great Planet Earth, often unfocused and befuddled in my thinking, Murt approached any problem or project with superb organizational skills that belied his quiet, unassuming bearing. He knew where he was going; he knew what he would be doing. And I? Oh, I might get to my goal eventually and be able to accomplish it with some degree of flair. But as my friends often said, *'What joy in the ride!'*

"Murt was not a touchy-feely sort of man. His manner was brusque at times, but when intimacy was required he was a big, old bumbling Teddy Bear who had a heart so soft that any distressed soul could melt away their troubles after they had confided in him. And I? I was of the type that my wide-open arms caressed everyone within reach, and then the stream of consoling words would follow, and the world of all those even peripherally concerned would eventually come up *'dew-pearled',* as Browning was wont to expound when he tried to define the little neglected and abused orphan, Pippa.

"Murt and I were as different as black and white, daylight and darkness, yin and yang and a hundred other comparatives. To have come from the same womb could be described as an anomaly at best. Where he had his feet solidly on the ground, I had my head in the clouds. Despite these vast differences, we both loved each other. Murt had told me in his quiet way that he had always been so proud of me. I had come close to tears once when he had tweaked me: *'I know you must have been given part of my brains. The Good Lord gave you way too many.'*

"I, in turn, had told Murt on countless occasions that he had done a marvelous job in raising Anastasia. For a man to understand the intricacies of first, a little girl, and then the surging demands of a prepubescent child and finally a pimple-worried teenager and lastly a beautiful young lady who had fallen in love right before his eyes—I praised him and extolled the practical manner in which he had met all of these circumstances. He took no claim for my praise of him. His only remark? *'Alicia! You must have forgotten out-of-hand all those telephone calls to you over the years when I fumbled about and asked dozens of silly and very uncomfortable questions. You haven't forgot that, have you?'* Naturally, I had not forgotten any of his calls, and I would always love and respect him for including me, even peripherally, in the rearing of Anastasia—even long distance.

"Murt and I drank our coffee without much conversation. If strangers had been able to view us at the breakfast table, it is likely that they would have said that we appeared to be a couple married for thirty-plus years—now at the mumbling non-communicating stage in our marriage. We heard Anastasia in her room and knew that she was preparing herself for the first day of our Grand

Opening.

"I had not asked him to do so, but Murt got up from the breakfast table, rinsed his coffee cup and then began to prepare my breakfast. He knew I was a cook of little repute. And he knew exactly what I had always eaten for breakfast when I came home: one egg, scrambled lightly in butter, two pieces of bacon—crisp, crisp, crisp—, one piece of Mrs. Baird's light bread, toasted, and mayhaw jelly. These were my comfort foods when I returned to Walkamile, and I had become spoiled rotten over the years by my brother's strictest attention to detail. To me, his actions proved to be one of his endearing qualities.

"Five minutes later Anastasia came bounding into the kitchen. She was dressed in her chenille robe, hair still in curlers, and no make-up at all. Her feet were engulfed by oversized floppy, fluffy pink house shoes which appeared to be half as large as a wash tub. She pranced gaily but awkwardly over to her father and gave him the lightest peck on his cheek and then she bent near me and gave me an air kiss. Despite her attire, she was as fresh and as lovely as I would have wished myself to be at that age. She announced her wishes in just two words: *'Orange juice!'* and then proceeded to pour herself a glassful.

"We had less than two hours before the ceremonies started. The first day, September 27, would entail our being *'kissy-kissy'* with the town officials, those governmental bigwigs—both state and federal—and those wonderful persons who had awarded me the grant in the first place. I definitely knew how to play the game: I would be cool and formal with the town officials who had not contributed one stinking minute or shekel to the cause of this cultural center; (I thought of the old saying that said in effect, *'those who have the most give the least.')* I would acquiesce to the state and federal officials without kowtowing to them, and I would extol the praises of those who had awarded me the privilege of the grant. To have said all of this and to follow through with it without stepping on anyone's toes would be an accomplishment of the first order. Laughingly, I reminded myself that I certainly could not wear Anastasia's floppy pink house shoes.

"September 28, the second day, would be the day for all the residents, former residents of Walkamile and a few honored guests. The program would be informal, and agreeable participants would be allowed to present brief anecdotal histories of their families. That had been the purpose of the letter I had sent out more than a year ago. I would have to wait and pray that this planned scenario would come off without a hitch. I had scheduled it from 9:30 AM until Noon in the hopes that the promise of a catered lunch would break up any long-winded, over-zealous speaker. *'We shall see!'* I reminded myself."

Chapter Thirty-Eight

Mavis Murray:

'I never eat anything that has eyes!'

"After my mother's death, I had chosen to remain with my grandmother, Leah Philbin, and see to her daily needs. After Ruth's death (Ruth being her only daughter), she seemed to go downhill with each passing moment. My Uncle Jeremiah was no real help though he did send some money each month to my grandmother, and he never came home anymore. I think I can understand why: out of sight, out of mind. While my mother was alive, it was not unusual for Uncle Jeremiah to make his presence known at least during the Christmas holidays. Then, on occasion, when the oilfield business hit a slow period, he would come home and stay several weeks. These were the periods I recall from my childhood when the adults carried on in their private conversations and whispered confidences.

"In a short time, I became accustomed to my grandmother's odd behavior: her continuous shuffling about throughout the house, her constant agitation as she carefully inspected any room before entering it, her obvious detachment as she looked over her shoulder and to either side of her as she roamed about. Even her jerking motions and trembling hands were earmarks of her unease. I was saddened to see these indications of her mental impairment as it took deeper root. Despite what I had learned from my mother on her death bed, I chose to treat my grandmother with kindness rather than with the scorn I would have lumped upon her had I not known the truth. I could not heap punishment upon someone in whose shoes I had not walked.

"My grandmother seemed incapable of accepting any tokens of kindness. Rather she would rebuff any overtures of that nature and stiffen when, and if, I made any physical contact with her: a hug, a loving touch, or whatever. Even a smile from me would be met with a look of pure distrust. To penetrate her world with any offerings of conviviality was to be met at the gates of her castle by barrels of boiling oil being rained down from above. Though I felt hopeless at times, I continued to try to reach some inner part of her soul. I longed to ignite some deeply entrenched vestige of what may once have been a happy person.

"Perhaps my most frustrating moments came at meal times. She refused to eat anything that I may have prepared for her. *'You know I don't eat squash!'* Or: *'I never eat anything that has eyes!'* Or: *'This syrup has strychnine in it! You taste it first!'*

"My own frustration had almost reached a bursting point when I discovered by accident a ruse that would allow her to eat my food without her usual refusals. As I would bring each bowl or plate of food to our table, be it breakfast, dinner or supper, I would invent some clap-trap remarks that would throw her off her usual gambits: *'Dear Mrs. Massey brought over this fine dish of chicken and dressing today.'* Or: *'Miriam Goldman sent these wonderful butter beans over by the Good Doctor this afternoon.'* Or some other idiotic example. The poor soul would eat whatever I then set before her, often asking for seconds. This charade hurt me deeply, but if it happened to be the only way I could get her to eat—then so be it!

Sadly, most of the characters I used in my devious lies to her had been long dead.

"Five years and two months after my mother passed away, my grandmother died quietly in her sleep. She had truly lived an agonizing life what with my Grandpa Philbin's abuse of both my mother and my uncle. As a collateral to their abuse, my grandmother was a victim by having to witness his abuses. I had formed my own opinion when my mother had died what with her deathbed confession. I know my grandmother must have carried a heavy load of guilt with her to the grave. I had hoped that somewhere along the line she had found a method to forgive herself. Only she knew.

"Over the years her mental deterioration had contributed to her physical decline, but I prayed that somewhere along the way a spark of peace had touched her spirit. Whether she had ever faced up to her own feelings of guilt or not was an unknown. I don't know because we were never able to talk about it. The abuse was always a subject that had been shelved in the back recesses of our minds—my mother's, my uncle's and my grandmother's. I had only become privy to it when my mother had told me the truth on her deathbed. Before that I had only suspected that something horrific had brought my family to ruin. In a way, I had filed away the elements of this destructive behavior, perhaps selfishly so. My inattention even on a limited basis was the only defense mechanism that I possessed as a child and later as an adult.

"I was able to get in touch with Uncle Jeremiah at a pumping station outside of Kilgore. When he finally came to the field phone at the station, I had to shout to him. At the time it seemed ludicrous that I would be yelling at my grandmother's only son that his mother had died. With the clanging noises going full blast in the background, I was only able to hear him say: *'I'll be there tomorrow.'* Then our connection went dead.

"Two days later Uncle Jeremiah and I went to Walkamile Funerals and arranged for my grandmother's funeral. He overspent as people are wont to do in times of deep grief, and a passing thought of what my mother had told me about my Grandpa's burial tugged at me deeply. But I let it go. I had to. My Grandpa had been buried without any formal fanfare, without the luxury of a proper casket, without anyone at his funeral showing any degree of grief. And my grandmother would be buried beside him at the Cedar Grove Cemetery in a fine mahogany casket lined in a delicate pink sateen material. And she would be attired for her trip to her eternal rest in a handsome dress that she would not have been seen wearing in public had she had her druthers. The irony was over the top, but I was not paying for the funeral.

"Uncle Jeremiah and I found my grandmother's will in her black traveling trunk. She had always kept the trunk locked and had announced that the best thief in the county could not pick its lock. In three or four minutes Uncle Jeremiah had opened the lock with a handy little device that was attached to his pocket knife! When he was successful, he looked at me, smiled and said: *'I'm the best thief from another county!'* His sudden levity brought a lessening of our tensions and gave us both some relief from our personal grieving.

"Uncle Jeremiah and I had been awarded all the property and possessions by our grandmother. When we learned of this, as stated in my grandmother's will, we had to be a bit surprised. Uncle Jeremiah likely hit the nail on the head when he told me that my grandmother would never have left anything to Ruth, my mother. He said the reason was real obvious. *'Your Grandma didn't want Ad Murray to get his hands on anything that was hers. That's all, really!'* Perhaps he was right. Despite what had happened, and despite the fact that Ad Murray had disappeared after he did what he did to me, my grandmother knew that my mother would take him back in a Mexican minute. My mother was that way. She never had a clear head when it came to matters of the heart, and she would readily sacrifice those she loved in her irrational pursuit.

"I stayed on where I had been all my life. Uncle Jeremiah still sent money to me each month, and he told me that I should improve myself. *'You have a good mind. When I'm gone there won't be none to take care of you. Go to school! Get smart and be a teacher. You can always make a livin' at that.'*

"Uncle Jeremiah was right. I went to Sam Houston all year long for three years to study to become a teacher. Uncle Jeremiah helped me with the costs. When I graduated, I came back to Walkamile and got a job teaching 3rd Grade. For the first time in my life (other than my first seven years of life before Ad Murray entered my comfortable little world), some stability and happiness have returned to me. I feel that I am now a vital part of our community. And—I plan to leave behind all the specters that I have met along the way. For my own well-being and for that of my Uncle Jeremiah, I have opted to allow the sleeping dogs to lie. Any other action would be criminal on my part and would further sully the spirit and essence of my mother and my grandmother, and they would bring my Uncle Jeremiah to his own ruin. He's all I have left in my world, and I plan to protect him."

Chapter Thirty-Nine

Bob Renner:

'Come on in! The water's fine.'

"At a point in time it almost becomes funny when you finally stop and think what a fool you've been for such a long time. One year, at our church's Easter Service, I heard the preacher use the word *'epiphany'* and I said to myself: *'Bob, you'll never have any use for that word. Forget about it! The preacher's just usin' a big word to impress us poor country hicks.'* Well, I was mighty wrong! I went home and got out the old Webster's that was so ragged that I didn't think I'd ever come across *'epiphany'* but I did. And the meanin' of that word has been with me ever minute of my life since that Sunday.

"The day Anna introduced me to Charity Chambers in our office was my epiphany though I didn't fully recognize it until she was hired by Anna and come to work for us. That day I had rushed off like a fool on a fool's errand and had said to Charity that I hoped she would come to work for us in the next thirty minutes. Leaving the office, I just forgot about the young lady and put her out of my mind because Koskobe and me had always left the hirin' stuff to Anna. I had enough to contend with on my messy plate and didn't

give a whit whether a pretty girl or a three-legged dog took care of
the other parts of our operation. Sayin' all of this now and believin'
all of it—well, that's two different things. But, like I said, my
epiphany started the moment Anna had said, *'Bob, I would like you
to meet Charity Chambers.'* Strange, strange how these things come
upon a person.

"Two days later Charity Chambers came to work for us. I knew
that Anna had put down the benchmarks for the things that she
would be doin' on a daily basis. Other employees had come and
went, and Anna was never happy with any of them. The first few
days a new employee was on the job everything went *'swimmingly'*
as Anna often bragged. Then, like boredom or laziness had set in,
the new employee let little things slide, then other more important
tasks fell by the wayside—and then chaos ruled the day accordin'
to Anna. I was sort of used to this because I was the sloppiest
person in the world as far as I was concerned. I knew it, but I
somehow managed to work around it. Findin' somethin' on my
desk was like the old game we played as kids—I think we called it
Treasure Hunt.

"A week or so passed, and I paid no attention to what was goin'
on in the office. Wrapped up in special projects, makin' on-the-spot
decisions at jobs in progress, eatin' always on the run and racin' in
and out of the office, forever on the phone—this was my life. I
didn't pay much attention to the things around me. Koskobe, busy
as always, could have been a hundred miles away from me instead
of in his office down the hall. We seldom took the time to interrupt
each other unless we happened to be workin' on the same job. Anna
only bothered me if some client was unhappy about somethin' of
importance or somethin' new sounded worthwhile. Then one
mornin' I come strollin' into the office, got my usual cup of coffee
and headed for my office at the back. When I walked into my own

space, I almost didn't recognize where I was. The place looked like somethin' out of one of the business magazines we got from office furniture places. On my desk was not a single piece of paper. A desk pad was neatly centered on the desk. It looked brand new. There was an office-style lamp with a green shade on the left side of the desk pad. The telephone had been placed behind my desk on a credenza which matched my old desk.

"I couldn't imagine where all my junk had disappeared to. My junk was what kept me workin' almost day and night, sometimes six days a week and even on some Sundays. Then I noticed a metal file cabinet placed to the right of my desk. At that point, I heard laughter outside my office door, and there stood Anna and Charity almost bent over double as they laughed. Well, all I could say to myself was that they knew somethin' I didn't. And they seemed to be gettin' a kick out of that fact.

"Though I wasn't mad, I did give them the best glarin' look I could muster. *'Come on in! The water's fine. And tell me all about it.'* I was tryin' hard to act unhappy with what I had found.

"Anna spoke first: *'Blame me, Bob. Two or three days ago I told Charity that we needed to get you organized. We did. How do you like it?'*

"For once I couldn't think of nothin' to say. Then I asked cautiously, *'Where's my stuff?'* And that's when the epiphany really came into being full force. Anna recommended that I spend the next couple of hours with Charity so that she could explain the filin' system she had set up for me. I reluctantly agreed, and as she went over the filin' of my *'stuff.'* I was amazed at how easy gettin' to somethin' could be. It all made sense to me, and I could put my finger on anything in less than a minute.

"Anna left us to our devices with her usual passin' remark: *'Bout time you got yourself organized. My next project for my little baby brother is gettin' him a wife.'* If I had been able to look at myself in a mirror, I know my face would've been redder than the reddest of beets. Charity, I noticed, looked away so that she wouldn't betray her own embarrassment.

"As I said, it can almost be funny when you stop and think what a fool you've been, and I don't think I'm talkin' about the junk that used to be on my desk every day, if you get the drift of my meanin'."

Chapter Forty

Anna Renner:

'A golden egg upon a silver platter.'

"After I learned what a palindrome actually was, I paid little attention to my name. Of course, when I worked at The Ordnance during World War II, my co-workers insisted that I needed to get married so I'd no longer be bothered with a name that you could read frontward and backwards. I just laughed at them good-naturedly with a stock reply: *'What if I married a fella by the name of Otto? Why, I'd be Anna Otto.'* This usually ended our little discussion about marriage, at least for the time being. They had no idea that *'Otto'* was one of our family names.

"Mama died during the war, and Daddy insisted that I stick with my job at The Ordnance where I was making good money for a woman at that time. When Koskobe and I had been at home during that time, neither one of us wanted to return to our wartime duties: Koskobe to Louisiana and me to Houston. Our little brother, Bob, was still at home helping Daddy, but he would be called up before the war ended. Daddy would then be left to hold down the fort. In a short span of time my world, Koskobe's world, and Bob's and

Daddy's world had been dramatically changed. I had always heard that war wasn't just about the killing. How true!

"When the war finally ended in late 1945, I, in effect, became the mother hen for the Renner clan. I returned home from my job at The Ordnance, and Koskobe and Bob were both discharged from their military obligations the following year. I was still plain old Anna Renner, but I had gained a measure of worldliness and *savoir-faire* during my years with The Ordnance. I had learned to swear like the proverbial longshoreman; I had learned to drink beer and love it in the process; I had tried smoking cigarettes but found them extremely distasteful; I had learned to bowl and roller skate; and I had discovered that I had an innate affinity for bookkeeping and numbers. In a way, I guess you could say that some of my rough edges had been smoothed out a bit, but that I still had an edge to me. I hope that makes sense.

"Daddy didn't last long after all of us came back home. Koskobe and Bob sort of assumed the burdensome duties that Daddy had been involved in before all of us left home. We evolved from Daddy's carpentry work into a competitive construction company with almost all of the bells and whistles that anybody could desire. Daddy tried to be intimately involved in the daily operation at first, but his heart was never fully given to the day-to-day demands of such an enterprise as we had become. He pined away before our eyes, and in 1950 he passed away. I hope he realized that he had left a credible legacy in two fine sons, a fine daughter (I trust) and that he imparted knowledge to the three of us allowing us to function as a viable business. And I pray that he knew that a part of his legacy was the unbounded love he showed daily for our mother, Alla Renner. And for us!

"By hook or crook our business grew. Each year saw more contracts and projects come our way. It was almost as if we didn't have to seek them out. We discovered that our reputation had preceded us in the excellence of Daddy's work over the years. He had established his own foundation of excellence and honesty, and this basis needed no elaborate advertising programs. For this fact we were extremely grateful.

"Our biggest breakthrough came the day when Alicia Woodman, Ph.D., called Koskobe and handed us, quite literally, the goose that laid the golden egg. I think Koskobe got that old saying all screwed up when he had called it *'a golden egg upon a silver platter.'* Regardless, either expression gets across the meaning of Dr. Woodman's telephone call. All we had to do was to produce the desired results she had outlined.

"From the late months of summer, through the autumn and winter of 1974 and again in to the spring of the following year, then the summer, we geared all of our goals to the fateful September 27 date. Watergate had, in a most unusual way, prodded us to meet our guarantees with Dr. Woodman. The sham and artifice, the delusion, the devious nature of our country's leaders—all these, and the other elements of Watergate—made us want, in a desperate fashion, to uphold Daddy's ideals of excellence and honesty. Then President Ford took the reins in August just as we were starting, and we all seemed to give a collective sigh of relief that there actually was at last a person of great integrity in this country. Whether the integrity lasted or not was not our immediate worry. We had a job to do.

"A golden event which affected all of our lives, both on the home front and in our business endeavors, happened to be the day that Charity Chambers came to work for me. Honestly, I gave not a whistling thought to any long-range plans for the young lady. Over the years I had hired one young lass after the other, and successively each of them had departed eventually for one reason or the other. In all cases, they had contributed very little to our company—at least nothing that would benefit us on the whole.

Charity Chambers was a different story, however. She apparently had not come on board just to draw a paycheck.

"During the interview, I had explained the duties which I expected her to perform on a daily basis. Only one of the prescribed duties had been met with a tinge of negativism: answering the telephone, if necessary. I somehow picked up on a shy streak in the young lady when this was mentioned to her. I assured her that there would be nothing to it at all once she had done it several times. And matters rested there.

"Within three weeks of Charity's being on the job, the change in our office was remarkable, for lack of a better word. Our workplace took on the appearance of something out of a slick publication advertising office furniture and supplies. Everything about the office seemed to be in its rightful place, and the entire office took on the guise of a place where all of us favored spending our time. Wild flower arrangements seemed to come forth out of the clear air; ivy plants once tangled and dusty glistened with their green tones in the dappled sunlight streaming through the windows; ash trays in the waiting area of our office seemed to clean themselves; magazines for clients to read while they waited for an appointment were neatly stacked and always up-to-date; the coffee room was always spotless, and it seemed that the coffee was always fresh; a floor lamp was situated near an overstuffed chair in the little entry hall giving a subtle hint of a homey atmosphere. Someone was having a great time doing what she was doing, and that someone was Charity Chambers! I could not have been more pleased at how quickly she had assumed more responsibilities than I had required.

"Then one day I had challenged her in a positive sort of way to see if she could get my little brother Bob on track with the mess in his office. Of course, she had done that and more. He had looked forward, after their first meeting, to have her come in every day and get him started on the right foot. Months flew by, and even though I truly had not given any thought to the happening that occurred—it happened. Bob and Charity had fallen in love. I didn't give a whistle about the age difference. Bob was absolutely sappy, almost like a little puppy, and Charity took on an aura of near bliss as she performed the most menial of tasks around our office. I had succeeded in spite of myself in getting Bob to find the right woman. Charity had to be the right ticket. Strange, strange are matters of the heart!

"Bob and Charity were married exactly one year to the date that she had come to work for us. They both continued to work at the office together. In my mind, I could visualize that one day in the future Charity would take over my position, and I would go to the country and dabble my toes in the creek near to our home. I savored the thought. There were even days when I had to restrain myself from throwing up my hands and yelling out to anyone who would listen: *'I quit!'* But I hung on because my work was my life.

"September 27, 1975, was upon us. Koskobe and Bob had driven to Houston a week ago and had spent the better part of a day at Foley's in downtown Houston getting all decked out in new togs. *'I bought the whole nine yards!'* Bob had explained to me when he returned from Houston. They had decided not to go to Huntsville after all. And me? Well, I had a good morning dress that I could wear the first day, and the second day I would be plain old Anna Renner and mix and mingle with all the homefolk. I had seen Charity's outfit for the first day, and it was a vision of swirling colors in rustling swaths of an ethereal organdy. *'Ah, youth!'* as the poets say. But forgive me! I wax poetic!"

෨

Chapter Forty-One

Alicia Woodman, Ph.D.:

'Faire ce qu'il faut.' (Do the right thing.)

"Murt and Anastasia were kind enough to herd me to the Walkamile Cultural Center about 8:30 AM. And I do mean herd! Flibbertigibbet that I was known to be, I was a bundle of nerves. I was talking a mile-a-minute and was running about the house like a chicken with its head cut off. Why I reacted this way to something I must have done a hundred times over in the past, and successfully so, is always beyond me. But—the butterflies do come and visit one's gastric regions; the throat becomes dry as a genteel Southern lady's powder box; random and completely unassociated thoughts flit hither and thither and detract from the practiced message at hand. And one's organizational capabilities fly out the window like a fly that has been trapped for days on end inside one's home. Ah, well! Thank the Good Lord for people like Murt and Anastasia! They were there, rock-solid, to give me the golden opportunity to disembarrass myself of my anxieties.

"The Cultural Center's maintenance man, John Hopkins, met us at the entryway. John Hopkins was a sturdy, reliable, no-nonsense Walkamilian who had retired from the military and had moved to

Walkamile after the war. I wanted desperately to call him Johns Hopkins, but I felt that he would not entertain the true meaning or the gist of my pathetic humor. We exchanged cordial greetings with him as he acknowledged us as invited guests at the entryway door. He was dressed to the nines, almost an icy formality to his bearing as he greeted us. Anastasia had whispered to me that he looked like a stuffed penguin except for the fact that he wasn't dressed in black and white.

"In what I had designated The Grand Hallway, the area that someone first views after entering, my precious photographs, enlarged and enhanced and each one bearing my personal stamp of approval, were systematically placed on either side of the vaulted space. Each depiction had been framed or matted and was displayed in such a fashion as to bring out its strongest point. Some had been hung from the wall while others had been situated on standing easels. There was a pristine orderliness to each of them: an old sepia of Walkamile (likely from the 1850s) in the days of the river craft traffic, the original courthouse built in 1911, the present-day courthouse which replaced the old one when it burned in 1966, a panoramic picture of two of the cemeteries located in Walkamile, a photograph of The Gully, apparently taken in the waning minutes of a setting sun—and finally—Anastasia's startling photographs of The Red Clay Cliffs which she had taken only a short time ago with Robert E. Massey's assistance. Interspersed among these were formal portraits of city leaders spanning the community's inception to the present. Some of the older portraits were amusingly stiff and formal but added much to the display.

"Anastasia and Murt had not seen any of these photographs before this moment. In a sense of fair play I had to "herd" them on to our destination—past the scurrying workmen, past the scampering ladies who were seeing to the last-minute touches of floral arrangements as well as the catering needs in the expansive kitchen. And some of the bigwigs were starting to approach the entryway. There seemed to be an excessive amount of to and fro activity which could either be a good sign or a bad omen. At the gymnasium's side entrance, several ladies from the Walkamile Garden Club were registering each guest. Each guest would be requested to sign in on the pages of a leather-bound album which eventually would be made into a display for the cultural center.

"As we entered the gymnasium, we were startled to note that a good number of the guests had already taken their designated seats. Our mayor, Ray Don Overstreet, approached us rather aggressively, I thought, and after extending his greetings and good wishes, he handed me a note which he informed me had been delivered to him about fifteen minutes ago. He had stressed this fact excessively as if to vaunt his importance. The vellum note was folded and the typewritten message read: *'Unavoidably detained in Houston. Please accept my personal apologies. And I offer my heartiest congratulations on your coup!'* Below the note was another message handwritten: *'Telephone call from Governor's Office, received 8:00 AM. Marybelle Withers, Secretary, Mayor Overstreet's Office.'* I was quite amused (and irritated somewhat) that the Governor's Office had not contacted me instead of the Mayor. But in the scheme of things it mattered not. Allow the Mayor to have his measly fifteen minutes of fame.

"I smiled when I read the note. My immediate urge to say something a bit snide was counterbalanced by my Southern good manners which had somehow kicked in the moment I arrived at Murt's home the day before. But I did think things not worth repeating aloud: *'So . . . the good Governor Dolph Briscoe was 'unavoidably detained.'* Bless his heart, I thought. He had not offered anything to this project other than a token mention of the cultural center in a speech he had made. In the last election he had not carried Walkamile and his presence or non-presence would not cast a pall on the proceedings. *'Not a whistle of a difference,'* as they say up in Massachusetts. Perhaps I should have invited Michael S. Dukakis, my own Governor. Oh well, I thought as Murt, Anastasia and I took our places at the long table under the basketball scoreboard. My best effort would be to downplay this occurrence and just proceed and do the right thing. As the French say: *'Faire ce qu'il faut.'*

"Minutes later, we were joined at the long table by Koskobe Renner, Anna Renner, Charity and Bob Renner. Each of them could have just stepped out of the pages of a fashion magazine. I was a bit taken aback when I first saw Koskobe: he could easily have passed for his father, Arppra, when he was at the same age. Bob, on the other hand, appeared to be a miniaturized copy of his father. And Anna gave off an air of a woman being in full control of herself and the conditions around her. Charity was a vision of loveliness. Before they all got seated there was much hugging and handshaking and meaningful exchanges of greetings. This latter part would never have occurred in my Massachusetts milieu, and I enjoyed every bit of it. To be hugged by two handsome fellows was not an everyday occurrence for me. In addition to this, I had taken great delight in working with all of them over the past year and more. They were extra-special people of an ilk that one does not come across too often in life.

"Our program, planned to the letter of the law, was a masterful stroke of organization. Being so far away, I had relied heavily on Anastasia and Murt in establishing the time slots for each segment of the program. There was no way on Planet Earth that I wanted to bore the Hell out of those sitting in the gymnasium's bleacher seats; and I did not, for one minute, want any of those attending to think of this program as a self-aggrandizing praising of me. Far from it! I wanted this to be about Walkamile, and in the course of the flow of the program, I would accept the occasional tidbits of praise which might come my way. But if I had my eventual say in the matter, I would see that any over-praise was down-played to the nth degree. This was all about Walkamile! This was not about Alicia Woodman, Ph.D. This was more about the dedicated work of people like Koskobe Renner and his entire staff at their construction company as well as the innumerable unsung workers who gave of their time without expecting anything at all in return.

"The ceremony opened with a flag ceremony in which the national flag and the Texas flag played the prominent roles; first, the Pledge of Allegiance, then the National Anthem, then a rousing rendition of *'Texas, Our Texas!'* A minister representing the Council of Walkamile Churches then delivered a brief prayer of thanksgiving. And we were off and away into the heart of the program.

"It is hours later—late on the Saturday afternoon of the first day of our celebration. Murt, Anastasia, Robert and I are seated in Murt's den. Each of us has a program in front of us, and we are critiquing the events of the day. We have all shed our dress-up duds except for Robert who had no opportunity to go to his apartment.

"I believe that the realization that we have all made it through what we now deem to be one-half of the end celebration has finally dawned on us. We all have in differing degrees endured more than a long year's work. One more day to go. A year ago I would not have dared think of this time. It was only a mythical date in the future circled on my desk calendar in red ink. A Red Letter Day, I suppose. There were too many obstructions to face and too many catastrophes biding their time. But we had been fortunate. We had so many quality people who gave unselfishly to pulling this thing off, and we had avoided these selfsame obstructions and an out-

and-out catastrophe. It had all come together like a giant jigsaw puzzle of five-thousand pieces.

"We had playfully castigated all the politicians that we had been able to do without running them out of the county. The city officials, from the mayor down to the city council members, were only there because they were invited and wanted to use the Grand Opening as a stage for their own advancement. They had not escaped our sharp tongues. Nor had the county officials, from the County Judge to the Precinct Commissioners and to other elected ones—we categorized them about the same as the city officials.

"We all agreed that the representatives from the consortium that had granted me this fabulous opportunity in the first place were gentlemen to the core and possessed not one ounce of self-importance. Their humility in all cases was striking. They were truly a blend of what is so excellent about our great country. Their last names reflected that so magnificently: *Armanzio, McDougal, Obrednegun, etc.* How the local officials could not see this and use it for their own career benefit and enhancement in the future was beyond all of us. We were in agreement that the humility of these consortium representatives flew completely over the heads of the local officials. They had failed to see the beauty in their names or what the names represented. Anastasia had suggested that '*a potpourri of humility*' would be descriptive.

"Without a doubt we were quite impressed by our U.S. Representative Charlie Wilson who had come down from Lufkin. He gave a very brief congratulatory speech about the cultural center and the '*esteemed Dr. Alicia Woodman*' which exaggerated my importance, I thought. But his remarks were sincere and were well-received by the guests. I had thought to myself that if I were twenty years younger, I would cast my net for him. He was a real looker, handsome, his face with sculpted good looks—tall and slim—and he had the eyes and the smile that immediately ensnared the person lucky enough to be talking to him. When I was introduced to him, I must confess that I took a sneaky look at his left hand to determine if he had on a wedding ring. I was unable to make that determination in my brief moment of introduction. I could not imagine any woman of good sense not voting for him whether she be of Democratic or Republican or Independent persuasion. I have always believed that politics and running for office are actually beauty contests in disguise! He was a winner in this genre. I told Murt later in an aside: *'Mr. Wilson will be around and about in Washington for a good long spell. He will bring many good things to our area in years to come.'*

"Anastasia shattered my day-dreaming as she asked a question which I knew would eventually be asked. The question could have come from anyone, and I felt relieved that it had come from my niece rather than from some belligerent resident. *'To what extent do you think those who have agreed to offer bits and pieces of their family's history will go in their elaboration?'* The simplicity of her question belied the complexities behind the question. The rest of us remained silent as we mulled over a sensible response to Anastasia's question. Prior to my arrival in Walkamile just one day ago, I had only received token information from quite a few families: dates of birth, dates of marriage, that sort of thing. No real anecdotal material.

"As is usual with me in circumstances of this sort, I burst out with my own opinion. *'There will always be uncomfortable episodes in the lives of all families even in a small community such as Walkamile. Of course, in a small place where everyone knows everyone's business before it happens, these episodes are often known by most of the people but are not necessarily talked about, except in private. I can't imagine Mavis Murray, as an example, standing up in front of her friends and neighbors and telling of her rape by her supposed father, about his disappearance and about the questionable death of her grandpa. Oh, we've all heard stories, and not a one of us knows if there is any truth in any of it or not. There will be those who shall provide us with rusticated histories of their family—and rightfully so, I'm afraid.'*

"Robert immediately added his own perplexing situation to the mix when he spoke of his own Grandpa Massey. *'There is no way I'd stand up and tell the world about my Grandpa Massey and the negative things he got involved in long ago. Even though he told me some of these things, I think I should have sense enough to hold them private. None of it would benefit anybody. It would hurt some people and would not serve any purpose—history or not.'*

"There was the matter of Micah Abraham Jessup which we had not addressed so far. *'What Micah plans to do is his own business. You know I'm referring, of course, to the Jessup boy—God! He's not a boy anymore. He's a grown-up! I see no harm in allowing him to relate the history of his Grandpa Jessup, that grand old man we all loved so. But when Micah starts on his upcoming marriage to a white woman—oh dear! I'm not sure Walkamile is ready for that! Those of us in this room today could easily accept it and go on with our lives. But the others? I worry. But this dedication of a cultural center should mean 'cultural', and 'cultural' should mean 'diversity' and we all should have sense enough to get along. My Lord, some of these issues are hundreds of years old, and we're still tossing them around like they're hot coals or hot potatoes.'* Proverbially, I was about to fall off my soap box when Murt rescued me.

"Murt spoke softly with overtones of studied conviction in his voice. *'Over the long life of this community there have been tragedies the like of which we may never see again. Let us hope that we can dwell on the good things—the things that bring laughter to* us and even some things that bring tears to our eyes. Each of our families should be able to find enough good things in our past lives to share with our own neighbors. We should not feel compelled to drag out all the dirty linen and air it in the form of a purging, repentant confessional. We can leave that to the revivals which sweep through here every now and then. Where is the like of Brother Billy Heart when we need him so?'* Murt gave out a low chuckle at his question.

"What Murt had said made more sense than all of our other comments combined. He had an innate way of slicing off the fat and getting to the sweet meat of any situation at hand. Tomorrow would bring out only the sweet meats. I would see to this in my introductory remarks. September 28, 1975, would be a day of celebration of the lives that had been led in our little community of Walkamile from the time it was a Trinity River port until the present day when we were all involved in the dedication of a cultural center whose cornerstone was based solely on diversity. Our individual roads had led all of us here. The very essence brings to my mind the words of Plutarch: *'When men are arrived at the goal, they should not turn back.'* God! He said that centuries and centuries ago, I thought to myself.

"The fact that Micah Abraham Jessup had in confidence shared with me his upcoming marriage to a white woman would, in no way, deter me from my long-sought goal. September 28, 1975, was upon us. We would not turn back. We all had come too far. Our goal was within our grasp."

☙

Chapter Forty-Two

September 28, 1975: 10:00 AM—12:00 Noon

'All of us, even in our shortcomings, are capable of love.'

"Where on earth had I heard the old adage, *'Today is the first day of the rest of your life'?* Yesterday I could not have under any figment of my own imagination remarked that we were in the penultimate stages of our endeavor. Remember, I was being herded about by my faithful brother, Murt, and my loving niece, Anastasia. They were my earthbound saviors on this day. I might need heaven-sent angels before the day was over.

"I had come out of all the goings-on of that day with minimal scratches, and all I had to do today was be myself. Today would be less formal than yesterday. We all would be involved in more one-on-one encounters (which I adored); and I would feel that I was an integral part of the Walkamile Community again. Today would be a series of refreshing encounters for me. I would come alive as I spent more time with so many different people that I had hardly had the time or opportunity to acknowledge yesterday. The potential negativism we had hashed and rehashed in Murt's den after yesterday's Grand Opening Ceremonies had been dismissed by one and all. Today was a new day ripely ready for those of us who were willing to meet it head-on. I was looking forward to all of the hullabaloo with great relish.

"Practically all of the local churches had agreed to hold their regular Sunday services at an earlier hour so that their congregants could attend today's festivities. Even the large church in Rogersville had told its congregants to come to church early. The minister had told me yesterday that he would make his Sunday sermon *'short and sweet for the not too fleet.'*

"Our program was to begin at 10:00 AM sharp, and the first order of business was a speech (if you can call it that) by me. I had fretted over this for months: what to say, how to say it; do I have humor in it? Or, because it is the Sabbath, should I be a bit restrained? For me the main focus should be that I come across as down-to-earth, which indeed I was. I had no one at Harvard to give me advice. One must reflect that my cohorts at Harvard are from other parts of the country—nay, world—than I, and what may be acceptable to their own standards in their home communities would offend the Living Hell out of my Walkamilian friends and newly-acquired acquaintances. So . . . in this backwater of my desperation I went it alone and traveled to the end of the proverbial limb as to my final decision. My speech would not be so much about me but about what I hoped would be shared experiences—with a dash of humor sprinkled here and there.

"At 10:00 AM on the dot my now good friend, Koskobe Renner, took the mike and, per the program, gave his brief speech before introducing me. He had, with an inborn sense of modesty, introduced himself and then began:

'Now that you know who I am, let me make it abundantly clear that today's events have nothing to do with me. They are about Walkamile. I am not important. Today's attentions are about happenings in all of our lives that have made this community what it is today. We are a proud and dynamic little community. But there

are so many things that have brought us here. I would like to share a few of these really ordinary things with you. Hold on! Our lunch is two hours or more away. I hope two things: that you ate a good breakfast and that you went to an early church service. I could ask for a hand count, but I won't because I might suffer from some embarrassment as would some of you on one of those scores.

'My father, Arppra Renner, was the son of Otto and Alla Renner. We all had names that were palindromes. You might ask me: 'What's a palindrome?' Well, it's a name or word or sentence that you can read from front to back and from back to front, and you end up with the same old person or word or sentence.

'Now I don't know if my Grandpa Otto did all of this on purpose. He probably did once he married a woman named Alla, my Grandma. But my daddy, Arppra, didn't have any idea what a palindrome was until, as he told us many times—until he was told this by a young lady in his 8th Grade class. That young lady was none other than our esteemed guest of honor today. But before I introduce her formally, you might wonder what in the name of God's Green Earth am I doing with a name like 'Koskobe'. I've wondered that myself a hundred times over. There's a reason. And I'll be happy to tell y'all about it later. Now to more important business. It gives me the greatest pleasure to present to you one of my newest friends, my family's friend, a friend to Walkamile forever and indeed our most famous former resident—Alicia Woodman, Ph.D.'

"*Oh, my God!*" I thought. The applause was thunderous, and I had so hoped that this whole mess would not be about me. I couldn't blame Koskobe, however. He really had done himself proud with his enchanting speech, but I wish he had toned down his overblown rhetoric a bit. But—what the hey? I'd have to tone it down myself.

"I approached the mike and motioned for the applause to cease. Thank God, it did in short order. In my best professorial manner I began: *'Do allow me, my dear friends and newly-found acquaintances, to tone down my good friend's use of the word 'famous'. I am not famous, and I don't intend to be. But I have become a friend of Koskobe Renner and his extended family. And the Ph.D. after my name shouldn't bring any fear to one or more of the lovely skunks that inhabit the woods in and around Walkamile. All it means is that I kept my nose stuck in books for many, many years. From now on—I am simply Alicia to the grown-ups and Miss Woodman to the children (I know you will insist on this for the sake of good manners).*

'And I shall remind you that Koskobe Renner is wrong about something. This event is all about him and the countless others who have contributed so unselfishly toward the amazing success of our endeavor. For that I am grateful. It is about all of you. And I am in awe of you all. You are very special in my heart!

'More than a year ago I was blessed to receive an open-ended grant from a wonderful group of people who are striving mightily to preserve the culture of this great country, America, region-by-region. I am humbled by the fact that they selected me. Some of you were fortunate to meet those gentlemen yesterday; and I trust that those of you who did realized the impact of their diverse origins. That is what has made this country great, and, in my opinion, will continue to offer sustenance to our very lifeblood in the decades to come.

'Now, when I use the term 'open-ended' I must remind you that I could have named any town in our great country with a population of less than ten-thousand and such a center would have been built there. But no! I gave it absolutely no thought when making my decision. I had only one choice: Walkamile!

"The applause first came in ripples, and then the entire gymnasium thundered as people both clapped and stomped their feet rhythmically. The hurly-burly must have lasted minutes—not seconds. Many of those seated at the tables clinked their knives, forks and spoons against their water glasses as a form of approbation. I motioned for it to stop and continued: *'I chose Walkamile because Walkamile will forever be in my blood. That day in his father's 8th Grade class that Koskobe spoke of a bit earlier, is a part of Koskobe's heritage, and mine, that we both embrace. On that day the late Miss Lohan, the teacher, became excited when she was registering our names in her grade book. She mentioned the word 'palindrome' and noted that she knew of three palindromes: Arppra, Otto and Alla. This incident is a part of Koskobe, a part of me and a part of Walkamile. And I'm sure there are similar anecdotes each family present today could recall as a part of their own heritage. If so, embrace them; if not, talk to the old-timers in your family. They can be a store of wonderful stories from the past. These precious people are the fountains of our oral histories.*

'There is one legend about me that I would like to share, and rebut, and then I shall turn the mike over to other far more interesting Walkamilians. When I was a schoolgirl, old enough at least to walk to school by myself, I had to pass by several homes on the way which, for whatever reasons, the owners kept savage-looking dogs in their front yards. Naturally, I was the object of their undivided attention as I traipsed by. On occasion one of the dogs would come tearing out of the front yard through a hole in the fence or through a gate left carelessly ajar. Really, I had no defense mechanism at all. I suppose I could have hit them with my book satchel and then run like the wind for safety. But surely they would have overtaken me and wreaked havoc upon my person.

'So . . . I decided that I would talk to the dogs in question much as I would talk to a person. I would look them straight in the eye and tell them how handsome they were (if the dog was a boy dog), and I would tell the females how lovely they were on this fine morning. I would then ask them to walk with me and protect me while I was in their territory. That's where the legend started. I think my brother, Murt, must have started it. Brothers are known to do things like that.

"(Sustained laughter from the audience). 'Today, I want to set the record straight. I am not a dog whisperer. I was a foolish schoolgirl who was scared to a point within an inch of her life. It's a wonder that each dog I ever confronted with my silliness had not torn me apart limb from limb. They did not, as you can see. Why what I did worked, I'll never know, but it did. It could have been that I was so brassy and forward with how I handled the situation that the dog reasoned that I must be a terribly dangerous creature not to be messed with at all.' Again the audience applauded, and I even heard several whistles from the more rowdy young men in the bleachers. It appeared everyone was honed in to my every word. I had kept their interest for a time being at least.

'Enough about me! I have put that legend to rest, I pray. The first Walkamilian to speak after me will be a young man who has done himself proud in so many ways. All of you know him. You see him almost every day in his assigned position. I know him because he is affianced to my dear niece, Anastasia. May I present Robert E. Massey?' Again, the ripple of applause as Robert took the mike from me. His face had turned four shades of crimson, but he was smiling broadly as he came to the microphone.

"He began: 'Thank you, Aunt Alicia. I may call you Aunt Alicia prematurely, I hope.' After the good-natured laughter subsided, he adjusted the microphone, looked about to all areas of the gymnasium and then spoke distinctly. *'There must be some of you here today who remember my Grandpa Elbridge Massey. He was the rural postman for many, many years, and he knew everyone and he knew where everyone lived. Though I will not confess it publicly, I am sure that he knew a good amount of everyone's personal business. In those days there would not have been a need for AAA and its routing and maps. Grandpa Massey had all the mapping in his head: 'go down past the big oak tree on your right, turn left at the next little pathway and go past the little branch that crosses the pathway, then a hundred yards or so to the twin cottonwood trees, and you'll find the Such-and-Such house.' I can almost hear him give instructions now to someone.*

'Grandpa Massey was also a handy repairman or a supplier of a needed tool or a deliveryman used by someone at the beginning of his route to send something of importance to someone else at or near the end of his route. He also was a drug dealer.

"Nervous laughter filled the air, and Robert Massey waited to let his pronouncement sink in before he interrrupted: *'Imagine that! A drug dealer! He delivered prescriptions from Carter's Drug Store to people on his route and, in turn, brought in handwritten notes to Mr. Carter about some medication that Mrs. So-and-So needed tomorrow. Today, as you can imagine, all of this would be against the law, and Mr. Carter and my Grandpa would be hauled into court, tried, and likely sent up to Huntsville or to an outlying place of confinement. But not back then! Those were different times— times that all of us hold in our memory. These are our gifts of heritage. These are the things that make us what we are today. We have become what we have become because of these small, everyday acts of random kindness. Kindness in those days was reciprocal.*

'And—Grandpa was both a bus company and a taxicab. It was nothing for children to ride from the farthest end of his route to the home of an aunt or uncle in town, spend a week in town and then catch a ride back to the country with Grandpa. And Grandpa ran a delivery service for fresh garden vegetables: okra, corn, watermelons, cantaloupes, berries, peas, beans, potatoes, onions—you name it! And we talk about our fresh produce today! In season with all the fresh vegetables—what more could you ask for?

'And Grandpa was a psychiatrist and a psychologist who had a receptive ear for those who needed to vent their ailments, real or imagined. He listened to all and sympathized with each of them. If this were done today, the authorities would be out and about checking his diploma to make sure that he was qualified to offer psychiatric opinions. His opinions were only commonsense undertakings. Nothing else!

'My own Daddy told me about the time that Grandpa had transported a pet rabbit from a house out in the country to a horse doctor in town. As you have already suspected—yes, the rabbit got loose when Grandpa made one of his stops, and Grandpa and two or three young boys spent almost an hour chasing the rabbit before they caught it.

'I think it might be just right for us to return to those old days. This beautiful Cultural Center reminds us of those days; and the large extent of the credit must go to Dr. Alicia Woodman—my soon-to-be-aunt.' The applause rippled throughout the gymnasium once more before Robert introduced Charity (Chambers) Renner.

"As Charity came forward, I looked over to where she had been sitting with Bob and the others. Bob's face was literally and figuratively aglow in the pride of the moment. Looking at him, I sensed that they were one happy couple. Charity cleared her throat and then spoke in a high-pitched voice with which I had grown familiar over the past year or so when she had answered the telephone at the construction company.

'I wish today to honor my late father, Matthew Chambers, who died years ago in the tractor accident which all of you know of, I am sure. And I honor my mother, Verity, who had been my Rock of Gibraltar before I fell in love and married Bob Renner. Bob now guides my Ship of State. So far we have not crashed our boat upon the Rock of Gibraltar. But seriously—the person to whom I owe a debt of gratitude today is someone who is no longer with us—my mother's late brother, Stace Wellborn—my much beloved uncle.

'I'm sure most of you know the basic details of Uncle Stace's short, sad life. He stayed with my father for over twelve hours in the field where my father died. Now, let me make this clear upfront—this is not a pity party. This is a celebration of a unique life—that of my Uncle Stace. Uncle Stace developed many unsolvable problems over the years, and at the door to desperation in how to face these problems twenty-four hours each day, my mother had to make a very tough decision. Uncle Stace had to be committed to a mental institution. Without my saying it—it broke our hearts.

'During his long stay at the institution, the only improvement was that he became more docile in his individuality. We are unsure if this was a result of the shock treatments he received during his confinement. It may or may not have been according to the staff of doctors there. Regardless, he ceased verbal communications. He closed himself off into a world that only he could understand. Ultimately, Uncle Stace was returned to us to be cared for at home. At first there were some problems, but in a short time he settled in to a stable routine at home. He became, in effect, a member of our family again.

'I could tell you a hundred stories about Uncle Stace before he was placed in the institution, and I could easily relate to you as many stories about him after his return to us. But I must tell you one story which portrays Uncle Stace in a light that is both difficult for me to understand and equally problematic for me to relate to you. It is a powerful story of an animal's bonded trust in a defective human being—a story of extraordinary love. We had witnessed an earlier episode that Uncle Stace once had with our outdoor cat, Pesky. That encounter, as dramatic as it was at the time, pales in comparison to the one I plan to tell you about now.

'My mother, Verity, was returning home one day from work when she came upon a little black and white creature lying at the side of the road. At first she thought it was a little kitten. Stopping her car, she got out and discovered to her surprise that it was a baby raccoon. Getting a towel she had in the trunk, my mother wrapped the little creature in the towel. It had hissed at her weakly as she picked it up and she had smiled at its sassiness. Then she proceeded on home with the tiny creature riding in the front passenger seat swaddled in the towel.

'She brought the tiny critter into the kitchen where Uncle Stace and I were sitting. Without any hesitation, Uncle Stace took the raccoon from my mother and carefully inspected it. My mother immediately telephoned Jaggers Forsythe, a veterinarian who lived nearby. He told mother how to care for the raccoon after they had mutually agreed on approximately how old it was. It had to be less than three weeks old, they had decided.

'To get to the beautiful point of this story—Uncle Stace assumed one hundred percent care and feeding of this little bugger. My mother and I utilized a sort of sign language to indicate to him how often our newly-found resident was to be fed, burped, et cetera. We also talked very distinctly to each other about the little kit's care so that Uncle Stace would feel included in the decision-making. Words were not really needed. Uncle Stace became a model in his surrogate parenthood status, and he allowed me to name the baby Cocoon. He had laughed out loud when I told him of the name. The *creature thrived under Uncle Stace's ministrations. Where we saw Uncle Stace, we saw Cocoon. If we saw Cocoon sidling into a room, Uncle Stace was never far behind.*

'To my mother's shock, she came home one afternoon from work and found the bottom drawer of Uncle Stace's chest-of-drawers pulled out. Inside was Cocoon the raccoon reposed and apparently quite happy in her bed in the drawer. Uncle Stace changed the towels which he used as a mattress substitute almost daily. From that moment on Cocoon was an intimate member of our small family, dictating unwittingly how our household was to be run each day. She continued to sleep in Uncle Stace's room in a cage my mother had bought in Beaumont, or quite often in Uncle Stace's bed if he so chose. My mother had remarked with a sense of feigned exasperation one evening while we were doing the dishes: 'What, dear Lord, have I got us into?'

'Cocoon was an absolute delight, unpredictable and capricious, frustrating us much too often, however, with her rambunctious antics. Uncle Stace was her Daddy—and she would totally ignore my mother and me if we attempted to chastise her for her frequent misbehavior. She would sidle off to her Daddy posthaste, climbing up his pants leg with deliberate speed to receive his protection, staring at us defiantly the whole time. Uncle Stace would look at us both and smile enigmatically.

'Uncle Stace refused our offer of leather gloves to wear when handling her as she grew by leaps and bounds. Though she nibbled at his fingers and especially his toes if he were barefoot as an attention-getting device, she performed these actions gently, not once giving him a severe bite. Innately she seemed to know the boundaries which not one of us had ever formalized.

'About two years after my mother had found the tiny creature on the highway, Cocoon disappeared. Uncle Stace was as bereft as *any parent who has lost a child. He moped about for weeks on end, and there was no consoling him. In the silence of his world, he searched the woods to the rear of our barn on a daily basis, always near sundown when raccoons are known to begin their nightly foraging. We prayed that he would not lapse into an earlier mental mindset which had brought on so many of his problems in the past. His face, once animated with the joy of having a little bundle of energy to tend to, took on aspects both dull and blank. And my mother and I worried so. The veterinarian informed my mother the raccoon's disappearance was not surprising. It was, he said, a natural instinct that bade Cocoon return to the wild. He had cautioned us that it was even more likely that Cocoon would never return.*

'Over a year and half had elapsed since Cocoon's exit from our lives, when, late one evening near sundown, my mother chanced to look out our kitchen window toward the barn at the back. Uncle Stace was sitting on the steps of the barn's first floor entrance. He appeared stiff—sitting up very erect and almost motionless. Two or three feet away from him a full-grown raccoon was approaching in what appeared to be a careful and calculated fashion. Uncle Stace did not move. The raccoon climbed up on the steps to his left side and with a studied deliberateness began to smell his trousers first and then his right arm. The raccoon next half-stood and placed one paw on his right cheek and held it there for a few seconds. Uncle Stace had closed his eyes, not in fright apparently but in acceptance of the animal's overtures. It was a moment I'll never forget. The animal next placed its paws on each of his closed eyes and then with a delicacy of motion smelled his face. The final action by the raccoon was to place a paw on Uncle Stace's lips and hold it there for a brief time. Without any prompting, other than from its own

instincts, the animal departed with the same care that it had come to the barn in the first place.

'*My mother and I thought this special scene was over and done with. We both knew in our heart of hearts that the raccoon was Cocoon, now fully an adult creature. No wild creature would dare attempt something like this. We were both taken aback only moments later when Cocoon returned with three feisty little ones following her in a single file. The three little kits were glorious to behold. Cocoon turned to the first kit and, nudging it with her nose, pushed it toward Uncle Stace who was still in his immobile state. With an amusing and exaggerated effort, the first little one climbed the steps and clawed its way up Uncle Stace's right leg into his lap and placed its paws on his face one at a time. My mother and I started crying when we realized that Cocoon, in her own inimitable way, was bringing her own offspring to pay tribute to someone that she obviously loved and respected.*

'*The next two little ones were nudged, one at a time, by Cocoon, and they repeated the exact scene that had occurred with the first one. Their movements were as clumsy as those of the first kit and equally amusing for us to see. My mother and I were turning into complete bawl bags as we watched. Cocoon basically got the attention of her little ones either by an imperceptible movement or a vocal signal understood only by them. Whatever the mode of communication, the four creatures disappeared in a single file formation into the woods behind the barn, back to their own world in the onset of twilight.*

'*Cocoon had likely repaid Uncle Stace for the many hours he had spent in being her surrogate Daddy. And she had gone to extreme measures to have her kits meet their human Grand-daddy. Even in the early dusk of night, my mother and I could see Uncle Stace's face. It reflected a tranquility of a sort that he probably had never experienced. There was no doubt in our minds that he was fully at peace with the world which he knew and with himself.*

'Forgive me for taking so long in telling you this. But to me, this true story is about love, unconditional love. It has no boundaries. Whether any of us is deficient, physically or mentally, it is still possible for us to give love and receive love. Please take this story with you and place it in your heart and know that all of us, even in our shortcomings, are capable of love. Love of this sort is a major part of all the families here. Too, it is the cornerstone of our heritage. Cherish it, and God bless you all!'

"I don't think there was a dry eye in the place. Charity had touched a nerve in all of us with her compelling story of her Uncle Stace. He had come across as a worthy individual in that family's heritage. The entire audience, men, women and children alike, stood and applauded as Charity returned to her seat. Bob embraced her for a long time before she took her seat. I gave a fleeting thought to Matthew Chambers and the horrific death he suffered. Today, if he were living, he would have been so proud of Charity, a most worthy daughter. I looked straightway to Verity, her mother, and as our eyes locked, I do believe she was thinking the same thing as I.

"I was brought back to the moment at hand when I heard Koskobe Renner's voice: *'We are extremely proud of one of our former residents who moved to Houston after completing the 8th Grade in the Rogersville School. He lived with his Aunt Audie and graduated with highest honors from Wheatley High School there four years later. We are even more proud of him for receiving scholarships to Dillard University in New Orleans where he graduated with high honors. He now teaches at the university level in Atlanta, Georgia. May I present our good friend and good Walkamilian, the son of Mrs. Matronella Jessup and the late Isaac*

Jessup, and the grandson of a Walkamile legend, Mr. Abraham Jessup—I give you Mr. Micah Abraham Jessup!' A hearty round of applause brought Micah to the microphone.

'Thank you, Mr. Renner. I always thought my first name was unusual until I found it in the Bible. As a child, I looked in the Bible for 'Koskobe' and could never find it. I've always wanted to know your name's origins. Will you tell me at lunch?' Koskobe nodded as he laughed at Micah's levity. *'I beg your pardon—dinner!'*

'Today, as Mr. Renner made quite clear in his opening statement, I am not up here to talk of Micah Abraham Jessup. As an individual, I am not all that important. I am here to talk about heritage. My heritage! My heritage can be summed up quite adequately by a name other than my own: Abraham Jessup, my Grandfather. Mr. Renner mentioned my Grandfather in his introduction as a Walkamile legend. I wholeheartedly agree. My heritage also springs from the love I received from a very fine woman—my mother, Matronella Jessup—and her sister, Audie Spinner, my Aunt Audie to whom I owe so much.

'I think most of you here today either knew my Grandfather or, if you did not have the pleasure of meeting him, you heard of him and his long association with Doctor Goldman. I use the word 'association' for lack of a better word. Doctor Goldman and my Grandfather were two peas in a pod. Or you could say one was vanilla and the other was chocolate. Or one was the storm while the other was the calm before or after the storm. One healed with wise words and medications; the other healed with kind words and helpful ministrations. One touched upon the physical pain; the other touched upon the pains felt by the heart and soul. But . . . the combination of the two and their efforts over the years brought

solace and comfort (or comfort and solace) to many in our community.

'My Grandfather once told me that when they arrived at the scene of Matthew Chambers' tractor accident, he and the Good Doctor treated the situation as if it were a normal operating room procedure, taking the greatest care to provide comfort to Mr. Chambers and offering encouraging words to the family and friends gathered there. When the Good Doctor had done all he could do, he had, according to my Grandfather, made a most unusual statement: 'One for sorrow, two for joy' which my Grandfather did not understand at all. The Good Doctor had looked skyward and pointed out two buzzards floating about on the early morning thermals. One tends to view these creatures totally in a negative light. The Good Doctor had then proposed that Mr. Chambers' soul was on its wings heavenward, surely a thing of joy. My Grandfather had later asked the Good Doctor about his saying, and he had dismissed it as a rhyme he had learned long, long ago as a child. If I may repeat it:

'One for sorrow, two for joy; three for letter, four for boy;
Five for silver, six for gold—
Seven for a secret that'll never be told!'

'In summation of my opening, please allow me to state that I believe that Doctor Goldman and my Grandfather completed each other. One without the other was unthinkable. Over the many years they were together, I fully believe one could state that they were by definition, inseparable. You saw the Doctor, you saw my Grandfather. People came to expect this combination. I believe that a bond existed between them that was undeniably one that transcended the scope of a magnificent friendship, despite the

social mores in which they found themselves as players upon this stage called life, the bond was inviolable.

'From a standpoint of heritage, I could regale you with stories my Grandfather told me of his own grandfather's days of slavery back in Virginia with the Goldman family. Of course, theirs was not a perfect world as ours now is not, but my Grandfather did not waver in his belief that the Jessup family could have been worse off if they had been owned by others. In earlier days they likely had been chattels to others what with the name of Jessup.

'When the Goldmans migrated to Texas from Virginia in the aftermath of the Civil War, many of the emancipated Jessups remained loyal to them and followed them to this area. To those who did so, it was not a matter of slavery. It was a matter of survival.

'I would like to set one thing straight about my Grandfather's name—nickname, appellation, call it what you will—but it is a vital part of our heritage that carries with it a message of hope far beyond today. As you know, many in our community, black and white, conceived of my Grandfather as no more than a flunky for Doctor Goldman. The blacks who took pot shots at my Grandfather derisively said he was a 'white nigger' while others spoke of our family as 'uppity'. Both of these designations are so removed from the truth. We, in the Rogersville community, can be very tough on each other at times. By the same token, we can come together—as we have done here today—and pay honor to our place in a larger community and offer our services to a higher calling. We can also discard old prejudices as more and more of our young people aspire to attain academic goals thought impossible only a decade or so ago.' Not a sound could be heard in the crowd in the gymnasium. It was obvious from the abrupt stillness that had come over the audience that Micah Abraham Jessup was getting too near a most uncomfortable subject matter.

'The white people, as you must know, had several names for my Grandfather, among them 'Old Jessup' and 'Nigger.' These names were often used interchangeably. The first name, Old Jessup, seemed not to bother my Grandfather too much. I suppose he may have viewed it as an honorific because he had been in the community for so many years that many did view him as 'old'. I had always viewed him as ageless.

'My Grandfather once told me that he had dropped by the Renner home to pay his respects at the time of Mrs. Renner's death. He had been invited in by Koskobe Renner who seated him at their dining table and served him cake and coffee. Grandfather told Mr. Renner that his mother had been one fine lady who had always called him 'Mr. Jessup'.

'As you can see then, my Grandfather had many names. But do you know what? I'll tell you what! My Grandfather told me that 'Old Jessup' and 'Nigger' were just 'them never-minds'. Both these names he would answer to without reaction, but he once told me that the second one pierced his heart. He had told me to just get on with life regardless what people called me. Study hard was his admonishment. Get a good education and these shackles would be tossed aside, he had reminded me. Knowledge is power, he had said. How right he was! My Grandfather was much, much smarter than I had realized at the time. And his advice turned out to be timeless in its true worth.

'My Grandfather was, however, the perfect example of what humility is all about. He possessed a certain calm and grace within his spirit that would bring benefits to any of us here today. Even with this aura of grace, my Grandfather still yearned deep down to be considered an equal, though his outward manifestations did not reflect this at all. And I do think he reached a state of grace and *equality on his death bed. May I share an incident I witnessed that will back up my supposition?*

'When my Grandfather was nearing his last hurrah, the Good Doctor Goldman attended him with the most compassionate care possible. Doctors from Houston could not have provided finer care. He came by at least twice a day, sometimes more than that. The Good Doctor on one of his last house calls seemed a bit reluctant to leave and he subsequently engaged me in a conversation. Near the end of our talk, he had told me: 'Micah, I love Abraham like a brother.'

"Doctor Goldman's remark to me is etched forever upon my heart. This was the first time I had heard a white man call my Grandfather by his given name. Grandfather was comatose during this visit, but I whispered a prayer to God: 'God, I hope you allowed Grandpa the honor of hearing the Good Doctor call him by his first name. It would please him so!'

'My deepest and most sincere gratitude to all of you for listening to part of my heritage. Take your own heritage, embrace it, tuck away the private little anecdotes in your heart, and cherish all things family and all things community. These are the things that make our country great. These are the very things that create love, and I'm sure you can tell by now that I loved my Grandfather very, very much. Be well! And be happy! And I'll shut up and allow Dr. Woodman to invite us to 'dinner' as we say here in Walkamile.'

"Though Micah Abraham Jessup had skirted close to the edge of the thin ice, he had not fallen through. In fact, he had won over the audience with his poignant portrayal of his beloved Grandfather. The audience stood as one and applauded vigorously as he smiled and waved as he returned to his seat. I was relieved that he had omitted the announcement of his upcoming marriage to a white woman. I'm unsure how that might have been received from his Rogersville friends as well as the residents of Walkamile.

"I accepted the microphone from Micah: *'Micah is absolutely correct. We call the noon meal 'dinner' here in Walkamile. You may have noticed that you have been seated at tables with pristine white cotton tablecloths. There is a reason for that. It's your dinner table. The local fire department, headed up by Roger Stafford and his efficient crew, have been in our kitchen whipping up our vittles. Please proceed in an orderly fashion to the "Exit" sign to my left, and you'll be surprised to find a veritable cornucopia of food: fried catfish, hushpuppies, coleslaw, pinto beans, potato salad, and Mrs. Baird's light bread. When you return to your table, you'll find our Garden Club's lovely ladies, headed by Janelle Prescott, serving iced tea and coffee. Enjoy! The last part of our program will begin just after we have finished our lunch—I mean, dinner.'"*

Chapter Forty-Three

September 28, 1975: 1:30 PM

'Dear child! At the Feast of Ego everyone leaves hungry.'

"A few more hours to go and my dream would become a full-fledged reality standing right in front of me. To say that my feelings were mixed would be an understatement. To say that I had no feelings about the entire matter would be a lie. I was proud, in a humble sort of way, at what had been accomplished by a select few people. And I was honored? I had hoped that the heritage of all the good folk here today was the honoree. That was the theme I had steered this celebration toward, and I think each of the speakers in their own way had carried this message forward.

"Our dinner a success, the tables cleared and we were back at the planned program once more. Doctor Goldman's grandson, Patrick A. Goldman, had roused the audience with his anecdotal portrayal of his grandfather and, of course, Old Jessup. Patrick had made it quite clear that his grandfather and grandmother, like all of us, were flawed individuals who still made a difference to our community. He had praised Micah Abraham Jessup for his touching assessment of his grandfather who had been a part of his own life in so many ways.

"The Garden Club hostesses had continued to serve iced tea and coffee throughout the ongoing speeches.

"Mavis Murray and Myrtle Froman provided brief insights into what death and the subsequent tragedies of losing someone could do to an individual and to a family structure. Still, even in their renditions of their own lives in Walkamile, they visualized that these elements are a vital part of one's heritage. What they both had overcome after facing up to their own setbacks reflected their own true grit in response to their temporary defeats. Mavis had simply stressed: *'You can win out in the end. Just keep trying.'*

"I took it upon myself to announce that William Beatty Heart and family from Knoxville, Tennessee, had committed earlier to attending our celebration. However, they did not show, and no one had heard from them about their reason for not attending. I purposely did not cite the fact that no representative of the Clayton Dykes' extended family had responded to my initial letter. I certainly did not mention Harrison Dykes.

"I next iterated that so many fine citizens of Walkamile had contributed to the success of our Grand Opening festivities; and I proceeded to name the various individuals and organizations that had been a part whether minimal or not.

"Before I handed the microphone over to Anastasia, I made one last announcement. *'Will all of you please stand? In a moment of respectful silence, let us reflect upon those who have gone before us—who have paved the way for us—who have given us our most precious heritage.'* Once everyone was standing and had become quiet, I lit a graceful taper located next to a floral centerpiece. I allowed it to flame for a minute or so as all the attendees stood silently. Then I extinguished the flame with a bronze candle snuffer. The audience remained standing as Anastasia walked to the microphone.

"Anastasia had taken the microphone to introduce Reverend Miller Freeman who was to offer the closing prayer when a woman raced into the gymnasium screaming at the top of her voice. *'Dr. Woodman, help me! Help me! My little James needs you! He's outside there trapped in the yard by a dog—a mean lookin' chow! Help me! Help him!'* After her emotional outburst, she had collapsed on the gymnasium floor in front of the microphone where the Reverend Freeman was now standing. Anastasia raced to her side and lifted her from the floor into a sitting position. Someone asked if an EMT was out back with the firemen. *'Go find one. Quick!!'* an unidentifiable voice called out.

"Murt, Koskobe, Patrick, and Robert caught up with me and were at my side as I ran as fast as I could in the direction the woman had pointed. I could hear each of them telling me not to go near the dog. One voice coming from the crowd defined all of this as the responsibility of the policemen or the firemen or the Sheriff. None of these people was about, having confined themselves outside to the back of the gymnasium while preparing the lunch.

"Murt had caught up to me by the time I reached the exit. He grabbed my arm and temporarily restrained me. *'Don't do it! I'll get in my car and find the police. Don't we have a telephone in here somewhere? Let me and Koskobe handle it.'* I hardly knew, and at the moment I didn't care who was located where. Some driving force within me was propelling me forward toward the little boy. Even Robert and Patrick had caught up with me and urged me to let them handle it. But whatever was compelling me to continue on my errand of mercy overrode all the protestations of those who were around me.

"In the distance, probably about fifty yards ahead, I saw an opened gate and a cobble-stone walkway leading to the front door of a small cottage that appeared to be in a disused state. The gate was a part of a hurricane fence, but it was obvious that the gate and fence had seen better days. Inside the small yard a little child, a boy I thought, was sprawled out on the drying grass. He was crying, and his face, child-like and innocent, showed all the signs of a deep-set and desperate fear; and in front of him—snarling and growling with teeth bared—was a large red chow dog. It was quite obvious that the dog was giving no quarters to his newly-found quarry. It was a scene straight out of Hell as far as I was concerned. The child stood no chance to escape this predicament on his own. How he had wandered inside in the first place was a puzzlement. Where had his mother been?

"I told all those around me—Murt, Koskobe, Patrick, Robert and anyone else in hearing distance of my voice—to remain very quiet and still. *'Do not do anything foolish or sudden regardless of what is happening. You'll bring harm to the child and to me.'* With this admonition I walked very confidently toward the opened gate. There was a soft buzzing from those gathered nearer to the gate, and then they quieted as I had requested. I also noticed, with satisfaction, that the dozens of people who had gathered outside the gymnasium's exit were following my instructions. A pall had settled over the gathering as many of them stood with hands shading their eyes in the late afternoon sunlight. Even the children seemed to be hushed as my entrance into the yard unfolded.

"When I reached the opened gate, I entered the yard and with assured authority I closed the gate with exaggerated but natural movements, dropping the catch securely in place. The chow momentarily turned its large head when I made the clanking noise, teeth still bared, and snarled at me. The young child was still screaming which most likely was doing nothing to improve the situation. As I approached the dog, I began to talk to it in the manner of a strict English schoolmaster who is scolding a miscreant student in private. The dog's snarling face took on the visage of absolute confusion. Apparently he had never been called out to face the music for his actions. Now he was experiencing that very thing. And he was probably hearing words and phrases he had never heard before from a woman or man, for that matter.

"I spoke in low tones with the sternest voice I could muster. *'You're nothin', you red Devil! You think that you're the son-of-a-bitchin' cock-of-the-walk 'round here! You—you ain't nothin' but a piece of horse shit that finally gets rolled off by tumble bugs. Your big ass starin' me in the face with your crappy balls hangin' loose—now ain't you a proud one? Well, I tell you what I'm goin' to do—I'm goin' to walk over to that child and I'm goin' to pick him up and take him to safety away from you—you sorry sack of shit! That's what I'm goin' to do, and you ain't goin' to do a thing, you hear me, you lousy brute? You try somethin' and I'll yank out your balls and throw them to Kingdom Come in one fell swoop. And you'll be a ball-less wonder.'*

"I glanced toward the crowd that had assembled outside the gymnasium and had a brief but passing thought that they looked like a fresco painting on a castle wall that I had once admired in Europe. I couldn't remember where. What an odd thought! I walked with an air of conviction up the cobblestone pathway and stepped to the left and then proceeded toward the child. The red chow was viewing me with a look of exasperation and confusion as I neared the crying child. When I finally reached the child, I stopped and spoke to the dog: *'You are a Devil, a red Devil! You won't pick on someone your own size—oh no! You pick on the little ones, the helpless ones, the innocent little children—and one day there's goin' to come along a big old brute that's goin' to tear you for a new asshole! That'll be your day of reckonin' for sure. You hear me?'*

"With my last question the chow rose, adrift and seemingly puzzled as to where he should go and what he should do. Likely his better judgment kicked in and he trotted off rather cavalierly toward the smaller backyard. I picked up the child, still crying, and held him in my arms for quite a long time before I started walking toward the front gate. He had ceased his crying. I quietly asked the child his name. For the first time he smiled and replied like the child he was: *'Mama calls me Little James.'* I told him he could call me *'Aunt Alicia'* if he liked. He just hugged my neck tightly as we left the yard. I could feel his little body convulse as he tried very hard to contain what earlier had been choking, uncontrollable sobs of outright fear.

"When we reached the front gate, I closed it with a lot more confidence than I had when I had walked through it minutes earlier. In the distance I heard what might be termed a susurration, and I realized that the gathered crowd was talking, applauding and whistling. I first noticed Anastasia and the mother of the child. They were running toward me. Then Murt, Koskobe, Patrick and Robert came forward. I gave the child to his mother by simply saying: *'Here's your Little James. He told me that's what you called him.'* She did not have to thank me. Her eyes did.

"She took the child in her arms, and I overheard his little child-like voice whisper to his mother: *'That lady said bad words!'* His mother hugged him tighter and shushed him with clucking noises only a mother can make.

"Reverend Miller Freeman then stepped out of the gathered crowd. He deferentially looked at me and asked: *'Dr. Woodman, do you think we could pray now?'*

"I laughed as I answered him: *'My dear Reverend, do you mean to tell me that you haven't been praying the whole time I was in that yard?'* Of course, he knew full well that I was tweaking him.

"Reverend Freeman gave a prayer of thanksgiving, short and sweet, and it was closed out with a lot of *'Amens'* floating upon the Indian summer air. And then the applause began all over again, first a ripple and then a steady thundering. Deep down I felt, that despite all I had done to make this celebration about Walkamile and its heritage, a part of it was indeed about me. My heart throbbed warmly, and I felt wholly accepted. I was still a Walkamilian. I even smiled as I recalled the little boy's whispered confidence to his mother that I had used bad words. I would not soon forget the childish assessment.

"On the way to Murt's car, Anastasia interrupted my pleasant reverie with an apparent statement of fact and a question: *'Aunt Alicia, you truly are a legend—you are a bona fide dog whisperer! Were you ever afraid?'*

"I had by accident looked skyward as Anastasia asked her question. I counted them—seven buzzards circling lazily in the pristine blue of the September sky. Carefully pointing them out to Anastasia, I then answered her as cryptically as I could: *'Dear child! At the Feast of Ego everyone leaves hungry.'* If she had paid attention to Micah today, she would know what the seventh buzzard represented: *'a secret that'll never be told.'*

❧ *FINIS* ❧

Acknowledgments

To those friends who read an early draft of the manuscript and gave their voices to its possibilities:

Betsy Duncan
Joan Miller (and her book club friends)
Beverly Norman
Betty and Allen Peebles

And to Tamara and Peyton Walters who generously did the same but also gave the novel its title.

And to the Reverend Doctor Charles E. Cravey and his wife, Renee, at Headlight Press, who coddled the novel through to publication.

৯

About the Author

Henry Wyath Gurley is the author of four books of poetry and has been widely published in regional and national poetry magazines and books. He presently has one book of poems awaiting publication. *An Untold Secret: A Journey Home to Walkamile, Texas*, is his second novel. *I Looked Out Tilt*, his first novel, was published in early 2008. He is presently at work on his third novel tentatively entitled *The December Fiction.*

He was born and raised in Ace, Texas, a small farming community on the Trinity River in Southeast Texas, but has lived in Montgomery, Texas, since 1996. Retired from an insurance brokerage firm since 1989, he spends his time reading and writing. He is also active as an auxiliary committee member of the Kurth Memorial Library in Lufkin, Texas.

ॐ

.